Seven Short Stories
of the **Vietnam War**

Sarge Lintecum

Seven Short Stories of the Vietnam War

Sarge Lintecum

Print ISBN: 978-1-54393-048-1

eBook ISBN: 978-1-54393-049-8

To Leslie Nan
My Best Friend and
Love of My Life

And to My Family, Friends and Fans
for Being Good Medicine for My PTSD

TABLE OF CONTENTS

ACKNOWLEDGMENTS

A special thanks to my sister, Norva Meyer, for her support and help with early editing.

My sincere gratitude to my editor, Remy Benoit, at http://www.niquahanam.com/writing -- Gentle Editing, for her excellent work and her patience with my malaria damaged brain.

AUTHOR'S NOTE

Throughout history soldiers have tremendously suffered from the realities of engaging in war. This suffering is obvious in journals of the ancients; in the journals of Napoleon's soldiers fighting the harsh winter in Russia; in mud smeared letters from World War I trenches; in journals from World War II. Over the centuries this heart and soul pain has been known by many names including Soldier's Heart, Battle Fatigue and Post Vietnam Syndrome. By 1980 this terrible burden borne by veterans came to be known as Post Traumatic Stress Disorder, and even yet there is still difficulty faced by veterans in having it properly treated by the Veterans Administration. In these stories I have used the modern term Post Traumatic Stress Disorder to clarify what the soldiers and then veterans experience and to note the angst, nightmares, and other related problems veterans and their families live with each and every day.

EDITOR'S NOTE

For many years it has been my privilege to help our veterans tell their stories; to help them put words to paper to try to make those who have never been there have some idea of the verities of war.

Not one of us who has never known war, combat, bombs raining down on their fields and homes can truly understand the horror of what we are often so quick to send our young off to experience. No one who experiences war ever comes back the same.

When they come home they often find that they feel they no longer fit in; that their families cannot understand their pain, their screams in the night, their attempts to find release of this pain in ways that too often just worsen it.

These stories offered by Sarge Lintecum are among some of the most heartrending, revealing, and soul-tearing accounts of what experiencing war really means that I have ever had the privilege of helping bring to the page and to you, the reader.

As these characters tell their tales, those tales are not here for you to judge; they are here to make you deeply consider what you are doing when you accept all that you are being told by those so willing to send soldiers into a living hell. They are here for you to share, to learn from, to help you look beyond the send-off parades into the hearts and souls of what this will mean to your sons, daughters, wives, and husbands as they are put into survival positions where all "civilized" rules of life are suspended and replaced with annihilating the enemy.

Let these stories help you truly consider what it means to put your loved ones on the front lines.

These stories are Sarge's gift to bring that home to you.

Remy Benoit

FORWARD

Although these stories are fiction they are based on my experiences during my three tours of duty in Vietnam. Even the story about the Viet Cong soldier is based on things that I saw in the boonies that the enemy had built and things that the enemy did while I was there. I served in Vietnam from 1966 to 1968, twenty-six months, and I was able to see Vietnam from three very different assignments.

My first tour of eleven months was in the jungle with the 101st Airborne Division as a combat infantry squad leader doing mostly search and destroy missions. My second tour was at E Company Support Battalion, at the base camp of the 101st Airborne Division, and my third tour of duty was as a security guard with the elite Saigon Machine-gun Patrol.

I have tried to show with this book how very different tours of duty in a combat zone can be, depending on to which job the soldier is assigned. My three tours ran the gamut from living in the jungle for weeks, and even months, at a time hunting men; living in a hotel with maid service in Saigon as an elite security guard, guarding the MPs and escorting Generals and other VIPs through the streets of Saigon at night with my machine-gun jeep. This being a work of fiction I was able to create plots that hopefully made the stories more exciting.

Sarge Lintecum

1 - BOONIE RAT

Boonie Rat in the Jungle in 1966

CHAPTER 1

ARRIVAL IN NAM

It was September of 1966 when Wayne Cox stepped off the commercial jet. The humidity was so high that the air seemed thick. He was in Vietnam. Even though it was a commercial flight, it was loaded only with army guys going to Vietnam. Wayne's first breath of Vietnamese air shocked him. The smell of the air was so strange that he didn't think he would ever get used to it.

All of Wayne's belongings were in his duffel bag, which he picked up from a pile on the tarmac in Phan Rang, Vietnam. Phan Rang was the in- and out- processing station, as well as the base camp for the 101st Airborne Division where Wayne was to go through a two-week intensive training program called "P" (preparatory) training to learn about booby traps and other dangers from both the Viet Cong and the jungle itself. These two weeks of training were important, but the main reason for keeping the soldiers in the rear area for two weeks was to let them become accustomed to the heat and humidity before being sent out into the jungle.

Otherwise, they would not be able to keep up on a normal day in the boonies (jungle), and heat stroke would have them dropping like flies, not to mention having to deal with the Viet Cong.

Wayne was from Indianapolis, Indiana, and he had only been in the army for six months before being sent to Vietnam. The training that he had received in the states had been intense, and considerably shorter than non-wartime training. The parachute jump school, where they taught the soldiers to parachute from planes, was shortened from six weeks to only two weeks. Wayne normally would have wondered why wartime soldiers were receiving only one-third of the training given to peacetime soldiers, but the intense training was too vigorous to allow the soldiers to have time to think of things like that.

Wayne had known that he was going to fight in Vietnam during his stateside training, and because of the intensity of the training, he had known that he couldn't remember everything he was being taught. Wayne's solution was to ignore parts of the training that did not directly apply to combat. As a result, he could shoot many weapons with deadly accuracy, but he had no idea what the chamber pressure or the muzzle velocity of any weapon was. And, luckily, as it turned out, the subject of chamber pressure or muzzle velocity never would come up in the jungle.

"P" training was nothing like stateside training. Everything taught here would be applied in the jungle and could save Wayne's life. He appreciated the special jungle warfare classes, and he paid very close attention. In "P" training they tried to teach the new soldiers who had just gotten to Vietnam everything they would need to know out in the boonies.

The Vietnamese were very good at using what was provided by the jungle as weapons against their enemies. They made things like punji stakes, a simple sharpened stick of bamboo stuck in the ground at an angle with the sharpened end up, so as to give a scratch or puncture wound to the lower leg. To make a simple stick stuck in the ground a serious weapon, the Viet Cong would put water buffalo dung on the sharp end of the stick. For some reason, water buffalo dung would cause a very dangerous infection that couldn't easily be stopped and had to be treated very soon in the rear area, or the leg would be lost. With one sharpened stick, they could take a soldier out of combat as surely as if they had shot him.

Wayne was taught that anything in the trail should not be stepped on, be it rock, vine, leaf or root; if stepped on, it could be the trigger for a booby trap. He learned that the only safe place to step in a trail was in the footprints that were made by the soldiers in front of him, because that was the only part of the trail that was proven not to blow up when stepped on. It was obvious that everyone was doing this, because there was only one big, wide set of tracks.

The large number of booby traps that could be made out of things easily found in the jungle was astounding, not to mention booby traps that exploded. The Viet Cong made a wide array of exploding booby traps, from something as simple as a shotgun round in a piece of pipe to anti-personnel land mines. Then there was the dreaded Bouncing Betty that exploded twice, once to blow the land mine up out of the ground and up into the air, followed by a big explosion while the mine was up in the air, giving it a much larger killing radius. Anything could be a booby trap, and the more inviting it was, the more dangerous. The soldiers were taught that a basket of fruit sitting like an offering in an abandoned village was probably going to explode when moved.

They were also taught that if they got separated from their unit in the jungle, or were captured and escaped, to always travel east until they reached the South China Sea, where being found by Americans was more likely.

They were instructed that the best time to try to escape if captured was as soon as possible. The longer a GI was in captivity, the less likely it was that he could escape, because the Viet Cong would be taking him to more secure areas with more VC.

While the days in "P" training were full of jungle warfare classes, the nights were free. Wayne used the free nights to find some short-timers who were soon to be on their way home and who would let him hang out with them, so he could find out what it would be like out in the jungle. The stories were horrifying. They told him of combat assaults on American compounds where the Viet Cong would use wire as a tourniquet to stop the blood flow to their arms and legs, so that if they got an arm or leg blown off they could keep crawling forward and get close enough to throw a grenade before they bled to death. They had stories about hookers with razor blades in their vaginas, and small children blowing themselves up with a grenade when they got close to GIs. Wayne didn't know if these stories were true or not, but he listened intently.

The barracks were row after row of big tents with the canvas walls rolled up, each lined on both sides with army cots with mosquito nets. The only entertainment at night was at an enlisted man's club or bar. Also, at night everything was dark. The enlisted man's club was the most "well-lit" place in the compound. It had a single light bulb with a rain cover hanging under the eave of the club. In contrast with the surrounding darkness, this one bulb made the club look like the Las Vegas of the entire camp. Inside the club it looked like a wild scene from an old western movie, without the barroom brawl. There was always some serious partying going on in there.

The crowd was a mix of hardened combat veterans, guys assigned to the base camp, and new troops—newbies—just arrived in Vietnam. They all seemed to have one thing in common—they were all partying like there was no tomorrow. This level of partying seemed natural, though, because some of these men would not make it home alive.

The two weeks of "P" training were going by fast as Wayne spent day and night learning about jungle warfare from classes by day and war stories by night. The day classes were filled with necessary information on how to survive Charlie and the boonies. The classes were in a jungle setting. One classroom was a Vietnamese village, but with bleachers to one side. The trainees practiced "clearing a hooch" of booby traps, and if you didn't find all the booby traps, you were considered to have been blown up. Wayne was very proud and a little relieved, after his turn, not to have blown himself up.

In the Jungle with Full Combat Gear

CHAPTER 2

THE JUNGLE

Sooner than Wayne wanted, the day came for his first operation in the jungle. Everyone was issued everything that they would carry in the "field"—the jungle—including a backpack, weapon, ammo, canteens; and then each man got one case of C-rations. One case of C-rations was a three-day supply of food for one GI. There was a huge bonfire to throw the cardboard and trash from the C-rations into. In a matter of minutes everyone was transformed from trainees to combat soldiers. Wayne would still have to earn the respect of the others because he was new to the jungle, so everyone called him "Cherry."

The weight of Wayne's backpack was disturbing, considering that he would be climbing mountains, fording rivers and streams, and chopping his way through thick jungle while carrying it on his back. Some of the extra weight was because Wayne had been issued the M79 grenade launcher, and the rounds (bullets) weighed one half of a pound each. The good news was that the rounds exploded on contact with the target, and they had a three-meter killing radius.

Wayne was also issued five shotgun rounds and five smoke rounds. The shotgun rounds held twenty double aught buck bearings and came in very handy when the jungle was too thick to fire High Explosive rounds. The HE round, when fired, would spin from the rifling in the barrel and, after two hundred and fifty revolutions, arm itself and then explode as soon as it hit something solid. In thick jungle, the HE rounds were no good because they would only be partially armed when they hit something solid, and as the round bounced back to where it was fired from, it would often complete arming itself and explode near the guy who fired it. The smoke rounds were for signaling air power as to exactly where the enemy was and, more importantly, to exactly where the Americans were.

Once everyone was all packed up, they were briefed that this would be a search and destroy mission and that they were to shoot to kill. Then the troops formed a line, and the order was passed back to move out and to keep spread out. It was important to keep the column spread out so that one grenade, mortar round, or rocket could only kill one or two soldiers.

This was it. Wayne was now in combat with real people trying to kill him and, even more frightening, Wayne didn't know if he could kill another human being or not. He had been trained to kill. Almost every day of his training they had been led in a chant while running, saying over and over again, "Kill, kill, kill, kill…."

They traveled cross-country for several miles until they came to a trail, and then they followed the trail deep into the jungle. Wayne had to constantly correct the distance between himself and the soldier in front of him. This would eventually become automatic, but for now it was a constant problem. Fear directed most of his attention to the jungle on his left and on his right, looking for the enemy. It wasn't so bad if he got too close to the soldier in front of him. He, and everyone behind him, would get to stop for a few seconds until the proper space was achieved. However, when he fell behind, he would not only have to go double time to catch up, but all the guys behind him would be pissed at whoever had fallen behind because they all would have to hurry and catch up as well.

It didn't take Wayne long to realize that even in the best-case scenario—no contact with the enemy—traveling through the jungle, or "humpin' down the trail," was torturous on its own. For the rest of the day, the soldiers followed the trail through streams and valleys and over some pretty serious hills. Just before sunset, they climbed one more hill and set up their night perimeter around the top. The officers, radio man, and others of importance slept in the center on top of the hill, while Wayne and the rest of the peons formed a big circle around them. Each guard position around the perimeter was manned by four soldiers for the night. A trip flare wire was stretched close to the ground across the front of each position about ten or twelve meters out, and a claymore mine was set up before the trip wire to blow up anyone who set off the trip flare wire. If the flare went off, it would light up the entire area like it was daytime. Then the guard would set off the claymore mine, and whatever—or whoever—had set off the trip flare was no longer a threat.

One soldier at each position had to be awake at all times. Wayne's first time alone on guard duty was very frightening. He could see nothing in the black jungle because the jungle canopy blocked out even the faint starlight, and all he could do was listen intently to all the jungle noises and try to tell if any of them could have been made by something as big as a human. As exhausted as he was, he had no trouble keeping awake—fear kept his eyes open wide and staring into the darkness. Wayne was amazed at how many noises there were at night in the jungle. The jungle, at night, had an entirely new population of critters than in the daytime, all crawling and creeping about. Wayne was relieved to make it through this first night in the jungle without setting off his claymore mine because of a snake or something.

By first light everyone was up, had finished eating breakfast, and was busy breaking camp. Wayne had had a can of cling peaches and a canteen cup full of coffee and hot chocolate mixed together. Wayne didn't like coffee, but he needed the caffeine. He didn't want to be looking for Charlie through sleepy eyes. Everyone called the Viet Cong "Charlie" because on the field phone (backpack radio) you would say words for letters, so Viet Cong or VC was "Victor Charlie," and that became shortened to "Charlie."

Word was passed around that they were going into an area where a lot of enemy troop movements had been observed and for everyone to be on full alert. Nothing eventful happened by noon, when they stopped at the side of the trail to eat lunch. Wayne wanted a warm meal, so he opened a can of beans and franks and got out a heat ration bar. Before he opened the heat ration packet, another soldier at his guard position told him to use C-4 and tossed Wayne a chunk of the plastic explosive that he had just torn off of a rectangular yellow clay-like block. The last thing Wayne wanted to do was to ignore the advice of a seasoned boonie rat.

"Don't worry, it won't blow up," the soldier told him, "but you have to keep moving your canteen cup around, so the flame doesn't stay in one spot. C-4 burns with a very hot flame, and it will melt metal." This was the first time Wayne lit a chunk of plastic explosive with a match; it made him feel very uncomfortable, even though he knew that it would only explode with another explosive, like a blasting cap. The C-4 burned very hot, but he was careful and kept moving his canteen cup over the flame. He was amazed at how fast the beans heated up.

After the lunch break they moved out again, and after an hour on the trail, a smell began to fill the air. Word was passed back that a village was ahead. The GI behind Wayne was a short-timer, and he confirmed that it was definitely the smell of a village. Wayne was surprised at how far away the village was from when they first started smelling it because it took a long time to actually reach the village. When they got to the village, the tiny community of grass huts was completely deserted, and the order was given to burn the village to the ground. Flames and smoke towered above the little village as the line of soldiers continued down the trail that had brought them. Wayne wondered what the villagers would do, way out here in the jungle, with no place to live.

Just outside the village, a few thousand meters up the trail, a shot rang out. Everyone dove off the trail and took cover in the jungle beside the trail as a barrage of shots resounded through the jungle. Word was passed back that the front of the column was pinned down by a sniper and for the M79 to move up to the front of the line and to report to the captain. That was Wayne with the M79 grenade launcher, so he made his way up the trail, keeping low. As Wayne rounded a turn in the trail, another shot rang out and Wayne heard the bullet cut through the air past him. "Get down!" a GI yelled from the side of the trail, and Wayne hit the ground hard. He low-crawled the rest of the way to the captain and reported in. The Captain pointed out a boulder on the side of a small hill where the sniper was, and Wayne estimated the distance to be two hundred and eighty meters.

The M79 had its advantages over the other weapons—the same advantage the Native Americans had over the cowboys. Wayne could shoot in a high arch, like an arrow, and drop a round right behind the boulder and take out the sniper. That's just what he intended to do. He fired a round and carefully watched it go. It looked just like a golf ball, and Wayne tracked it so he could make a correction on the next shot. Wayne had worked as a caddy at the local golf course back home, so he had a good eye for following a golf ball and knowing where it hit so he could find it. The shot was close, but it exploded in front of the boulder. He had to put one behind the boulder to have a chance of killing the sniper. He made a correction on the next round and it exploded in just the right place, to the side of and behind the boulder. No more was heard from the sniper. The captain had them move carefully to the hill in case this was an ambush, or there was another sniper. When they reached the body behind the boulder, Wayne looked down into the open eyes of the dead sniper but, just as the horror of the situation started to sink in, a cheer went up. "The cherry has a body count! The cherry has a body count!" Wayne was the hero of the day, and that was the last time anyone ever called him a cherry. Wayne would now be known as Cox.

Everyone was known by their last name because in the rear area everyone's last name was clearly printed above their right jungle-jacket pocket. The captain confirmed to Wayne that he now had a body count and that he had earned his CIB (Combat Infantry Badge) because the sniper's last shot was directed at him. He patted Wayne on the shoulder and told him that he had done a good job. Wayne just wished he hadn't seen the dead man's eyes.

Within a week, two of the squads in Cox's company were already down to three men. Cox felt lucky that the squad he was in still had four men. A squad is the smallest element in the army. The size of a squad depends on what the squad does. A squad can be as big as nine or ten soldiers, but in the jungle, they ranged from only four soldiers all the way down to two soldiers. The only reason that the squads would go below four men was soldiers being killed, wounded, or medevaced out of the jungle sick. The importance of having four men at each position was that at night each man would get three-quarters of a night's sleep, or six hours. With three-man positions, everyone would get only two-thirds of a night's sleep, and with two-man positions, which was very common, each man would get only four staggered hours of sleep. Then, of course, there were the exceptions to the rule, like when Charlie would attack at night, or have you pinned down all night, or you might be on an all-night ambush, or a forced all-night march to "surprise" Charlie. In these cases, the soldiers would get no sleep at all.

Everyone became very excited as word spread that the mission would end the next day. They were all in good spirits, and the day cooperated by providing no contact with the enemy. In fact, a day in the boonies couldn't be any better than this day. During the heat of the day they came to a stream, and the captain had the men set up a perimeter with the stream going right through the middle. Everyone got a turn swimming in the deep part while the others guarded. No one had had a shower since "P" training, so the swim was a welcome relief. Some of the guys just swam and frolicked in the water for their turn, while some brought a bar of soap and used their turn to bathe. Cox just swam, and even did a cannonball off of the root of a tree up on the bank. This was the most refreshed that Cox had felt the entire mission, and the swim left him feeling a joy that was rare for the boonies. It was the joy a young boy would feel. The kind that made you squeal with glee—but that would not be a proper way to act for a man with a CIB.

That evening they set up camp on top of a small hill, and everyone settled in for another night of guard duty–interrupted sleep. Cox had done his first guard duty and was sound asleep when a claymore mine exploded on the other side of the perimeter. Firing broke out around the perimeter as the sleeping soldiers went from sleep to full alert with the aid of a big dose of adrenaline. There was a lot of confusion, and soon everyone was yelling, "Cease fire!" as word slowly spread above the sound of the bullets. It was very easy to get everyone to start firing; one shot or explosion would cause everyone to fire, but to get them all to stop was much harder. This was partly because the noise of the firing was hard to communicate over, and partly because firing was so much fun.

Soon a sergeant came around to each guard position and told everyone what had happened. Harris was dead. He had been taking his turn on guard duty for his position and he had gone out in front of his position to take a dump, but he had not gone out straight, so he had gotten out in front of the position next to his. The guard there had heard him out front, thought he was Charlie, and he had set off the claymore mine, killing Harris. This news seemed to hit everyone hard. They all knew that Charlie was trying to kill them and that the jungle was trying to kill them, but Harris's death had made it clear that "friendly fire" might beat Charlie and the jungle to it.

The excitement level had been tempered by the death of Harris, so the first order of business was a Field Cross Service. The Field Cross was a ceremony for fallen brothers performed in the boonies. The fallen soldier's rifle was stuck bayoneted into the ground with the dead soldier's helmet on top. The ceremony usually consisted of a few kind words and a moment of silence in honor of a friend. Brooks cried through the whole ceremony. No one had said anything, but Cox figured that Brooks was probably the one who set off the claymore mine. At first light they moved out, with Harris in a body bag on a makeshift stretcher. Cox was glad that he didn't have to help carry Harris's body, because he didn't think he could have done it without crying.

After the ceremony, they carried Harris until they found a clear, level area big enough to land several Hueys in. Soon they were being picked up for an amusement park–like helicopter ride. Cox loved helicopter rides with everyone sitting in the open doorways with their feet dangling out on both sides of the helicopter. And then, when they were coming in for a landing, everyone with something to hold on to would step outside the Huey and come in riding the landing rails. Somehow the joy was gone from this helicopter ride. Cox could only think of Harris and how Harris would never see his family back in the States again. At the end of the helicopter ride, they were all deposited in an even bigger open area than they had been choppered out of. It was obvious it had been someone's home, because a bombed-out farm house was right in the middle. This was their forward base camp—that is, it would be as soon as they finished building it.

Cox's First Forward Base Camp

CHAPTER 3

THE FORWARD BASE CAMP

Row after row of pup tents were set up for each company. Cox teamed up for the two-man tent with a guy in his squad who he had become good friends with, a guy named Phil Johnson. Johnson was from Boston, and Cox got a kick out of Johnson "talking funny." They set up the tent, but that was just the beginning. With a two-man pup tent, they had to crawl in and lie down because there was not enough room to stand up. So, as instructed, they started digging a foxhole inside the tent. From just inside the walls of the tent, they dug straight down for three or four feet. They leveled the floor and then dug a trench from the front of the tent to the back that was two-feet wide and two-feet deep. This made two daytime couches or two nighttime beds, one on each side of the ditch, and the ditch provided a place to put their feet while sitting on their beds.

Next, they dug a small trench around the outside of the tent to lead rainwater away from the tent, so no water would get inside the tent and down into the foxhole. They were now protected from enemy fire while they slept, and they had a good bunker to fight from just in case the base camp was attacked. As Cox looked around, he saw a miniature city of pup tents, plus big tents for the officers, and the supply tent and even a mess hall tent. He was amazed at how fast the open field had been turned into a forward base camp. Cox and Johnson got settled into the tent and each sat on their "bunk," but it wasn't long before they realized that it wasn't much fun sitting in a hole.

A sergeant came around passing out paper, pens, and envelopes, coming just short of ordering everyone to write home. Both Cox and Johnson wrote a letter home before coming out of their tent to check out the base camp.

The base camp had every modern convenience, except they weren't modern, and they were far from convenient. It even had a shower.

Forward Base Camp Shower

The first place that Cox and Johnson went, after writing home, was to the bombed-out farm house that had been turned into a club with a big cooler full of warm water and warm cans of American beer. Well, they had everything but ice, and it didn't seem to matter. Cox and Johnson totally enjoyed a warm beer sitting under a parachute awning that provided shaded seating beside the bombed-out farm house. Most of the house was completely bombed out, but a back room was pretty much intact. The "bartender" sat on top of the cooler as Cox ordered two beers. He hopped down and opened the cooler and fished out two Miller High Life beers. Cox took the beers to the table out under the parachute and laughed as he told Johnson that even though they were living the low life, the bartender had given them high life beer. Despite the fact that it was a very lame joke, Johnson laughed.

Cox was ready to go as soon as he finished his beer because his mind kept wondering about what happened to the family who used to live here. They must have been proud of their home. Even after being bombed out it was still better than the grass hooches that many folks lived in.

Cox Ordering Beer at the Club Stocked with Free, Warm Beer

This was to be a three–day stand down or break from combat. The bombed-out club, the warm beer, and the primitive shower—none of that was looked at negatively because, compared to the boonies, this was heaven.

At night they even showed segments of movies between the projector breaking down and the film breaking. But again, none of this mattered to the soldiers; it just provided a chance to yell and chant and throw things at the poor soul who was running the projector. They never did get to see the end of the James Bond movie that was showing that night. Right in the middle of the movie, someone from an adjoining company area fired a hand flare into the audience, and it scattered the movie viewers as it crashed into a very recently vacated bench.

The hand flare was a metal cylinder about a foot long and of a two-inch diameter. To fire it you would take the cap off the top and slide it onto the bottom of the cylinder. The inside bottom of the cap had a spike sticking up that, when slammed into the bottom of the flare, set it off. Flares were meant to be fired up into the air, and the lit flare would have a small parachute to let it drift slowly to the ground while lighting the entire area. However, when fired along the ground, it became a fun weapon.

Well, so much for the movie—a big hand flare battle erupted between company "B", or Bravo Company, and Cox and Johnson's Company "C," better known as Cobra Company. Normally, "C" Company would be called Charlie Company, but "Charlie" was already taken by the enemy, so they were officially Cobra Company. The "Great Hand Flare Battle of 1966" was soon over, and Cobra Company won. Two pup tents in Bravo Company were burned to the ground, and only one was burned in Cobra Company. The best part of the hand flare battle was that no one got in trouble, no one tried to stop it, and no one even tried to find out who was involved or responsible; it wasn't even officially mentioned. I guess they knew that boys that may die tomorrow play very hard today.

All too soon the party was over, and they were packing their backpacks to go back out in the boonies. This time the helicopter ride didn't turn out to be as much fun, as they were delivered to a hot LZ. Hot meant that they were receiving enemy fire as they came in for a landing; and landing, to the helicopter pilots, meant swooping down just close enough to the ground to avoid broken bones before swooping back up again. For

Airborne troops, the chopper pilots knew they were trained to land hard, so at a hot LZ they would come even less close to the ground before swooping back up. The troops were highly motivated to get out of the chopper, because if the chopper swooped back up and you were still on board, you would be guilty of desertion under fire, and they could give you the death penalty for that.

Being under fire, the chopper pilots didn't swoop low enough, and one of the guys suffered a broken ankle and was medevaced right back out again. When Cox heard about this he was just a little bit jealous because he knew that the pain of a broken ankle was not nearly the amount of pain that humpin' in the boonies would give you every day. In a few years, the design of the combat backpack would be changed to put the weight of the backpack on the hips instead of the shoulders; but for now, the excruciating shoulder pain was just part of the job.

Cox and Johnson leapt from the helicopter and hit the ground hard. They were receiving heavy enemy fire from small arms and mortars, so they and the others from the chopper headed straight to a clump of trees for cover. Cox could hear the bullets ripping through the air all around him as he ran. Just as they were entering the clump of trees, they heard a huge crash.

The squad leader, Sergeant Kelly, yelled, "Chopper down!" and he ordered the squad to secure the crash site. They had to leave their cover no sooner than they had gotten there and go back out into the middle of the open area where the chopper was lying on its side and bullets were as thick as mosquitoes in the air. They circled the downed chopper, and the medic tried to help the crash victims as everyone else pumped as much lead as they could into the surrounding jungle. The only way they could use the downed chopper for cover while in a crossfire was to lie down with the chopper behind them, like spokes coming out of it, and fire like hell into the jungle.

A Cobra gunship—heavily armed helicopter—had arrived, and it began decimating the edge of the jungle with rockets. The noise was deafening, but somehow, above it all, Cox heard the thud and looked to the side in time to see Johnson lying lifeless the ground. Johnson's helmet had rolled away from his head, exposing a clean bullet hole in one side of his head;

and the other side of his head was completely gone. Cox didn't remember anything more until he "kind of woke up" sitting on the ground and holding Johnson with the captain standing over him and ordering two other soldiers to take Johnson away from him. Cox was covered with Johnson's blood, but he was too dazed to notice for a while.

The gunship had run off the enemy, and everyone was running around trying to help the wounded. They had been hit very hard. The next few days were a blur to Cox and, despite being offered a clean uniform several times, he would not take off the bloodstained clothes for two days. He did not want this mission to end because he knew he would have to write Johnson's parents the letter that he and Johnson had promised each other. He also owed a visit to Johnson's parents, but Cox didn't think he would live long enough to go home and keep that promise—and he didn't even care.

Cox didn't talk much after Johnson's death, and he seemed to always have a mean look on his face. When they would engage the enemy, Cox would fight savagely and fearlessly, trying to extract some revenge for Johnson at every opportunity. But with every Viet Cong he killed, he was disappointed that it offered no relief. The new replacements that came to replace the dead and wounded never got to really know Cox. He was unable to risk losing another friend, so he had none. Cox would never return to "normal," but he did become a little less antisocial, and he was promoted to Sergeant E-5 and made a squad leader. Now he was called Sergeant Cox, and that was just as well, because "Wayne" had died with Phil. Sergeant Cox made a good squad leader. He knew what to do in every situation, and he was definitely "combat hardened."

Sergeant Cox and his squad were breaking camp at their guard position one morning when the all-too-familiar sound of Charlie's AK-47 barked out above the noise of the jungle and everyone hit the ground. It soon became clear that Charlie had hit and run, because no more was heard from the AK-47. The captain came over right away and had Sergeant Cox take two squads and chase Charlie. They moved out at once. They had gone only a few hundred meters when they spotted Charlie ahead just in time to see him disappear into the thick jungle. Sergeant Cox didn't like this at all, and he suspected a possible ambush ahead, so he passed the word along to the others to be extra alert. When they got to where Charlie had disappeared into the jungle, they went very slowly. It wasn't long before they came close to the edge of the jungle, where it opened into a big clearing. On the far side of the big clearing was a hill strewn with boulders. This looked bad. This was a perfect place for an ambush.

Sergeant Cox called up the RTO (radio man) and called in an air strike on the hillside across the clearing. Then, before the jets could arrive, Charlie opened up, unexpectedly, from both the right and the left flank of Sergeant Cox and his men. Everyone hit the ground and crawled into a rough line, alternating directions of fire to both flanks. The radio man said the jets wanted a white flare on the enemy, so Sergeant Cox chambered a white smoke round and dropped it right in the middle of where the firing was coming from on the right flank. A plume of white smoke rose toward the sky, and he fired another white smoke round to the enemy on the left flank. Then the earth shook. A jet had dropped something that made a very big explosion on the right flank and then another on the left and one on the hill in front of them. The smoke rounds had done their job well. Those two explosions marked the end of the enemy fire, and, after a half a minute or so, Sergeant Cox called a cease-fire as he noticed there was no longer any incoming fire. Two more explosions happened, one on each side of the squad, after the cease-fire but before Sergeant Cox could call off the air strike on the radio.

Then they divided into squads and checked out both flanks where the enemy had fired from and found a dead Viet Cong on the left flank and nothing on the right. Then they checked out the hill. The side of the hill facing the clearing was really torn up from the jets, but on the back side of the hill they found a tunnel coming out. Sergeant Cox had the cave blown up with a half-block of C-4 to prevent it from being easily used again. Sergeant Cox figured that the other end of the tunnel had let out behind one of the boulders on the ambush side of the hill. And that if they had chased Charlie out into the open clearing, one or two VC would have opened up from behind the boulders to draw them further out into the clearing, and the VC would have ducked into the tunnel and come out on the other side of the hill. Meanwhile, the main force of Viet Cong would have opened fire on the Americans from both flanks, and that would have been very bad if this happened in the clearing without cover. They had foiled a well-planned and deadly ambush.

For the next few days, they hunted Charlie without much success. Then, after having patrolled half the day, the captain had them reverse direction, and they returned to the exact camp where they had camped the night before. They were all shocked to find that every hole that they had dug the night before, be it for burying trash or for taking a crap, had been dug up by Charlie. Anything that Charlie could use against American troops that had been thrown out or lost was now in his hands. Charlie had been following, and the American troops were constantly losing stuff. A magazine of M16 ammo slips out of an ammo pouch as a soldier slides down a steep hill, and Charlie has ammo for the M16 that he took from a dead American. This was not good, and it kind of pissed everyone off to know that Charlie had been playing with them.

They camped at the dug-up site again that night, and early the next morning they were off; only this time they were expecting Charlie. They found a good place and set up a rare daytime ambush. Sure enough, two hours later, along came three VC following the trail right to the ambush site. They only had one old rifle between them, and they were very thin and ragged-looking. One VC was walking on the trail to follow the American boot prints, and the other two were, one on each side of the trail, looking for anything the GIs had dropped. Someone started firing when the three men were in the ambush area, and it sounded like a war started.

The Viet Cong looked like one guy with a BB gun could have taken them out, but enough lead was pumped into them to kill fifty men. After the bodies hit the ground, the firing continued, and the bodies did a jerky dance of death until the firing stopped. To the amazement of everyone, one of the VC was still clinging to life when they came down to check out the damage done. Stewart put an M16 round in the VC's forehead and walked away.

No one said a word, but anyone with revenge issues had to feel better after that. There was a thin line between combat and murder, and no one spoke of it, because after a while it was all the same—combat of course.

The jungle would take its toll on the GIs even when Charlie was lying low. Everything from mountain-climbing accidents to illness from a thousand sources would constantly deplete the ranks. Sergeant Cox was about to be taken out of action by a terrible threat in the jungle. Not by a tiger or a snake or by Charlie, but by the lowly mosquito.

Pleased to be Anywhere other than in the Jungle, even the Hospital

CHAPTER 4

THE HOSPITAL

The next day Sergeant Cox felt very bad as he went down the trail, and he asked to see the medic. The medic told the captain that Sergeant Cox had malaria and needed to be medevaced out. The jungle was thick, but they finally got to a place where a hole in the jungle, big enough for a helicopter to land. Soon Sergeant Cox was being loaded onto a chopper, and up they went. He held on long enough to know that the chopper had not received incoming fire as it took off. Sergeant Cox was relieved, not for his own safety but that Charlie was not in the area of his troops on the ground. Sergeant Cox slipped into unconsciousness.

He woke up in the hospital in a real bed with clean white sheets. He started to look around at the other beds in his ward just as his high temperature sent him back into unconsciousness. That was enough for him to know he wasn't in heaven. When his fever broke, he still slept for two days. It seemed like his system was trying to catch up from weeks of sleep deprivation in the jungle. When he did catch up on his sleep, he felt weak, but good, considering what he had been through. The relief of being out of the jungle was tempered by his concern for his squad still out in the boonies.

Sergeant Cox lived for the next hospital meal. Real food, even army food, was so much better than C-rations. In the jungle, when Sergeant Cox would get re-supplied with his case of C-rations, he always ate the good stuff first. Then, when all the good stuff was gone, he would be stuck eating meals like canned pork slices in their own juices, which back home he would have considered to be a poor-quality dog food. No more fruit cocktail, pound cake, or beans 'n franks until the next re-supply.

Cox was six feet tall, his body weight was down to one hundred and thirty pounds and he looked like walking death, but there was nothing wrong with his appetite. As relaxing as it was having nothing to do but eat and rest, Sergeant Cox told his doctor that he needed to get back to his squad ASAP. But the doctor said that because of his body weight, he would have to be sent to a convalescent center in Cam Ranh Bay for two weeks. Sergeant Cox objected and told the doctor that his squad needed him, but the doctor would have none of it. The doctor told Sergeant Cox that he couldn't send him back into the boonies at his low body weight and that he would be more help to his squad when he was healthy. A convalescent center sounded like an "old folk's home" to Sergeant Cox, but he knew he had never been as thin as he was, so he resigned himself to a two-week tour of duty at the convalescent center.

Sergeant Cox was transferred to Cam Ranh Bay by helicopter and, for the first time, he rode in a chopper that had doors and no machine-gun-ners; and he didn't like it. But, as uneasy as being unarmed made him feel, they arrived at Cam Ranh Bay without receiving any enemy fire.

After a few days of eating and resting, he ventured out onto the compound and discovered a dirt road that led through a thin strip of jungle and down to the South China Sea, which Sergeant Cox could see through the gap that the road made through the strip of jungle. The trees in the thin strip of jungle were full of monkeys, and he stopped to watch them for a while. Then, when he broke through the jungle strip, he was amazed. He came on a scene that he would have thought was California if he hadn't known better.

Skiing, Boating, Swimming, and Sunbathing at Cam Ranh Bay

Sergeant Cox had never seen anything like this in Vietnam and, for just a brief second, he wondered if joining the infantry might have been a big mistake and that maybe he should have asked to be trained to be a life guard.

The two weeks went by fast at Cam Ranh Bay, and then Sergeant Cox boarded a helicopter to be flown back to his unit, a full eleven pounds heavier than when he had arrived. This helicopter Sergeant Cox liked much better than the last one. This one had no side doors and had an M60 machine gunner on each side. He was glad to get back to his unit without being shot at, and the two M60s made him feel safe. The helicopter brought Sergeant Cox to the forward base camp, where he was equipped with his full combat gear. He would be going back out in the boonies the next morning on a resupply chopper. This gave him time to write letters home.

The next morning Sergeant Cox was standing by the helicopter that was to take him back out in the boonies before the crew even got there. He had to wait for the chopper to be loaded, which seemed to take a long time to him. Finally, the chopper lifted off, and Sergeant Cox strangely felt like he was going home. He had missed his men and the excitement level of the boonies. In the hospital, he was just one of many nobodies, but in the boonies, he was a leader of men, and he made life and death decisions almost daily.

CHAPTER 5

BACK OUT IN THE BOONIES

When he arrived at his unit in the boonies, they were set up in a perimeter around the landing zone and were waiting for their resupply and hoping for mail from home. Everyone was glad to see him, but even more glad that the chopper he came in on also brought resupply and mail from home. Then, after packing the new supplies into their backpacks and reading and burning their mail that had come in on the chopper with Sergeant Cox, they were ready to go. They were instructed to always burn their mail after reading it because if Charlie got the mail he might write to their folks. No one had ever told them what Charlie would say to their parents if he wrote to them, but those were the orders: read and burn your mail. Then the moment came.

Moving Out Down the Trail, or Humpin' in the Boonies

It was time to move out, and Sergeant Cox had never felt as at home in the jungle as he did when he gave the order, "Move out, and keep it spread out!" There was something about going from high school to war, where life and death decisions were made almost every day, that had changed Sergeant Cox from a boy to a man. His squad felt a little safer with Sergeant Cox back on the job.

McKinney, Stewart, and Jackson were Sergeant Cox's squad, and they were all excellent boonie rats. McKinney was from Oklahoma, and he spoke slowly as if he was always planning ahead what to say. He had red hair and freckles, and he was over six feet tall. He was a good rifleman, and Sergeant Cox could, as with all of his men, depend on McKinney in hard times. Stewart was from Ohio. He was to go home in a month and a half and was getting more anxious the shorter he got. He was not only a short-timer, he was also short in stature and patience, and he hated to be pinned down. He would rather charge the enemy over open terrain with no cover than to be pinned down in one place. He had black hair and seemed to need a shave twenty minutes after shaving. This was unusual because most of the guys hardly needed to shave at all. And then there was Jackson. Jackson was from Mississippi, and he spoke with a slow southern drawl, but that was the only thing slow about him. He kept two M16 magazines taped together end to end so he could reload very fast in a fire fight. He was a black man with very dark skin. He was thin and tall, and moved like a cat when traversing rough terrain.

The first few days were very hard for Sergeant Cox while his body adjusted to the tremendous workload of humpin' in the boonies. But the boonies weren't into waiting, so, on the third day, within an hour of starting out in the morning, they started smelling a village. Half an hour after that, Sergeant Cox really felt right at home; they were pinned down by sniper fire coming from the village.

Sergeant Cox and his M79 grenade launcher were needed again. The M79 grenade launcher was called the commander's "hip-pocket artillery." The captain called for Sergeant Cox and his M79 to move to the front of the column. They were receiving enemy fire from several of the hooches in the small village. Sergeant Cox found cover where he could get a good shot at the first hooch. He needed to put an HE round through the window, so it would explode inside the hooch. They had been receiving fire from two or three of the hooches, but when the first round from Sergeant Cox's M79 exploded inside the first hooch, not another shot came from the village. The Viet Cong fled out the back of the village and were gone—all except the Viet Cong who was in the hooch that Sergeant Cox had fired into. He was still there, and he was dead. Killing was not so much for revenge for Johnson's death now as it had been; it was just part of his job, and Sergeant Cox always tried to do a good job.

Usually in the States when you went visiting and no one was home you would leave a note, but leaving notes was not a military thing to do, so they searched the deserted village and then burned it to the ground.

The next day they were moving around the side of a hill when a big firefight broke out. The enemy was on the side of an adjacent hillside and had already taken cover. Soon after diving for cover, the Americans returned fire. Two men had been hit before getting to cover, and the medic crawled past Sergeant Cox's position on his way to tend to the wounded men. It looked pretty much like a standoff, although the Americans had a decided advantage in firepower, so the captain called in a Cobra gunship helicopter. The enemy was too close to call in the Phantom jets, but a gunship could blast the enemy without creating enough shrapnel to threaten the American troops.

The firing back and forth continued until the gunship arrived. It was awesome! The gunship opened up with a big machine gun that fired M79 HE rounds all hooked together in a belt. Yes, the rounds that explode when they hit the target, each with a three-meter killing radius. The Cobra gunship blanketed the hillside where the enemy was with a wide path of M79 HE rounds, creating so many explosions that nothing could survive in its path.

As the gunship worked out, the Americans kept their sights on the enemy hillside and shot anyone who came out from their cover and tried to run away. It was a massacre—wait, that's an unacceptable military term—it was a great victory. Of course, anyone who walked across the enemy hillside and saw the aftermath of the Cobra gunship's work would have thought it was a massacre.

They walked for a day and a half and found themselves in a forest with a very tall canopy. They were following a pretty big and well-traveled trail but hadn't engaged any enemy. Then they all heard it coming—that whistling sound that they all had made as children playing war to simulate a rocket before the explosion. It was artillery, and it was American artillery—friendly fire. Everyone dove to the ground except Sergeant Cox. His backpack was so heavy with extra HE rounds that he had trouble getting back up if he was laid out on the ground, so Sergeant Cox just squatted down. A barrage of explosions happened in the treetops above them, raining shrapnel down on the troops below. The ground right in front of Sergeant Cox was hit by a big piece of shrapnel, throwing dirt all over him. That was right where he would have been laying if he had hit the ground like everyone else. Realizing that he was okay, Sergeant Cox looked to his left and saw that McKinney was hit. His leg was pretty bad.

"Medic!" yelled Sergeant Cox, but the medic was busy with two men in the front of the column who had also been hit. A third man was dead. The captain had obviously gotten through on the radio to stop the bombardment, because the explosions had stopped. Sergeant Cox had already made a tourniquet from his bandana and was tightening it with a stick above the torn-up part of McKinney's leg. McKinney was pretty shook up, so Sergeant Cox tried to soothe him with some kind words.

"You son of a bitch, you've gone and got yourself a million-dollar wound. You son of a bitch!" the sergeant said, grinning down at McKinney. McKinney grinned back through the pain. Everyone wanted a million-dollar wound. That was a wound that got you sent home, but could be fixed so you ended up pretty much back to normal.

They found a clearing, and the captain had a crew with machetes chop down a few narrow, but tall, trees to make a landing zone for a medevac chopper. The dead man and the three wounded men were soon lifting off in the medevac chopper, and Sergeant Cox would never see McKinney again.

That night they set up an ambush on a major trail. They set up the perimeter in a big circle with the trail going right through the middle. The two positions that were directly on the trail as it entered and again as it left the perimeter were given a night vision scope. Sergeant Cox's position was one of the two directly on the trail. While Sergeant Cox was taking his turn on guard duty, he stared into the night vision scope until he thought he would go blind. Back then night vision scopes were new, and not very good. They were called starlight scopes because they used the faint light from the stars to light up the view through the scope. But the view looked like a totally snowy or static television screen. You couldn't make out what anything was unless it moved. If something moved, you would see a part of the static move, and you could clearly see the outline of whatever was moving. When whatever was moving stopped, it became invisible again.

Sergeant Cox had been staring through the scope until he was starting to need to take frequent breaks from staring at the static. He would look away and squeeze his eyes tightly shut and then return quickly to looking through the scope again. Just as he returned to looking through the scope after a short break, there was Charlie slowly coming around the bend in the trail. Then there were two more VC, and then three all in a row. Their outlines were unmistakable in the starlight scope. He could see their slanted hats, and they each were definitely carrying weapons that Sergeant Cox assumed were AK-47s. Sergeant Cox waited until it became clear that there were only three of them and, when they were close enough, he set off the claymore mine that was set up in the middle of the trail and opened fire. The open fire part was unnecessary, because the claymore took out all three VC. Nonetheless, as usual, everyone opened fire from every position around the entire perimeter. Sure enough, they found three dead Viet Cong, and they all three had AK-47s that would never be fired at an American again.

The next day was their last day of the mission, and everyone was excited because they were going to the rear base camp at Phan Rang. This was the Las Vegas of rear areas for the 101st Airborne. They were in for some serious party time.

CHAPTER 6

THE REAR BASE CAMP

The chopper ride to the rear base camp was a joy—no incoming fire, and beautiful scenery all the way. As usual, as soon as they got to the rear area the pens, paper, and envelopes were passed around for everyone to write home. Sergeant Cox knew that they wanted everyone to write home before they were all loaded. The rear area meant some serious partying was in order. They didn't need stamps to write home, because the postage was free for the troops. They simply wrote the word "Free" on the envelope where the stamp would go.

The rear base camp at Phan Rang was a huge round compound that was divided in half. Half was the air force and half was the 101st Airborne. The difference was striking. On the air force side, they had paved streets and concrete barracks with an air conditioner in each window. The paved streets were lined with football-sized rocks that were, for some unknown reason, all painted white. The NCO (Non-Commissioned Officers) club had ice cold beer and live entertainment.

In contrast, on the 101st Airborne Division side they had dirt roads with no painted rocks, wooden barracks, tents with no air conditioning, and the club was a dump. Granted, it was a standing-room-only dump, but a dump nonetheless. The beer was all the American brands, but "toned down" in alcohol content from six percent to three-point-two percent. That might have worked on the air force side, but on the army side they made up for the low alcohol content by drinking twice as much. This way, they figured that they were point-four percent ahead. The attitude on the air force side was much more laid back than on the army side. The army guys coming in from the boonies were into some serious partying, and they played rough.

Sergeant Cox kept mostly to himself but braved the crowded club to get drunk every night. He mailed a letter to his high school buddy that he had written out in the boonies. He had written the letter and then he had reached out and grabbed a hand full of jungle leaves and stuffed them into the envelope with the letter. Then on the back of the envelope he had written, "Free sample of Vietnam jungle inside!" His friend back home, Bucky, would get a kick out of that.

Sergeant Cox was now a short-timer, and he would be going home soon. He had one more month to go before his tour was up. Being a short-timer made you special to the other GIs, but it also had a dark side. There was no shortage of stories about short-timers getting blown away just days before they were to go home, like the probably made-up, but often repeated, story of the jet taking troops home and crashing. So, a building paranoia was often a big part of being a short-timer.

The shorter Sergeant Cox got, the more frightening it was for him. Now it was time to go back out in the boonies, and Sergeant Cox knew that if anything was going to happen to him to keep him from going home, the jungle was where it would happen.

This was to be a three-day mission and, for the first time since his first mission, Sergeant Cox dreaded going out in the boonies. They loaded onto the choppers, and Sergeant Cox hoped that the LZ wouldn't be hot. They landed without receiving any incoming fire, and soon there he was, heading out down a jungle trail and into the unknown once again.

The entire first day they expected to get hit, because signs of Charlie were everywhere. Then they came upon a trail that intersected with the trail that they were on. The trail that they came upon was big. It was twice as wide as the trail they had come in on, and it was well-traveled. The big trail even had thin bicycle tracks. This was how the Viet Cong moved big loads that were too heavy for a man to carry—letting the bicycle carry the weight.

The captain stopped the column while he called in to report the well-traveled trail. They must have told the captain over the radio to check out the big trail, because that's what they did. They hadn't gone very far when the two explosions happened. Sergeant Cox and his men were back in the column, but he knew it was a Bouncing Betty booby trap from how close the explosions were apart—first a small explosion, followed closely by a big one. A Bouncing Betty was an anti-personnel mine that exploded once to throw the big explosive charge up into the air, where it then exploded again. When an explosion happens from just below the surface of the ground, like with a land mine, the blast goes up from the ground in a "V" shape. You could be lying on the ground fairly near the explosion and the main blast would miss you. You may go deaf from the explosion, but the shrapnel would likely miss you as well. But an explosion several feet above the ground would spray shrapnel in every direction, and it would have a much bigger killing radius.

The word was passed back that Private Cole had been killed and for everyone to take cover at the side of the trail. Soon they heard the sound of a chopper, and Cole's body was taken away for his last chopper ride. Everyone was, of course, on full alert as they began moving out again. They moved much more slowly because now the path was being checked closely for booby traps. They were on the big trail for over an hour when the point man opened fire, emptying a twenty-round clip from his M16. The point man had seen a unit of Viet Cong coming down the trail toward him. When he opened fire, the Viet Cong turned and ran back up the trail the way they had come. The entire column started running down the trail, chasing the Viet Cong.

Usually a full backpack was a good thing—lots of food to eat and nothing in short supply. But to run with full combat equipment was not fun. They ran until Sergeant Cox thought his heart would explode, and then all hell broke lose. They had been led into an ambush from AK-47s and mortars, and when Sergeant Cox reached the front of the column, he found a terrible sight. It was devastating to see so many dead and wounded Americans.

The ambush site was strewn with bodies, and many were crying and moaning. One GI was screaming because he had looked at his legs and they weren't there anymore. Soon he was quiet, but he died with a look of horror on his face that Sergeant Cox would never forget.

Two squads chased after the Viet Cong, but soon returned without any success, while Sergeant Cox did anything he could to help the medic tend to the wounded. The medic was frantically busy while shouting directions to Sergeant Cox and several other non-medics who were helping him, mostly by stopping the bleeding with tourniquets while the medic worked on the worst wounded who would die without quick attention. This was a very bad day in the boonies, and that was saying a lot, because even a day with no contact with the enemy was a bad day just because it was so painful and exhausting.

They had immediately set up a perimeter around the ambush site while the wounded were tended to. Sergeant Cox's hands were shaking badly, but he was able to work around that to help his wounded brothers. One GI, Private Michael T. Mills, made Sergeant Cox promise to tell his parents that he loved them, and he even wrote down their address before dying in Sergeant Cox's arms. "James and Rosa Mills" was written in shaky handwriting, followed by their address.

These boys had been turned into hardened combat soldiers, but most returned to being boys as they died. They just wanted their moms, and that was one thing that Sergeant Cox could do nothing about.

The rest of that day everyone was very solemn, but the next day they all were mad. They wanted revenge for their fallen brothers. It was a good thing that they never came upon a village that day, or the My Lai massacre might have had a different name.

There were a lot of Viet Cong in this area of operation, and daily contact with the enemy went on for the next three weeks. This was the longest three-day mission that Sergeant Cox had ever been on. It lasted for three weeks and two days, until finally they were chopping a hole in the jungle big enough for the choppers to land. Everyone was fairly relaxed, but as soon as the choppers arrived they started receiving enemy fire from all sides of the American's position. They were surrounded. The extraction helicopters were unable to land because of heavy enemy fire, so two Cobra gunships were called in.

Word was passed around the perimeter to throw yellow smoke grenades if you had them. This defined where the Americans were, and the gunships began a devastating attack on the surrounding area. This was a very close call. If the Americans weren't being extracted that day, they would have probably been wiped out, because the enemy had them completely surrounded: and this was not Viet Cong, wearing black pajamas and carrying antique rifles; they were NVA, with uniforms and AK-47s, and they were nearly as well-equipped as the Americans.

The Cobra gunships were a godsend; well, to the American troops, that is. The gunships delivered a thunderous attack on the enemy positions. Soon the extraction helicopters could come in, and no one was glad to get out of there more than Sergeant Cox. When Sergeant Cox reached the chopper, the door-gunner reached out to help him aboard and, as he pulled Sergeant Cox up, he shouted in his ear, "You guys were in a world of shit out there!" he said with a big grin on his face. Sergeant Cox grinned back, and the chopper lifted off. They received some sporadic enemy fire from below as they rose up out of the jungle, but no one was hit, and the joy of getting out of the boonies began to sink in.

They were flown to the rear base camp at Phan Rang and, as they were getting settled in to a real bunk, in a real tent barracks, the captain sent for Sergeant Cox. The Captain told him that he would not be going back out in the boonies in three days with the others. He was to spend the next five days at the base camp, and on the sixth day he would be going home. Sergeant Cox was numb. He was surprised that no great feeling of joy swept over him, he just felt numb. His thoughts had returned to his dead friend Phil Johnson.

Sergeant Cox got drunk at the club every night except one. That night he stood in a long line until two o'clock in the morning. The line was to call home. This was only possible because of a network of ham radio operators that stretched halfway around the world. They would all hook together to establish a link to the US, and the closest operator to the soldier's home would call his parents and patch them through. The only difference from a regular phone was that everyone at both ends of the conversation had to say "Over" each time it was the others turn to talk, so the operator would know to throw a switch to reverse the direction of the transmission.

When Sergeant Cox heard his mother's voice on the phone his eyes began to stream tears, but he managed to not let it bleed over into his voice. He told his mother that he was coming home, but that he had to stop in two other states before he could come home. This made her cry, but he explained that he had to keep his promise to speak to the parents of both his friend Phil Johnson and of Private Michael Mills. Sergeant Cox felt that it wouldn't be fair for him to go home before making good on his promise to his two brothers who would never feel the joy of returning home from the Vietnam War. His mother was proud of her son, despite her tears.

One Last Look Before Going Home

Time passed fast. Sergeant Cox had said his goodbyes to everyone, and he was to report to the out-processing station. He couldn't shake the feeling that he was deserting his squad, Stewart and Jackson, who were already back out in the boonies.

A driver showed up with a jeep and drove Cox to out-processing, where he waded through the sand until he came to a very special place. Just before the out-processing building was the "Gateway Home." It was a covered wooden walkway that led to the building. Hanging under the roof all the way down the walkway were shingles with the names of all the major cities in the United States and how many miles away they were. Sergeant Cox paused in front of the walkway and turned to have one last look before stepping from the sand to the wooden walkway. This was the last time his feet would ever be in Vietnamese sand. As he walked down the wooden walkway, he found his hometown on a shingle, and he knew that he was only eight thousand nine hundred and twenty miles from home.

8,920 Miles from Home

II - E Company Support Battalion

CHAPTER 1

VIETNAM

The year was 1967, and it was Tony Wilson's time to do his tour of duty in Vietnam. He had been trained for combat and had requested a combat assignment, but for some reason he had been assigned to E Company Support Battalion where he would be a guard on the perimeter of the rear base camp of the 101st Airborne Division at Phan Rang, Vietnam. Wilson had a nagging feeling that his uncle Steve, who was a congressman, may have had something to do with it, even though he had told his family that he wanted no string-pulling from anyone. Tony was determined to join the army and serve in combat in the Vietnam jungle even though his family was against it. His mother had told him that he did not have to serve in the military at all. His uncle Steve could make sure that he was not called up, but Tony wanted to prove himself without help.

When he joined the army, at the recruitment center he had signed up for everything necessary to be a combat soldier out in the jungle fighting. He had signed up to be a combat paratrooper. He had chosen light weapons to be sure to be in combat, and the recruiter had told him that by making these choices he was assured to be in combat. But this was not to be.

Despite this change in assignment, he could still get a taste of combat because part of his job was to help protect the surrounding villages. His unit set up occasional night ambushes and patrols outside the perimeter of the base camp if Charlie was in the area. But this was an assignment for which anyone out in the boonies would trade a limb.

Wilson was assigned a bunk and issued all the equipment that he would need. He was busy moving in when he met Rusty Littman. Littman was a combat veteran, and this was his second tour in Vietnam. Combat had had a bad effect on Littman in a way that made him frightening to the other troops. When Littman came into the barracks, he walked straight to his bunk on the end next to a wall. Wilson's bunk was the only one next to Littman's, and Wilson now knew that that was no accident. Littman pulled a set of chopsticks out from under his pillow. He opened his footlocker and started to poke around inside the top tray with the chopsticks while calling, "Here, Herman! Here, Martha!" Wilson looked away quickly and busied himself with his equipment.

Guard Tower Number 10
(FTA Means Fuck the Army)

Wilson was assigned a bunk and issued all the equipment that he would need. He was busy moving in when he met Rusty Littman. Littman was a combat veteran, and this was his second tour in Vietnam. Combat had had a bad effect on Littman in a way that made him frightening to the other troops. When Littman came into the barracks, he walked straight to his bunk on the end next to a wall. Wilson's bunk was the only one next to Littman's, and Wilson now knew that that was no accident. Littman pulled a set of chopsticks out from under his pillow. He opened his footlocker and started to poke around inside the top tray with the chopsticks while calling, "Here, Herman! Here, Martha!" Wilson looked away quickly and busied himself with his equipment.

Wilson only needed to look in Littman's eyes to see that he wasn't right in the head. Wilson had said "Hi" when Littman came in, but Littman had not answered. Wilson gasped as Littman drew the chopsticks up from his footlocker, and at the end of the chopsticks was a squirming big black scorpion.

"There you are, Herman, what a good boy," said Littman as he carefully placed the scorpion into an opened fruitcake tin in the top tray of his footlocker. Then Littman went back to rummaging around with the chopsticks, and soon came up with another, slightly smaller, shiny black scorpion.

"There you are, Martha, what a good girl," said Littman as he carefully placed the scorpion into the fruitcake tin with Herman and put the lid on the tin. The lid of the fruit cake tin had air vent slits that had been made by stabbing a knife into it repeatedly. After securing the lid, Littman removed the tray from his footlocker and pulled out a huge bag of pot. It must have been two or three pounds of pot in a big, clear plastic bag. Without speaking, he rolled three joints on his bunk and put the big bag of pot back into his foot locker. He brushed the spilled weed off his bed onto the floor and put the top tray back in the footlocker. Then he removed the lid from the fruit cake tin. The scorpions immediately started trying to climb out of the tin as Littman closed and locked the footlocker. He stuffed the joints into his jungle jacket pocket, stuck the chopsticks back under his pillow, and looked at Wilson. Littman's eyes reflected a body count that would make Billy the Kid jealous and give a cold chill to most others, now including Wilson.

"Hey," growled Littman, "touch my stuff and you're dead." He then turned to the door and disappeared. Wilson looked at the only other GI in the barracks and asked, "Who the hell was that?"

"That's Littman. You best leave him alone; everyone does, even the officers," said a young man of medium height with reddish blond hair.

"My name's Ross, Billy Ross," he continued. "Hey, I've got the new Beatles album on reel-to-reel tape, want to hear it?"

"Sure," Wilson said, and he went over to Ross's bunk. Ross had done a tour in the boonies before volunteering for a second tour at E Company Support Battalion. He wore the coveted CIB (Combat Infantry Badge) above his parachute jump wings over the US Army patch above the left pocket of his jungle jacket. Wilson had also noticed a CIB on Littman's jungle jacket.

Ross had a big reel-to-reel tape recorder that he had bought at the PX, and he put a reel on. The music was like none Wilson had ever heard; he had heard plenty of high-fidelity music, but this was stereo. As Sgt. Pepper's Lonely Hearts Club Band played, Ross explained that Littman had done two tours of combat in the boonies and that he had flipped out. No one wanted to upset Littman because they were afraid they would find a scorpion in their bed or boot.

Littman did his guard duty, and that was all he did. He was never called on for work details, and sometimes, Ross explained, they called on Littman to replace someone who was on guard duty. This was not because the guy he was replacing was sick or something, but because there was about to be a surprise inspection and none of the officers wanted to inspect Littman's footlocker. This also alerted the guys in the barracks that a surprise inspection was going to take place. They still had to stand inspection, but it was never a surprise. None of the officers wanted anything to do with Littman or his footlocker because of Herman and Martha. Ross went on to explain that Littman was the main suspect in an ongoing mystery.

Every now and then someone would find a hidden cache of explosives somewhere in the company area, usually in one of the sandbag bunkers that were beside each barracks in case of a mortar or rocket attack. It would always be enough explosives to destroy the bunker and do a considerable amount of damage to the surrounding buildings. The explosive cache usually consisted of a number of blocks of C-4 plastic explosive, a few grenades, and anything else that Littman could get his hands on that would make a big boom. Every time a new cache of explosives was found, they would call Littman to the First Sergeant's office and accuse him of planting the explosives. No matter how much the First Sergeant yelled, Littman would always deny it, and they could never prove that he had done it without his confession. But this all went to help Littman achieve his goal—to be left alone.

Rising Dust on the Perimeter Road Means a Truck is Coming

Wilson's first time on guard duty was the next night. The guards got their equipment together and climbed up into a two-and-a-half-ton truck that had bench seating on both sides of the truck bed facing each other. Littman was there, but he did not speak. They each had ammo cans that contained hand flairs and hand grenades that they bravely tossed onto the center floor of the truck, freeing up their hands to finish climbing over the side and into the truck. Everyone laughed and joked as they made their way around the outer perimeter road. But, as they dropped off one fresh guard and picked up the one tired guard being replaced at each tower, the laughing and joking slowly disappeared. The towers were triangle-shaped, with the point facing the enemy. They were heavily armored, with big iron plates on both front sides. There were sandbags covering the roof in case of mortar or rocket attack, with a sandbag bunker at the bottom of the tower. A tall, steep ladder was the only access to the guard position, and Wilson had to climb it with his ammo can containing the hand flairs and hand grenades in one hand, wearing his backpack, plus an M16 rifle slung over his shoulder.

He learned how to climb with the ammo can and all his equipment by watching the tired guard who he was replacing climb down the ladder. Then the truck left for the long, slow drive to the next tower, leaving Wilson alone in his fortress. He was very well-armed.

M60 Machine-Gun with Ammo Belt of One Thousand Rounds

The inside of the tower was boarded over from the front where it started, back about three feet to make a table surface for the M60 machine-gun. A direction finder—a round disc with a movable pointer—was attached to the tabletop with all the directions in degrees. By pointing the pointer toward the enemy and radioing in the degrees the pointer was on and the estimated distance to the target, the artillery guys would know just where Charlie was.

Out in front of the guard tower were two rows of concertina wire and then about a one-hundred-meter area totally cleared before any cover was available for the enemy to use. Wilson checked the bush line carefully with his field glasses (binoculars) and everything looked okay.

Before dark, gunfire broke out from the next guard tower down from Wilson's. The M60 was really working out, so Wilson got on the field phone and called in by turning the little crank handle in a circle, the whole time frantically scanning the bush line in front of his position for any sign of Charlie.

Field Phone Beside Guard Tower's Armor Plating

"This is Wilson in guard tower number ten. We have a firefight at the next guard tower to my south!" Wilson yelled into the phone. A surprisingly calm voice replied that it was just Littman, and that Littman almost always found something to shoot at while on guard duty. "Just ignore it, he'll stop before he runs out of ammo," the voice on the other end said. Wilson was amazed. If he were to fire even one shot, his field phone would be ringing, and a truck would be on its way to his tower and he would be in trouble, but Littman seemed to be outside of the military's control. Littman had spent seventeen months of combat in the jungle, and no one blamed him for the way he was. He had a Purple Heart and many other medals, and his body count was rumored to be huge.

The rest of the night went quietly by, and then, after daybreak, Wilson saw dust rising in the distance on the dirt road, kicked up by the truck coming to change the guards. He gathered up all of his equipment and was ready when the truck arrived.

When they got to the next tower where Littman was, Littman climbed into the truck without a word. He tossed his ammo can into the center floor of the truck, as everyone did, but in the same hand was a dead furry animal. Littman tossed the dead animal into the center of the truck floor after his ammo can. Someone asked if that was a weasel, and another guy, who seemed to know, said that it was a mongoose.

"It's a fuckin' Viet Cong mongoose," growled Littman. He had not only shot the mongoose, but apparently, he had gone through the two rows of concertina wire and brought the carcass back from outside the perimeter. Littman sat down next to Wilson, but never said another word the whole trip back to the company area. Neither did anyone else.

The next night, Wilson was taken off the guard duty roster to take part in his first night ambush. He was nervous as he gathered his combat gear and painted broad black stripes under each eye. This could be it—his first taste of combat. This was the first time he had felt that his life was in danger since he had been in Vietnam. He was glad that Ross was going on the ambush, and Wilson stayed close to him because he knew Ross had been in combat before. Wilson strapped his M16 over his shoulder and climbed into the three-quarter-ton truck with the others. Looking around at the soldiers in the back of the army truck, Wilson noticed how combat-ready everyone looked, but it almost looked like they were going to play war because their faces looked so young.

The truck took them out the main gate and soon dropped them off. They walked until dusk before they arrived at a good ambush site. They took their positions along a ten-foot-high ridge overlooking a trail. Wilson pointed his rifle at the trail below and looked down the sites. He knew from his stateside training that he was an excellent marksman, but he didn't know if he could actually kill another man when the time came. Wilson kept this to himself, as most combat soldiers do.

Night fell, and everyone was as quiet as possible. All attention was on the trail below. They would all stay up all night waiting for the enemy to come down the trail. The jungle sounds were very scary to Wilson, because he had had no idea how much noise the bugs and critters made all night long. Not only that, but he had no idea what was making the noises. This left him without a way to isolate and identify any sound that Charlie might make; this was an art that only a seasoned combat veteran would know.

To Wilson's left was Ross and to his right was Littman, and this was the first time that Wilson was glad to be around Littman. He knew that if the shit hit the fan, Littman and Ross would be good guys to be near. Wilson was between two combat veterans, and it made him feel as safe as it is possible to feel on your first night ambush.

The whole night, Littman didn't appear to move. He lay there in the prone firing position, looking down his sites at the darkness below. Wilson, on the other hand, was moving his head, scrunching his face and releasing it over and over again; anything he could think of that he could do without making any noise to keep himself awake. The night passed without Charlie coming down the trail, or Wilson falling asleep. At first light, they moved out to rendezvous with the truck. Everyone was laughing and joking on the ride back, except Littman. He looked really pissed, and Wilson heard him mutter under his breath, "Chicken shit, Charlie." Littman was actually pissed that he didn't get to have a firefight with Charlie. The very thing that Wilson had been terrified of all night long, Littman had wanted to happen.

Soon they were back in the compound and eating breakfast in the mess hall. Wilson couldn't help but wonder how the boonie rats could live day and night out in the jungle chasing Charlie for a confrontation. As frightening as the night ambush had been, Wilson had realized how lucky he was being assigned to E Company Support Battalion rather than being with a combat unit out in the jungle.

101st Airborne PX at Phan Rang All Decked Out for Christmas

CHAPTER 2

THE SMOKING CIRCLE

It was Christmastime, but you couldn't tell by the weather in Vietnam. In fact, there were no signs of Christmas, except at the PX. The PX was all decked out for Christmas, with two aluminum Christmas trees on the roof and a cardboard Santa face on the door.

The nights flew by fast, and soon Wilson was a seasoned veteran at guard duty. He had become good friends with Ross, and they spent most of their free time together. Ross, along with almost everyone else in E Company Support Battalion, smoked pot. Wilson had never smoked a cigarette, let alone pot, but after some coaxing he tried it with Ross. They went with several others from their barracks to a place where new barracks were being constructed, and they all sat down on the cement floor of a barracks that was yet to be built. They sat on the edge of the cement, and Ross pulled out a big briar-bowl pipe and a bag of pot, and started stuffing pot into the pipe. He lit it with a Zippo lighter and passed it to Wilson.

"Just breathe it in deep," he said, and Wilson inhaled the smoke. Wilson went instantly into a coughing fit. Everyone laughed, because coughing while smoking pot was considered not to be cool. Smoking pot was mostly a nighttime activity and, after a few weeks of late-night practice, Wilson was able to inhale the smoke without the humiliation of coughing up a lung. Ross and many of the guys that Wilson smoked with had done a tour in the boonies before coming to E Company for their second tour of duty. They told Wilson that the more combat they had seen, the more the pot seemed to help them deal with it all. Wilson, having never been in combat, found that it helped relieve his loneliness from being so far away from home, but he would never mention that to anyone.

One-day Ross came running into the barracks and quietly told Wilson to hurry to the PX because the new pipes were in. Every time new pipes came into the PX it caused a rush on the PX. Everyone wanted to have the biggest briar-bowl pipe that would hold the most pot. Smoking pot had many rules in Vietnam. No coughing was the first rule. Then it was uncool to, while smoking your personal pipe by yourself, let it go out. You were supposed to keep it burning to the very bottom of the bowl. To do this, you had to make the smoking part of your breathing, because pipes go out very easily. And the final rule was that when you were in a passing situation, never "bogart" (forget to pass the pipe). Ross reached for his jungle fatigue pocket as he turned his body, so the pocket was hidden from the other GIs in the barracks, and he pulled out a new pipe with a huge bowl to show Wilson. He quickly stuffed the pipe back into his pocket, and Wilson ran out the door to the PX. He had gotten to the PX in time to buy a briar-bowl pipe that was almost as big as the one Ross had bought. The size of the bowl was a status symbol, but that was his personal pipe; Wilson needed another pipe to share at the smoking circle. He bought another briar-bowl pipe for passing and returned to the barracks to show them to Ross.

That night word was passed around that there would be a smoking circle after dark. Wilson had heard of the smoking circles but had never been to one. It was very dark when Wilson and Ross arrived at the circle. The circle was just forming in the middle of a big field and, as they walked up, the guys made room for the two, and they all sat down. The idea of the circle was for everyone to watch behind the guys across the circle from them, so no one could approach without being seen. It was awesome.

There must have been twenty-five or thirty guys in the circle before they quit coming. Everyone pulled out a pipe and stuffed it full to over-flowing with pot. Ross told Wilson to break out his passing pipe, not his personal pipe. Then twenty-five or thirty Zippo lighters came out, and everyone began lighting their pipes. This was not easy because of how full the bowls were, but soon a glowing red dome crowned each bowl. Then, even though everyone had a pipe, they all passed their pipes to the GI to their right and began puffing on the new bowl. After several more tokes, they would pass the pipes again, and this would continue until the pipes were smoked to the bottom.

Inevitably, someone would cheap out at the PX and buy the cheapest pipe for their passing pipe. That would be the corncob pipe, and that would end up being a fun thing. As the pipes had been smoked nearly to the bottom, someone's corncob pipe would often burn completely through the bottom of the bowl and, in the pitch-black darkness, a big stream of sparks would fall into someone's lap. They would jump up frantically trying to brush off the sparks as everyone cheered to see such a light show in the pitch-black night. Everyone would refill and light the bowl that they had and begin smoking and passing again.

Suddenly everyone became quiet as word was passed that someone was approaching the circle. It was Sergeant Soretti, with a .45 caliber pistol holstered on his hip.

"Alright, what's going on here?" Sergeant Soretti asked in his "you're all busted" voice.

No one in the circle spoke, but all around the circle metallic clicking sounds erupted like a small round of applause as knives snapped open and pistol hammers were cocked. Sergeant Soretti froze in his tracks. He didn't utter another sound, he just started slowly backing up for four or five steps, and then he turned and ran off into the darkness. Now you would think that the circle would have dispersed after that, but they all just went back to smoking and passing, only now they were on full alert. Wilson was expecting a large number of MP jeeps to come storming up any minute, but no one ever came, and the circle broke up later that night just as it normally would have. The next day, Sergeant Soretti didn't say a word about the incident. Wilson had been mistaken; democracy can work in the army, but only if everyone is well armed.

Littman had been on R&R in Taipei, Taiwan, and he was now back. He was sitting on his bunk working, with a thin file, on a very big switchblade knife that he had bought in Taipei while on R&R. Littman closed the knife, and as soon as he let the blade go, it snapped back into the open position. He had filed off the locking bar for the closed position, so the knife would not stay closed. Next, he removed the hinged crossbar at the base of the blade. This crossbar was intended to stop another knife blade before it reached your hand when it came sliding down your blade toward your hand. Wilson watched as Littman finished working on the knife. Then Littman took a parachute rigger's knife holster and forced the closed switchblade down into the holster stretching the holster to accommodate a much larger knife than it was designed for. Parachute riggers were the guys who packed the parachutes for the paratroopers. They were the only people in the army who were allowed to carry a small switchblade knife in a holster, because they used them to work on the parachutes. Littman put the holster on his belt and stuffed the knife down into it.

Littman's Switchblade Knife

The knife must have been eleven inches long, but the holster held it closed. Littman's jungle jacket hid the holster and knife completely.

For days, Littman stayed by his bunk practicing a fast draw with his switchblade. He would stand still with his right thumb under the bottom hem of his jungle jacket, and he would use that thumb to very quickly raise his jungle jacket above the holstered knife. Then, as his hand was coming up, he would grab the handle of the knife sticking up from the holster and out would come this very long knife and, with a loud metallic snap, it would be open. Littman would hold the knife near the bottom, which made it look even longer. Once he had his quick draw down really well, he began drawing the knife at a calendar he had on the wall beside his bunk. In a week, Littman could do his fast draw and end up with the tip of his knife exactly where he was aiming on the calendar.

Not long ago, Littman having a knife on his person at all times and living in the next bunk would have been alarming to Wilson. But he had realized that Littman had never harmed another GI the whole time he had known him, and Wilson actually felt safer with Littman around. Wilson enjoyed watching Littman practice his draw, but once he had made the mistake of stopping beside Littman's bunk to watch him practice, and Littman had turned toward Wilson and whipped out the knife right in his face, with the very tip of the blade on the end of Wilson's nose.

One small drop of blood had appeared on the end of Wilson's nose, but he'd kept his composure, smiled at Littman and said, "Groovy, man," as he walked back to his bunk.

CHAPTER 3

THE STRIP

Littman must have been impressed with how Wilson handled the knife on the nose incident, because the strangest thing happened. Littman invited Wilson and Ross to go to the strip with him.

When you got a pass to leave the post, there were only two places you could go. One was the town of Phan Rang, and the other was the strip. The town of Phan Rang had plenty of bars and plenty of whorehouses, but the strip was closer to the post, and it was one block long with all bars on both sides of the street, and every bar was also a whorehouse. The army had "arranged" for the strip to be built there close to the post for the GIs. When they issued passes, they would hand out a condom with each pass. It was much safer to go to the strip because all the girls were checked regularly, by doctors, for VD.

Of course, Wilson and Ross accepted the invitation before they found out that Littman regularly went to the strip at night. This was bad news, because in order to go to the strip at night, they would have to go AWOL because the army only gave out day passes. But it got worse. Between the post and the strip, it was all boonies, with American, Korean, and South Vietnamese patrols and possible night ambushes set up, not to mention a possible run-in with the Viet Cong. Then, if you made it to the strip, you would have to deal with the South Vietnamese police who patrolled the strip at night. And how they would even get off the post was another question they dared not ask Littman. They decided that they were stuck, and that they had just better go along with it rather than taking a chance of getting on Littman's "Things to Kill" list. It was a "things" to kill list because it included several animals that Littman wanted to kill before he left the 'Nam. Being on Littman's list was much more frightening than getting in trouble with the military.

They met after dark at the edge of the company area, and Littman had a pistol holstered on his hip and two M16s slung one over each shoulder.

"Where'd you get those?" Wilson blurted out without thinking.

"Shut up!" Littman ordered, and he handed Wilson an M16 and gave Ross the pistol. "I'll do all the talking. Let's walk." They started off. "First, I've done this many times already, so we know it can be done. Second, if at any time it even appears that you two might get me killed out there, I'll cut both your throats." Littman patted his switchblade under his jungle jacket to emphasize his threat. "If we come in contact with anyone we freeze. It doesn't matter who they are, even Americans; if they see or hear us, they will fire first and ask questions later." Littman continued, "You guys just keep quiet, keep alert, and keep up with me and we're gonna have a good time tonight." That was the last thing that Littman said until they arrived on the perimeter at guard tower number one.

Littman called out, "Johnson!" A face popped up over the back wall of the tower. "It's me, Littman!"

"Okay, come on through!" the guard responded. Littman led them past the guard tower to the first row of concertina wire. Littman then lay down on the ground and began low-crawling on a little trail that snaked through the two rows of concertina wire. Wilson was just thinking this was definitely the craziest thing that he had ever done in his whole life when he came to the Claymore mine. Of course, to follow Littman's trail, you had to crawl right in front of the Claymore mine. What that guy wouldn't do for a little adrenaline, Wilson thought.

Claymore Mine – "FRONT TOWARD ENEMY" - Good Idea!

When they got through the concertina wire, they proceeded very slowly through the sparse boonies, trying not to make a sound. Every once in a while, Littman would freeze and listen for a while, and check his compass, and then they would pick their way a little farther. Wilson and Ross would do the exact same thing as Littman, whatever he did.

When they came to the strip, they stopped at the edge of the boonies and watched the strip for any South Vietnamese police activity. Littman knew just what bar he was headed for because he had a girlfriend there. At the strip, a girlfriend meant a prostitute who liked a GI and didn't charge him for her services. Wilson and Ross would have to pay. Littman lead them behind the row of bars and tapped on a window. A girl moved the curtains aside and looked out to see who was there. She smiled when she saw Littman, and she pointed toward the back door. Littman led them to the back door, and the girl let them in. Except for three candles, it was pretty dark, but they could see that they were in a bar and they had it all to themselves. Amazingly, exactly the right number of bar girls showed up, and the party began with everyone disappearing with their bar girl.

One by one the guys came out of their rooms with their girls, and they partied in the bar for over an hour until the front door burst open and a girl ran in yelling, "Police come! Police come!" As the police jeep pulled up and the police were coming in the front door, the guys grabbed their weapons and were going out the back door. Outside the back door, Littman reached into his jungle jacket pocket and pulled out a hand grenade.

He instantly pulled the pin and threw the grenade towards the edge of the jungle behind the strip as he yelled, "Hit the dirt!" They all dove to the ground, and the grenade went off with a huge explosion. Littman jumped up, and off they all ran.

"They won't be so anxious to follow us after that," Littman said as they ran. Sure enough, when they started moving through the boonies at slow speed, there was no sign of anyone following them. Littman knew that the South Vietnamese Police would catch and arrest them if they could, but that the police would never risk their lives to do so. It took a long time to cross the boonies to get back to the post, but the danger wasn't over yet. The guys were in the boonies in front of guard tower number one but being out front of the guard position was very dangerous. If the guard had fallen asleep, he might hear Littman call and wake up with a start and set off the Claymore mine.

Littman called out, "Johnson!" Johnson was awake, and he waived the guys in. One more crawl past the claymore mine and they were home free.

Littman climbed the guard tower ladder and handed Johnson a can of beer that he had brought back from the strip. Wilson couldn't believe that they were back safe on the post, and Ross didn't know what to think, but they both went back to the barracks with grins on their faces. All that had happened that night didn't seem to matter, because they were the only guys in the whole company that had gotten laid on a weekday night.

CHAPTER 4

GRENADE!

The next night Wilson and Ross had guard duty, and it was a hard-ship tour of duty. They were tired from being up most of the night before, and were they ever dragging ass the next morning when the truck came to change the guards. Ross was picked up first, and the next tower was Wilson's. It was extra hard to climb up into the big "deuce and a half" truck, and they both closed their eyes and tried to rest on the ride back to the barracks. Wilson and Ross didn't know who it was, but while picking up one guard he climbed up the side of the truck and tossed his ammo can into the center of the truck bed. Everyone heard it—the muffled but unmistakable sound of a hand flare going off inside the ammo can. To fire a hand flare, you took the cap off the top and put it on the bottom of the flare and then hit the bottom with the heel of your hand. A spike inside the cap of the flare would set off the flare when hit. The GI had accidentally left the cap on the bottom of the flare. The bad news was that in the ammo can with the hand flares were five hand grenades that were about to go off. "Grenade!" someone yelled, and it was unbelievable how fast the tired and napping soldiers emptied that truck. Then, almost immediately, the deafening explosion shattered the morning silence. They all were trying to see if everyone else was okay until it became clear that no one had been killed or wounded. Wilson climbed up on the tailgate of the truck and saw the damage that had been done. There was a three-foot-wide hole in the thick wooden truck bed, and as Wilson climbed into the truck bed, he looked down the hole in the floor. The only thing between the hole and the ground was the drive shaft, still intact and working fine. Of course, anyone who hadn't gotten out of the back of the truck in time would have been killed, but there was also an eight-inch hole blown right through the truck cab and through the back of the driver's seat. The driver would have been killed for sure if he hadn't gotten out. So everyone was fine and, strangely enough, no one was the least bit sleepy all the rest of the way back to the barracks. When the next guard was picked up, everyone yelled at him not to throw his ammo can, and a new rule was born. Now you would think that the new rule would be to never throw your ammo can into the back of the truck, but it wasn't. The next time Wilson had guard duty, everyone was throwing their ammo cans into the truck just as they always had done. The new rule was:

Don't forget to put the lid back on the top of your flares.

A few days later, Wilson was switched from the night shift to the day shift. He was used to the night shift, but the day shift made him feel safer.

He figured, "Who would attack a guard tower in broad daylight?" Plus, he had his nights free to party.

One-day Wilson spotted a truck coming around the perimeter road toward his tower. The truck went past without stopping, and Wilson saw Littman all by himself in the back. Wilson waved at Littman as he went by, but, of course, Littman didn't waive back; yet Wilson thought that Littman might have smiled just a little. Wilson knew that they were going to have a surprise inspection back at the barracks. He laughed to think how Littman had made the United States Army adjust to him. Wilson had been taught that there's a right way, a wrong way, and the "army way"—and now there was the Littman way. He watched through his binoculars as the truck took Littman to the next tower and exchanged him for the guard that was there.

It wasn't an hour before Wilson heard the machine gun fire from the next tower, and it didn't even startle him. He knew it would be Littman. He looked through his binoculars and saw Littman out in front of his tower with his M60 machine gun, firing it straight up into the air. Wilson couldn't tell from so far away what Littman was firing at, but Wilson was sure he would find out when the truck came to pick them up that evening. Sure enough, on the truck ride back to the barracks, when they picked up Littman he was sporting an eagle or hawk feather and talon on his helmet.

Littman's Trophy

Littman's Helmet

Later that night, Littman told Wilson that he had seen the bird circling above his guard tower and that he thought it was a vulture, and that the vulture thought he was food, and that that had pissed him off. So, he had brought it down with his "60" even though it was just a dot in the sky. Apparently, Littman believed in defending his guard position against any and all living things. Littman wore his bird parts in his helmet from then on.

They all three had the next day off, and the word spread that the sergeant was looking for some "volunteers" for a work detail. That meant that, if the sergeant saw you, you were "volunteered" and were on the detail. They needed to get out of the company area fast, and Littman invited them to come with him because he spent most of his time out of the company area. They took off and followed Littman around for the rest of the day. First, Littman took them to where the new barracks were going up, and it was clear that he came there often. This was where Littman practiced throwing his M16 bayonet. There was a telephone poll with a three-quarter-inch thick sheet of plywood leaning against it. On the plywood, drawn in magic marker, was the outline of a Viet Cong with a sloped hat. The face, heart, and crotch were all three just holes. Littman threw that sheet of plywood to the side, on top of two others just like it, and he had Wilson and Ross bring over a new sheet from a nearby stack. Littman took a magic marker from his jungle jacket and drew another "Gook," as he called them, on the plywood. He then put his back to the plywood and paced off six big steps. He did a military about-face and pulled an M16 bayonet out of his boot. His windup and throw looked like a major league baseball pitcher as he sent the bayonet spinning to the target. The bayonet sunk to the handle into the four-inch circle that designated the heart. The blade was very hard to get out of the plywood, so Littman assigned that job to Wilson and Ross. They had to work the blade back and forth, back and forth, until it worked its way out of the wood. Littman wouldn't give anyone else a turn until the entire four-inch heart area was nothing but a hole, and then he let Ross throw. Ross missed the entire piece of plywood, and his turn was over. Wilson didn't do much better. He hit the board, but the bayonet just bounced off, and Wilson's turn was over as well.

"So, what else do you want to do?" Wilson asked Littman in a way that made it clear that he didn't want another turn, and Littman got the message. Littman had brought a small rucksack that he picked up and threw over his shoulder, and they were off again to Littman's next destination. Littman took them to a base camp company area for a combat unit that was out in the field. He had them wait for him, and he went into the supply tent. Just as they were wondering if he would ever come out, he did.

He walked by them without stopping and said, "Let's go." They went to a very desolate place in the compound and came to a campfire area hidden by some bushes.

"Want some coffee?" Littman asked as he pulled a mess kit from his rucksack.

Littman filled a metal canteen cup with water.

"I'll get some firewood," Ross said.

"No need for that," Littman responded as he opened the top of his rucksack, exposing a stack of C-4 blocks. Littman tore off a corner of a block and put it in the fire pit. C-4 is a plastic explosive that makes a very big boom, and that's about all Wilson knew about it. So, when Littman lit his Zippo lighter and started moving it toward the C-4, Wilson dove for cover. Ross and Littman had a big laugh at Wilson's expense, as the C-4 burned with a very hot chemical fire. So hot, in fact, that Littman had to keep moving the canteen cup around over the flame or the heat would melt the bottom of the metal cup. Littman explained that he had been in the CO's office, and he had seen ten M79 grenade launcher shotgun rounds lined up on a shelf for decoration. Shotgun rounds for the M79 were rare in the boonies, and they were the only rounds that a grenadier could fire in thick jungle. Littman had snuck back into the CO's office and stolen the shotgun rounds. He had traded them to the supply sergeant at the combat unit's supply tent for six blocks of C-4, which there was never a shortage of. Now the shotgun rounds could do some good out in the boonies instead of being the CO's trophies. Soon they were passing around the canteen cup of C-ration coffee. Wilson had never been a coffee drinker. The drink of strong coffee almost made him shudder, but he resisted both the shudder and mentioning the bitterness to the other guys. He took a drink every time it was his turn and pretended to like it.

They spent the afternoon at the little camp talking about their lives back home, and then they were off again. No one spoke of the C-4, but Wilson and Ross knew damn good and well what Littman would do with it. Sure enough, not two weeks later, the First Sergeant called Littman into his office to try to yell a confession out of him. But that technique hadn't worked before, and it didn't even have the slightest effect on Littman.

No one heard much from Littman for two more weeks when, unannounced, he went home. He had gotten short and had not told anyone, not even Wilson and Ross. He had just packed his duffle bag and jumped in the back of a jeep and he was gone. The day after that, Wilson heard that at out-processing they had checked Littman's duffle bag and found two M16s, a pistol, and several knives. They had confiscated the illegal weapons and let Littman go on home. Wilson heard that Littman was going on a thirty-day leave and then he would be coming back to Saigon to be a security guard, and that was the last Wilson or Ross would ever hear of Littman.

A few days after Littman left, the sergeant stepped into the door of the barracks and yelled, "Atten-hut!" and everyone rushed to the foot of their bunks and snapped to attention. This was the first time that Wilson and Ross's barracks had had a surprise inspection without Littman being there, so this inspection actually was a surprise. Things just weren't the same without Littman. During the inspection, the captain looked at Wilson's bunk and open footlocker.

"Very good, soldier," the captain said. "Report to my office when the inspection is over." Wilson reported as instructed, and the captain told him that they needed a good man out at the pumping station and that he was that man. Wilson didn't know what to expect at his new assignment. Hell, he didn't even know there was a pumping station until now. He was to be a guard at the water-pumping station that pumped the water for the whole 101st Airborne Division base camp as well as the Air Force side of the compound.

CHAPTER 5

SANDBAG CITY

After giving the sad news to Ross and all the guys, Wilson packed his belongings and climbed into the waiting three-quarter-ton truck that would take him to the pumping station, or "Sandbag City" as it was called. It was a twenty-minute drive from the main gate of the base camp to the pumping station, and Wilson was a little worried about how far "out in the boonies" it was. As the truck pulled up to the compound, a guard opened the gate and they drove in. It was a sandbag city—a small compound with a two-story sandbag building in the center for the officers and sergeants, and bunkers at each guard position all around the perimeter. Four guys lived in each guard bunker. The bunkers were surprisingly big inside, with two double bunks, one on each side. The bunkers were constructed with railroad tie supports and structure, and with plywood board walls and ceilings. The outer walls and roof were covered with sandbags. The guard bunkers were half underground and half above ground, and each guard bunker had the guard station on top. The compound was right next to a small banana plantation, and one of Wilson's new roommates had an entire bunch of bananas hanging from the end of his bunk, and he offered Wilson one. Even though they were full grown, the bananas were only three or four inches long, so they looked kind of stubby, but they were sweet and delicious.

Wilson got moved into his new quarters and got to know Boone, Gillis and Hayworth, his new roommates. They seemed like good guys, and it took only minutes for them to invite Wilson to smoke pot with them. Well, all but Boone, or "Boonie" as the guys called him; he didn't smoke for religious reasons, but he didn't seem to mind at all that everyone else did. Wilson respected Boonie's choice not to smoke. It blew Wilson away when Boonie pulled out a bottle of mouthwash and passed it around. The other guys were very pleased, and when the mouthwash got to Wilson he smelled it. At first, he thought it really was mouthwash because it smelled like peppermint and alcohol, but Boonie told him that it was peppermint schnapps that his grandfather made and sent to him from Delaware, through the mail, disguised as mouthwash. Wilson smiled to think that Boonie, the one guy that didn't smoke, was getting them all blasted on booze.

Gillis was a quiet guy, but he always seemed to be glad to be included in what the others were doing. He was very big on writing home, and he wrote letters almost every day. His main concern was simply to make it back to Rhode Island alive. Gillis had brochures from a truck driving school, and it was his dream to attend the school and become a truck driver when he got back home. He seemed to know every move he would make after he got out of the army, and he spent a lot of time thinking about it. Wilson didn't like to think about what he would do back home because he thought it might jinx his making it out of Vietnam alive.

Hayworth, Wilson's other roommate, was from Iowa, and he had no idea what he wanted to do when he got home; he just wanted to make it home alive and take it from there. Hayworth was into music and he and Wilson liked the same groups, so they spent a lot of time keeping up with the latest songs that were being played back in the States. Hayworth was big, being over six-foot-three inches tall and of stocky build. He weighed over two hundred pounds, but he was not fat. He reminded Wilson of Dan Blocker, who played Hoss Cartwright on the Bonanza TV show. Wilson spent a lot of time listening to music with Hayworth and soon he felt like he was totally up on the music the folks were listening to back home.

Guard duty here was at night, and before Wilson went on duty, the sergeant told him that Charlie had been hitting and running lately, so to be alert for a big attack. Charlie used hit-and-run tactics on the perimeter of a compound to test the response time. He wanted to know how big of a response came when the GIs returned fire and how long it took for the air power to arrive, be it artillery or gunships. Then, once Charlie had the information, he could determine any weakness which he could take advantage of with a big attack.

Wilson sat in the guard position and took out two hand flairs, removed the caps, and slid the caps onto the bottom of the flairs so they were ready to fire. He placed the claymore mine detonator within easy reach, and loaded his M16. He was an experienced guard, so none of this was new to him.

It was just before midnight, and Wilson had been on guard duty for three hours and forty or fifty minutes when the Viet Cong opened up with an AK-47 right out in front of his position. One of the rounds hit a sandbag near Wilson and threw sand on him. Wilson set off the claymore mine, popped a hand flare into the air, and opened fire with his M16, all in just a few seconds. The flare made it bright like daylight as it slowly parachuted down to the ground, and Wilson scanned the terrain for Viet Cong, but saw nothing. By then, the sergeant and two others had shown up. Wilson popped the second hand flair and told them that he hadn't seen anyone out there while the first hand flare was lighting up the area. They all scanned the area out in front of the position in the light of the second flair, and the sergeant said that it looked like another hit-and-run. When Wilson showed the sergeant where the round hit the sandbag right beside where he was sitting, the sergeant smiled and told him that he had never been shot at that close, and he had been in-country for ten months. Wilson had no problem being very alert the rest of his time on guard duty that night. Adrenaline will do that to you.

The next night, Wilson was awakened in his bunk by a big explosion, followed by small-arms fire and then another big boom. He jumped into his pants and boots, grabbed his M16, and ran out of the bunker. He ducked down as another burst from an AK-47 chattered away, followed by another big boom. Then all was silent until everyone started yelling. Some were yelling to find out if everyone was okay, and one was yelling for a medic.

On the bunker beside the front gate, the guard, Phil Robins, was hurt really bad because one of the mortar rounds had hit his bunker while he was on guard duty. Within minutes, a Cobra gunship was in the air, shining a spotlight on the ground outside the compound. Charlie was long gone by then, it seemed, because the gunship searched for quite a while, but never fired a shot. Soon, a medevac helicopter was landing in the yard beside the officers' bunker, and Phil was flown out.

The next day, Wilson was on a work detail to replace sandbags that had been damaged by the mortar attack when word was passed around that Phil had died. The officers got everyone together and held a short service for Phil, and everyone was very solemn the rest of the day. This was all very frightening to Wilson. He wondered how the guys out in the boonies could go through stuff like this every day, and his respect for his old friend Littman grew even more.

A few days later, Wilson got to visit the base camp. He got ready and jumped into the back of a three-quarter-ton truck, and off they went. Wilson went to his old barracks at E Company, and there was Ross who, luckily, had the day off, too. The old friends talked and partied the rest of the day. Ross told Wilson that he was short and would be going home in eight days. The guys exchanged stateside addresses and went to the club for their last party together in 'Nam.

Wilson was very drunk when he returned to Sandbag City, and no one cared because getting drunk and getting laid was what a day pass was for. Time went by slowly on guard duty that night because Wilson was so tired. This was an excellent time for an uneventful night of guard duty, and that's just what Wilson got.

Wilson knew the exact day that Ross was leaving, but he couldn't get back to the base camp to see him off. Wilson stayed by himself that day, and even though he had Ross's address back in the states, he didn't know if he would ever see Ross again. Wilson was sitting on some sandbags and smoking pot in his briar-bowl pipe when Boonie came to talk to him.

Wilson Sitting on Sandbags Smoking Pot

Wilson spent hours out back of the compound, where they filled sandbags. This was where he would go to be alone. He would smoke pot and throw his bayonet for hours on end. Wilson had mastered throwing the bayonet completely, out of respect for his good friend, Littman. Wilson now could throw so hard that he could sink half the bayonet blade into a phone pole, just like Littman. Boonie asked Wilson if he would teach him to throw the bayonet. He said that he threw like a girl, and he wanted Wilson to correct this problem. Of course, Wilson was glad to help. He threw the bayonet himself a few more times, making mental notes as to exactly where his hand was during each phase of the throw, which foot he stepped forward with to throw, and all the things you never think of until you try to teach someone else. Then he had Boonie throw. Wilson thought that even a girl would be ashamed of throwing like that. Boonie was doing everything wrong. He was even stepping forward with the wrong foot. Wilson started correcting things about Boonie's throw, and within an hour Boonie was throwing like the famous Major League Baseball pitcher Sandy Koufax. Boonie was very grateful to Wilson, and he gave him an entire bottle of "mouthwash" as a thank you. After that day, Boonie would often join Wilson when Wilson went to throw his bayonet.

Having friends in Vietnam was kind of like life must be in an old folk's home in the states. Every so often, you would have one less friend than you had the day before—only in this case, because the friend, Ross, finished his tour of duty and went home.

CHAPTER 6

CHOPPER DOWN

Wilson and Hayworth both got a day pass on the same day, so they decided to go to the town of Phan Rang and check it out. They lucked out and were driven into town by Sergeant Thomas in a jeep because he was going to town to see his girlfriend that day. Sergeant Thomas drove like a Saigon cab driver, darting around anything that got in his way but, against all odds, they made it safely to town. It was eight-thirty in the morning when Sergeant Thomas dropped them off in front of a bar and told them to meet him back there at five o'clock and drove off. Wilson and Hayworth grinned at each other, and they busted into the bar in front of them like cowhands just off a long cattle drive. The bar girls grouped around the two, because they were the only Americans there. And the party began.

At five o'clock that evening, Sergeant Thomas came screeching to a stop in front of the bar, and Wilson and Hayworth were sitting on the steps of the bar, obviously very drunk.

They stumbled into the jeep, and Sergeant Thomas asked, "So, how'd you guys like Phan Rang?"

The guys cracked up laughing, and Wilson said, "We can only report on that one bar, Sarge. We stayed there the whole time, but we liked it just fine." Sergeant Thomas joined in the laughter, and they raced back to Sandbag City with the wind in their faces.

A few days later, Wilson was sitting on top of his bunker and writing a letter home when he heard a helicopter in the distance. It caught his attention because the sound it was making was not right. The motor was sputtering and cutting out. As it grew near, Wilson already had his binoculars on it, and he heard the motor cut out: and then it did not start up again. Wilson watched the chopper go into auto-rotate—a mode where the blades keep going without the motor to slow the rate of descent in a crash—but it hit the ground very hard nonetheless.

"Chopper down!" Wilson shouted as Sergeant Thomas came running out of his bunker. "It hit down real hard!" The sergeant had the radio man contact the base camp for help as he organized a squad to go out and secure the downed chopper. Wilson was among those chosen for the squad. They all loaded into a three-quarter-ton truck and raced out the front gate. It took just a few minutes to reach the chopper. It was lying on its side, and all four GIs on board were dead—the pilot and the co-pilot and the two door gunners. The squad circled the chopper with their backs to it, and they all lay down in the prone firing position to defend the crash site until help arrived.

Helicopters started showing up right away. One Cobra gunship circled the area for security as another chopper landed to drop off a work team to secure the bodies. They worked quickly, without saying much at all to each other as they put the four bodies into body bags, loaded them into the helicopter, and were gone. Then a third chopper came that looked like a mosquito, and it hovered above the crashed chopper and let down a long cable with several ends that the work team hooked to the downed chopper. Then the skinny mosquito chopper lifted the big Huey helicopter right off the ground and reeled in the cable until the Huey was right up under the thin body of the "flying crane helicopter," as they called it. Off the flying crane flew, and the crash site was cleared. They rode back to the compound, and no one said a word. Compared to the boonies, this duty assignment was very safe; and yet people kept getting killed. Wilson tried to just think of home.

Being in a rear area duty assignment was a lucky break for any soldier. So, when faced with death it tends to shake that feeling of being safe in the rear area. The guys out in the boonies were used to death. They had to learn to deal with it, but the only thing rear area soldiers could do was to try not to think of it, and that is just what Wilson did.

The next few days, everyone was busy replacing sandbags on the officers' bunker. One entire wall had to be completely replaced because the sandbags were rotten. Wilson enjoyed being on sandbag detail. It helped get his mind off the four guys in the downed chopper. He liked to fill the bags with sand, because it was soothing in its routine.

In Vietnam the army promoted smoking. Cigarettes were even included in the C-rations for the guys out in the boonies, and every fifty minutes they were required to give the soldiers a ten-minute smoke break.

"Smoke 'em if you've got 'em!" the sergeant would announce, and everyone would light up. Of course, Wilson didn't smoke cigarettes, but the good news was that no one seemed to notice or even care that, for ten minutes out of every hour, Wilson, and most of the others, would be smoking pot.

Smoking pot may seem to be a less-than-honorable pastime for soldiers in a war zone, but pot allowed the escape from reality that the alcohol in a businessman's martini provides without losing one's ability to react to an emergency if needed. Adrenaline cannot completely overpower or erase the alcohol high, so the soldier would not be able to perform efficiently in combat while drunk. However, when the first gunshot rings out, or the first explosion occurs, the pot high is gone, and the soldier is ready to react. When a soldier reacts in combat, it often leaves behind horrible pictures in the soldier's mind. These can be pictures of a burning village, of shredded bodies, of many terrible things that occur in combat. The combat soldier also carries a vivid picture of the face of every enemy soldier and civilian that makes up the soldier's personal body count. These are images that the soldier must carry with him/her for the rest of their lives. And this is one of the main causes of veteran suicide, and the reason we lose more soldiers/veterans to suicide than we lose in any given war.

Tony Wilson was now a short-timer." He had only a few days left in his tour of duty, so he had been getting everyone's home addresses and saying his goodbyes. He had learned a lot in his eleven-month tour, and it all added up to Mom and Dad's boy returning home a man. Most of all he had learned how much he had lucked out not having been assigned to jungle combat. Tony was a completely different person than he had been when he had arrived, but his parents and friends would still recognize him as his old self. Unlike Littman's family and friends, who would never again see in Littman the boy that went to Vietnam. The first thing Tony wanted to do when he got home was to call his uncle Steve in Washington. Not to complain about any strings that may have been pulled to keep him out of combat, but to thank him.

III - SAIGON MACHINE GUN PATROL

Machine Gun Jeep Team

CHAPTER 1

SAIGON

Johnny Stone had just arrived in Saigon for his second tour in Vietnam. He had been assigned to the 716th MP Battalion as a security guard, and his job would be machine gunner in charge of a gun jeep. His first tour he had done eleven months working in the motor pool of the 101st Airborne as a mechanic.

It was 1968, and the war was going strong. Johnny had a very good assignment being in Saigon. He never had to experience the worst of Vietnam like the combat infantry troops did; never had to live in the jungle and drink from the streams and rivers while expecting death with every step they took, day after day. He was grateful for this, but at the same time he was frightened to be in Saigon among throngs of people with no way to tell the bad guys from the good guys.

Johnny was just back from a thirty-day leave of absence at home in Indianapolis, Indiana. His parents had been so glad to see him, but they had had a hard time understanding why he would volunteer to go back again. His friends from high school were very impressed with Johnny's paratrooper uniform, and the fact that he was going back for a second tour made them even more impressed. Johnny wore his paratrooper uniform to visit his friends, and he looked more military than he had ever felt.

Johnny went to all of his old hangouts, and there were some of the same guys playing the same old school boy games, and Johnny was surprised at how much even the tough guys seemed to be playing children's games. He noticed that the tough guys were thinking on a "black eye and bloody nose" level, and that looked very silly to someone who has been in a war zone where thinking on a "life and death" level is the norm. Johnny thought that his paratrooper uniform made the bullies leave him alone, but it was really the look in his eyes that protected him from their kid games.

Johnny had a good time on his leave, yet the whole time he felt disconnected from it all. It was surprising to Johnny that by the time his leave was almost over he felt like he was ready to go back to Vietnam. When the day came, he made his tearful goodbyes and boarded the plane to return to his home away from home.

Once back in Vietnam and settled into his new Saigon home, the seven-story tall Capital Hotel where security guards manned the bunkers at the front on each side of the entrance, he went through orientation. The hotel was for elite troops, mostly MPs (Military Police), CID (Criminal Investigation Division), and folks like Johnny who guarded them when they were at work, as well as when they were off duty.

Johnny had a lot to learn, like how to talk on the radio with all the proper police codes. "Proceed to the Princess Hotel, code four!" "Code four" meant to go to the hotel very fast using the flashing red light and siren—this, of course, would be Johnny's favorite way to travel through the streets of Saigon. Johnny was issued a shiny black helmet with "SG" on the front. The "SG" stood for Security Guard, but the Vietnamese thought it meant "Saigon." He was issued an arm band for his left shoulder to wear on duty, along with the 716th MP's patch on the shoulder and another "SG" below that. He was also issued a police whistle, and Johnny could barely wait to get to someplace where he could try it out. When he finally did get to try it, the sound was ear-piercing and left your ears ringing. This was the best whistle that Johnny had ever owned. There was still a lot of "boy" in Johnny, and this was the part of Johnny that liked whistles.

Johnny's rank was Sergeant E-5, and he was assigned to be the machine gunner on a gun jeep patrolling the streets of Saigon at night. The gun jeep teams worked twelve hours on duty and then had twelve hours off. Johnny was in charge of his gun jeep, and he decided what weapons were on board. Johnny was trained as a light weapons expert, so he knew how to use each weapon. Of course, his M60 machine gun mounted on the dashboard in front of his seat gave an entirely new meaning to "riding shotgun."

Johnny's driver, Greg Bowlen, was also back in Vietnam for a second tour of duty. They hit it off right away and became good friends. Greg was from Illinois and Johnny from Indiana, so they both had similar mid-western experiences growing up. Greg had been in Saigon for almost two months, so he was able to bring Johnny up to speed in short order. They each had their jobs, and when they did them together they were a very efficient gun jeep team. Greg was the driver until the jeep stopped, and then his job changed to assistant machine gunner. He was responsible for keeping Johnny supplied with ammo and an occasional hand on the back when Johnny was firing on full-auto, so the machine gun didn't push Johnny back from the tremendous recoil of the weapon.

Johnny's home for the next six months would be a room shared with three other GIs in the Capital Hotel where all the MPs, CID, and other police lived. He would have it made on this assignment; and each day his bed would be made, his uniform would be cleaned and starched, and his boots would be shined. All these things would be done by the maid service. Johnny thought that this must be about as far away from combat as you could get without leaving the combat zone. The hotel was in Cholon, a predominantly Chinese suburb of Saigon. The first floor of the hotel was a huge nightclub with slot machines lining one entire wall and a stage for live entertainment. Vietnamese waitresses scurried about delivering cans of twelve-ounce American beer for fifteen cents each and twenty-five-cent mixed drinks to the thirsty GIs. A Vietnamese band played Beatles tunes from the stage, and you had to look at them to tell they weren't actually the Beatles. They had practiced the Beatles tunes until they could perform them flawlessly. They even sounded British.

Johnny was ready for his first night on the gun jeep. His job was to protect the MPs as they worked. If the MPs came under attack from the enemy, the gun jeep would move in and take over. Greg would stay two blocks behind the MP jeep, lurking in the shadows and waiting to spring into action. If the MP jeep pulled over to the curb, so would Greg to maintain the proper distance between the two jeeps. The gun jeep ran without lights, and the windshield had been removed and replaced with the dash-mounted M60 machine gun.

Greg's job, of course, was driver; but, when the stuff hit the fan, as soon as the wheels of the jeep stopped turning, Greg became Johnny's assistant machine gunner. Greg would grab an ammo can with a belt of one thousand rounds (bullets) all connected together. The assault bag that held the first load of seven hundred and fifty rounds was attached to the M60, and when those seven hundred and fifty bullets were gone, Greg would be right there with the belt of one thousand more rounds.

The work day (or night) began with an inspection with Johnny and Greg standing at attention in front of their gun jeep. This was Saigon and, like in any big city, there was always plenty of action, from fire fights to entire buildings blowing up—usually it was police stations that blew up.

Another job that the gun jeeps did was to escort VIPs who needed to move at night. Usually they were moving from one cocktail party to another. During Johnny's tour of duty in Saigon, he and Greg would escort both General Westmoreland and his replacement, General Abrams.

Johnny and Greg stood at attention as the officers inspected each gun jeep team to make sure that they looked "spit and polished" enough to drive on the abandoned streets of Saigon in the dark—Johnny never did understand why all the "spit and polish" was necessary just to drive around in the dark. After inspection, all the gun jeeps left the compound. They were on the streets for thirty minutes before they were to meet up with their MP jeep at a prearranged meeting place. Strict radio silence was enforced because the Viet Cong monitored all radio frequencies in Saigon. But regardless of this, each gun jeep had two radios; the regular Army jeep radio that had a very long antenna, and a Motorola radio under the dash. The gun jeeps hit the streets just before curfew, so the streets were full of people when Johnny's night of work began. The big problem that they had been warned to look out for during the time before curfew was someone tossing a grenade into the back of the gun jeep. So, as Greg would make his way through the crowds and traffic, Johnny would keep a very close eye on the back seat for grenades, as well as carefully watching all the people around the jeep. Then it would be curfew and the streets would become totally deserted except for the MP jeeps and the machine gun jeeps. About then, it would be time to start heading for the rendezvous place to meet up with the MPs that they would be guarding for the night. At the rendezvous place, the MPs would be waiting, and Johnny and Greg would kick back until the MPs were ready to begin work for the night.

Saigon Traffic Before Curfew

The rendezvous point was sometimes at the Continental Hotel and sometimes at an all-night snack bar that operated from a small trailer in a secure Korean military compound. It was the only place in Saigon that was opened all night selling food and snacks to the only people allowed on the streets at night.

Soon, everyone was ready, and the night's work began. As the MP jeep pulled out of the compound, Greg followed, but kept falling further behind until a two-block distance was between the two jeeps. The gun jeeps ran all night without any lights in hopes of being invisible until they were needed. Johnny had always loved convertibles and motorcycles, anything that put the wind in his face. On this tour of duty, Johnny would get all the wind in his face that he had ever wanted. The two jeeps had patrolled the streets of Saigon for about twenty minutes before the first call came into the MPs. The MPs red lights and siren went on as the MP jeep sped away. The chase was on. Greg followed suit, and they were on their way to their first emergency call. Johnny thought that nothing could be as much fun as racing through the deserted streets of Saigon at night with red lights flashing and the siren screaming.

Their destination was a dark alley in downtown Saigon. As they arrived, Johnny grabbed his M60 and lifted it from the dash mount. As soon as they jumped out of the jeep Johnny and Greg saw two MPs running toward a body lying beside a pile of trash in the alley. Johnny trained his M60 on the dark alleyway to provide security for the MPs. He walked out of the light and peered into the darkness as if he expected to be able to see something. The two MPs had knelt down by the body with their .45-caliber pistols drawn.

Almost at the same time, one MP yelled, "It's a GI!" as the other MP yelled, "He's alive! Get an ambulance!" He didn't look alive to Johnny, but Greg called in for an ambulance on the Motorola radio and then backed the gun jeep out of the way so the ambulance could get through when it arrived. The American GI had been mercilessly beaten by a gang of street thugs. The street gangs called themselves "cowboys" because of all the American western movies that were so popular in Vietnam. The cowboys were not known for their bravery, so finding a helpless GI in an isolated area and beating the GI to death was a fairly common practice. Johnny was shaken after seeing how badly the GI had been beaten, but Greg assured him that he would get used to that sort of thing after a while. The GI's face was so distorted from the beating that his own mother would not have been able to recognize him. Johnny, with his M60, and Greg went down the alley looking for the cowboys. They, of course, found nothing because the cowboys always disappeared after they struck. Having cleared the alley and secured the area, the guys kept an eye on the rooftops because that was the most likely place from which the enemy might attack.

Johnny had a license to kill. Any Vietnamese found on the streets after curfew were fair game, and Johnny was allowed to shoot first and ask questions later. This was the rule, but Johnny didn't think he would shoot someone just because he could; but having seen the beaten GI, for the first time Johnny thought that if he saw the cowboys he would have no problem cutting them down.

Soon the GI was on his way to the hospital, and they were once more on patrol. Johnny hoped for the rest of the night that he would see the cowboys. The rest of the night, however, was uneventful as the two jeeps patrolled the city. Then, just as Johnny was beginning to feel tired, curfew lifted and the streets once again filled with people in a matter of minutes. This had a refreshing effect on the gun jeep team, and they felt wide awake as Greg made his way through the crowd and Johnny, once again, kept a very close eye on the back seat and all the people around the jeep.

Johnny with a Substitute Driver and His New Mirror

CHAPTER 2

EXPLOSION AT THE POLICE STATION

Several nights of gun jeep duty went by without a major event, but on their fifth night of work Johnny had a substitute driver. Greg was driving another gun jeep for the night.

They had been on duty for several hours when Johnny spotted something. Johnny had the substitute driver stop and back up the jeep beside a Vietnamese military bus. The bus had big convex mirrors on both sides. With a mirror like that Johnny would not have to sit with his body turned in his seat so he could keep a close eye on the back seat of the jeep before and after curfew when all the people were in the streets. Johnny had the substitute driver position the jeep, so he could stand on the hood as he removed the side view mirror from the bus. He attached the new mirror to his jeep, and he now had a panoramic view of everything behind him with no blind spots and without turning in his seat.

The gun jeep team had a lot more leeway with their jeeps than was usually allowed in the military. They could make any changes, like the machine gun holder that Greg invented. Greg would come up with the new idea and the guys in the motor pool would make it for him. He had noticed that Johnny had to lean forward in his seat all night to keep holding the M60 machine gun. So Greg invented a holder for the machine gun that brought it back closer to Johnny. From then on Johnny was the only machine gunner without a constant backache. He could sit back in his seat and still keep the machine gun stable. Between the machine gun mount and the new mirror, Johnny and Greg's jeep was very well prepared for the streets of Saigon.

Most of the rest of the night with the substitute driver was calm until a call came in that there had been a gun jeep wreck. Johnny's heart sank as he heard the jeep number. It was Greg's. The wreck had happened across town, so Johnny knew that if they went to the scene he would be too late. Greg would be in the hospital, or the morgue, and the accident scene would have been all cleaned up. There was nothing Johnny could do. The rest of the night went slowly by, and Greg was all Johnny could think about.

When Johnny finally got back home to the hotel there was Greg grinning ear to ear. He had suffered a few bumps and bruises, but he was fine, and the gun jeep team of Stone and Bowlen would work together again the next night.

The next few nights were uneventful except for one GI prisoner of whom the MPs were frightened. He was one of those guys who had gone crazy from too much combat, and he would kill anyone who he felt had crossed him. So far the MPs knew of two Vietnamese guys and one bar girl who had crossed him and who he had killed on the spot. It was easy to disappear in Saigon, with its narrow alleys and maze like neighborhoods.

The MPs briefed Greg and Johnny fully on the prisoner. He was obviously crazy and needed help. He had flipped out and gone AWOL (Absent Without Leave) from his combat tour in the jungle with the 82nd Airborne paratroopers. He was one scary dude, so the MPs brought him back to the gun jeep, and Greg and Johnny took him to the MP station to be booked. Johnny and Greg felt sorry for this GI. But he really needed to be off the streets and getting help. Even though the MPs were afraid of the prisoner, he gave the gun jeep team no trouble on the ride to the MP station.

Vietnamese police stations back then had a problem. They kept blowing up. It was a problem that was very hard to stop because many Vietnamese police were actually Viet Cong, or Viet Cong sympathizers. They would smuggle explosives into work and hide them in the police station until they had enough to blow up the entire building. This happened a lot in 1968 Saigon, and it happened this time while Johnny and Greg were on duty. They were patrolling in Cholon when they heard the explosion. It was only a few blocks away, and it rattled the windows where Johnny and Greg were. Greg went into "code four," flashing red light and siren, and they were the first on the scene. It was bad. Greg was on the radio calling for help as Johnny ran to check on the outside security stations on either side of the entrance, but there was no hope for them. Johnny started helping the few people who were emerging from the rubble. He couldn't do much with only the little first aid kit that they kept in the gun jeep, but he did his best. Johnny was startled when a man who Johnny had already checked out and had thought was dead woke up pinned in the debris and started screaming. Johnny called Greg, and they started lifting the debris off of the man; but when they moved a big piece of a beam from the man, they saw that he was completely crushed in half. When Johnny and Greg saw the man was separated from the rest of his body at the waist and they heard the breath leave the man, they lowered the beam back onto the body; the man was now dead for sure. Johnny would never be able to forget the look in the policeman's eyes as he looked up at Johnny, screaming.

Several other ambulances, MP jeeps, and gun jeeps were arriving on the scene, so Johnny went and sat in his jeep, wanting to cry, but unable to. Greg was one tough GI, so he was still removing rubble, trying to reach someone still alive below. An MP captain who knew Johnny and Greg saw that Johnny was having a hard time, so he told Greg to get Johnny away from the scene. As they drove off Johnny felt better and was soon able to think of something else.

After Curfew Comes the Morning Rush to Market

Soon daylight broke, and the streets came alive. The shopkeepers opened their shops as merchants from the outskirts began bringing their goods to sell on the streets and in the open markets of Saigon.

Johnny and Greg were off duty and, instead of going back to their hotel, they went to the Continental Hotel, a well-known party place for GIs, and by ten thirty that morning they were both drunk. Bar girls and booze seemed to ease Johnny's mind. The bar girls would meet the GIs at the door and try to get the GIs to buy them as many "Saigon teas" as they could. A Saigon tea was not an alcoholic drink; it was usually just colored water, but it cost a lot more than the alcohol the GI was drinking. It was just a way for the bar owner to extract more money from the GIs. Johnny hadn't been much of a drinker, but from this day on he drank every day.

There was a lot going on the next week because General Westmoreland was being replaced by General Abrams, and the gun jeeps were used a lot to move VIPs around Saigon at night. They knew this was the case whenever they were called to the hotel where all the high-ranking military lived. One night there were three gun-jeeps all waiting to escort some high-ranking officers to their destination. The officers were late coming out of the hotel, and the wait went past twenty minutes. Considering the adrenaline level that the gun jeep job maintained, twenty minutes sitting idly by was about ten minutes too long. One of the gunners took out his .45-caliber pistol and started playing with it out of boredom. No one paid much attention until the gun accidentally discharged. The sound echoed off the building walls like a bomb had gone off. The lieutenant came running over to the gunner yelling, "Get him out of here!" to the driver, and the jeep sped off. The lieutenant told Johnny and Greg that they would be one of the gun jeeps that would be escorting General Abrams that night instead of the gun jeep that had had to leave. The guys only got to see the general at a distance because they were assigned to bring up the rear, but they were on full alert because if Charlie wanted to blow up gun jeeps, he must really want to blow up a general.

Johnny and Greg had escorted both Generals Abrams and Westmoreland before the week was over. This was a well-deserved break from racing from one emergency to another all night with the MPs. Johnny seemed to become more of his old self, and for this week the gun jeep team had fun on duty and off.

Two weeks later the gun jeep team had a surreal experience. They were following the MP jeep two blocks behind when the MPs received an urgent call. There was a disturbance in a hotel. When the MPs arrived at the hotel, Greg pulled over to the curb, closing the two blocks of separation from the MP jeep to one block. Hotels had to close and lock their doors at curfew, but the hotel bar could remain open to the people in the hotel for the night. The hotel door was open and the Vietnamese proprietor was standing on the sidewalk, screaming in Vietnamese and pointing inside the hotel. The MPs jumped out of their jeep and drew their nightsticks and ran into the hotel. The MPs had only been in the hotel bar for a few minutes when Johnny and Greg saw two MP helmets come flying out the hotel door. Shortly after that the two MPs were thrown out after their helmets. When the MPs had tried to break up the fight the GIs had removed the MPs helmets, taken their "Billy clubs" away from them, and lumped up the MPs heads with their own nightsticks before throwing them out the front door. When the MPs' bodies came flying out onto the sidewalk, Greg raced the jeep to the hotel door, and Johnny lifted his M60 from the dash board and ran to the entrance of the hotel. Meanwhile the discarded MPs were on the radio, calling in backup.

What Johnny saw in the bar reminded him of the old western movie cowboy barroom brawl scenes, only with American GIs instead of cowboys. Johnny knew that he would have to fire a burst from the M60 to have any chance of breaking up the fight. He was afraid that if he fired into the ceiling he might kill or wound someone on the floors above, so Johnny pointed his M60 up and put a short burst of machine gun fire into the top of the doorjamb. The result shocked even Johnny. Everyone froze in mid-punch, and all heads turned toward the door where Johnny stood. With that one short burst of machine gun fire, the fight was over. Johnny knew that many GIs would be in big trouble and he never had liked getting his own troops in trouble, so in a loud voice Johnny ordered everyone to go back to their rooms. The hotel bar emptied surprisingly fast and just in time, as three more MP jeeps with their gun jeeps came screeching to a stop outside the hotel entrance. After finding no one to arrest and realizing that in order to find those responsible they would have had to go door to door to every room in the hotel, the MPs decided to let it slide, and everyone left. Johnny felt proud that he had saved some of the GIs a blot on their military records. The disgruntled MPs were not pleased, but what could they do? And Papasan, the bar owner—well, he'd get over it.

The Motorcycle Cyclo in Saigon

CHAPTER 3

WHO IS THE ENEMY?

Every day off in Saigon was a new adventure interspersed with fear and excitement for Johnny. Wondering if the barber with a straight razor at your throat was going to shave you or cut your throat, or if the taxi driver taking you about town was a Viet Cong could really mess with your head. Saigon was, after all, the main R&R (Rest and Recuperation)—or, in civilian terminology, the main vacation—spot for both the Viet Cong and the NVA (North Vietnam Army). This, however, did not slow Johnny down.

In downtown Saigon, an off-duty GI had a lot to do. Just getting from one place to another was insanely fun because Johnny always rode in the motorcycle cyclos, where the passenger was actually the front bumper. The motorcycle cyclo driver would dart in and out of traffic at breakneck speed, making a ride to the PX (Post Exchange—or Store) more like an amusement park ride.

There were bars everywhere, and people selling everything that you could imagine. Not to mention the "Scientific Massage Parlor," where the beautiful women masseuses offered way more than just a massage; and almost every bar and hotel doubled as a whorehouse.

Johnny loved to interact with the Vietnamese people, especially the people who lived on the outskirts of town. He would spend hours talking to people using pidgin French and hand gestures. The Vietnamese were a warm and friendly people, and very patient. They would sometimes invite Johnny to have a meal with them. Johnny would never turn them down, no matter how unappetizing the meal might look or smell. He knew that monkey brains were a delicacy in Vietnam, but he felt safe from that dish because his high school had served cow brains once a week and he knew what brains looked like. He also had heard that they ate dogs and cats. Johnny thought this might even be true because he had never seen a dog or a cat on the streets of Saigon, but none of this really bothered him. The important thing to Johnny was to be respectful and polite, and to try to learn more about what the Vietnamese people were really like.

The next night Johnny and Greg were back on duty when the MPs they were guarding got a call about another disturbance at a hotel. This time it wasn't a barroom brawl. It was a GI who had smashed up the lobby and barricaded himself in his room. The MPs asked Johnny to come into the hotel with his M60 machine gun for backup because the GI barricaded in the room had claimed to have a machine gun.

When Johnny got to the second floor, the MPs said that they hadn't heard anything from the GI in the room for quite a while. They had decided to kick in the door and rush the GI, so Johnny put his back against the wall opposite the door of the room to keep himself stable if he had to fire the M60. Two MPs with a handheld battering ram stepped in front of the door, and with one hit of the battering ram, the door flew open. Johnny could see the GI lying on the bed and not moving.

At first everyone thought that the GI might have killed himself, but it turned out that he was just passed out from over drinking. He was unarmed, and no weapons were found in the room. However, in the closet, they found a stack of eight or ten ration cards. The GI was AWOL and had been living in the hotel for several months. The MPs suspected that he had been surviving by making a living on the black market. The MPs asked Johnny if he would transport the GI to the MP station for booking. Johnny knew that the MPs were not afraid of this GI, and that they were asking for the GI to ride in the gun jeep because they didn't want to risk the GI throwing up in their MP jeep, but Johnny said okay anyway.

The wind in his face seemed to revive the GI, and he seemed to be in good spirits. Johnny asked him what he was doing with the ration cards, and the GI went into a long explanation and even seemed glad to have been caught. The GI told Johnny and Greg that he would take a ration card and get in one of the tiny Vietnamese cabs and show the driver the ration card. Usually the cab driver would say, "You buy for me?" and the GI would be in business. Even if the cab driver did not buy black-market goods, he would take you to a cab driver who did. The drunken GI said that the cab driver would take the ration card and race off through traffic, darting from one lane to another to get the GI to the first PX as fast as possible.

While driving in very challenging traffic, the driver would open a tiny bottle and paint over the squares that would be checked at the PX when the rationed items were purchased, using a clear liquid that was invisible when it dried. About then the cab would come screeching to a halt at the first PX. Budweiser beer and Salem cigarettes were the most valuable black market PX items, so the GI would buy all of those two items that the ration card would allow. At checkout the clerk would check each square for the allotted items with a ballpoint pen, and the GI would take the beer and cigarettes out and put them in the trunk of the cab.

The cab driver would speed the GI to the next PX while taking out yet another tiny bottle and dabbing its contents on the ration card squares that had just been checked off. The second clear liquid would remove the first coating along with the ink check mark from the ball point pen. All that would be left would be a check mark–shaped groove that the pressure of the ballpoint pen had made in the ration card. The GI explained that then the cab driver would simply place the ration card on the metal dash of the cab and take out a Zippo lighter and, using the edge of the Zippo, would iron out the check mark groove, and the same ration card could be used to buy the same items again with a fresh coat of clear liquid from the first tiny bottle.

As the MP jeep reached the station, Greg closed in to turn over the GI to the MPs. While Johnny was walking the GI to the MP jeep to turn him over to the MPs, he told the GI that he should tell the MPs about the ration cards, and as Johnny walked away he heard the GI telling the MP all about the ration card scam.

Back on patrol and not a half an hour later, the gun jeep team found themselves racing after the MP jeep, code four, to the next emergency call. Johnny and Greg loved to use the flashing red light and siren. This call was about a reported gang of Vietnamese "cowboys" or a "teenage gang of juvenile delinquents," as they were called back in the States. They were smashing car windows and stealing anything they could find inside. There were six or seven of them, and as soon as they saw the MP jeep they ran around the corner and up an alley. The MPs waved the gun jeep in, and

Greg sped to the scene. Greg came to a screeching halt in the alleyway, and Johnny grabbed the M60 and stood in the center of the entrance to the alley. The assault bag that was attached to the machine gun held the usual seven hundred and fifty rounds. They were supposed to put a tracer round every seventh round not only to produce a bright red line defining the path of the bullets but also to produce a virtual light show. Johnny had put seven hundred and fifty tracer rounds in his assault bag. The tracer rounds were coated with phosphorus, and when they passed through the barrel the friction ignited the phosphorus, producing a glowing bright red line so you could see exactly where the bullets were going, and direct them much like you would a garden hose.

The alley was pitch black and Johnny didn't want the disadvantage of running into darkness after the cowboys, so he opened fire up the alley and emptied the assault bag of all seven hundred and fifty tracer rounds. What a light show! The red stream of rounds swirling down the alley, ricocheting off everything they touched, made both of the MPs gasp in delight. As soon as the assault bag was empty, Johnny flipped up the locking latch and let the machine gun barrel fall to the ground.

The barrel, lying on the ground, glowed with a dull red color at the base where the bullets had entered the chamber. Seven hundred and fifty tracer rounds in a row had created so much heat inside the barrel that it had ruined the barrel by erasing the rifling inside. Greg held the new barrel in place while Johnny flipped the locking latch back down into the lock position. Then Johnny popped open the top cover of the M60, and Greg was right there with an ammo can containing a belt of one thousand rounds. Greg slapped the end of the belt across the M60 as Johnny slammed the cover shut, locking the rounds in place, and the team began to move in slowly to clear the alley one dark corner at a time. Half a block down the alley the tracer rounds had started a fire in a pile of trash stacked against a brick building's wall, so this part could be cleared faster because of the light the small fire made. The gun jeep team let the fire burn as they moved down the alley into the darkness because it could not spread. The cowboys knew every inch of these alleys and were probably blocks away by then, but the alley still had to be searched. It took about a half an hour to clear the alley for two blocks. It was a rather intense half an hour for Johnny and Greg because they were busy finding out if they had chased the cowboys into the alley or been led down the alley and into an ambush. The cowboys were long gone.

The gun jeep team went back on patrol until a few hours later when the MPs got a call that an American GI was being held and tortured at a South Vietnamese police station. Of course, the South Vietnamese police were supposed to be on our side, but whatever the GI had done had really pissed them off. Four gun-jeeps were called to the scene, and since Johnny and Greg were already near the police station, they arrived first. The street in front of the police station was barricaded with concertina wire at both ends of the block. In the middle of the block was the police station with two concrete machine gun bunkers, one on either side of the front entrance, with machine gun barrels sticking out of each bunker. As Greg pulled the gun jeep up to the concertina wire, the gun-jeep team saw the two machine gun barrels turn to point at their vehicle.

Despite this, Johnny jumped out, grabbing his M60 from its holder. Johnny held the machine gun on his right hip as he walked over to the concertina wire, grabbed the wire with his left hand, and began pulling it out of the road so the jeep could enter the compound. The whole time, Johnny kept the barrel of his M60 pointing at the bunkers. The timing was perfect; as soon as Johnny had the concertina wire out of the road, an MP jeep, escorted by three gun-jeeps, came racing up and drove into the compound. Johnny felt some relief as he saw the two Vietnamese machine gun barrels move from him to follow the other gun jeeps as they entered the compound. Things were very tense as the MP officer stepped out of his jeep and walked toward the front door of the police station with an entourage of heavily armed troops. As they entered the police station Johnny saw the barrels of both machine guns in the bunkers slowly turn back to him and Greg. Inside, the MP officer and his men found the GI lying on the floor of his cell, badly beaten and unconscious. They were able to revive the GI, but he couldn't walk; so, when they came out the front door of the South Vietnamese Police Station, two MPs were holding the GI's arms, one on each side, and they were more or less carrying him with his feet dragging behind him. If even one shot had been fired, either inside the police station or outside, a tremendous firefight would have erupted between the two "friendly" forces. The MPs made their way back to their jeeps with the GI and went tearing out of the compound. When all the jeeps were out,

Johnny got back out of his jeep with his machine gun and put the concertina wire back across the street and the last gun jeep team drove off. When they got back to the MP station the GI was awake and able to talk, and Greg and Johnny were relieved to see that the GI would be alright.

Johnny and Greg's Saigon Home at the Capitol Hotel

CHAPTER 4

THREAT FROM WITHIN

In the Army one tour of duty in a combat zone was eleven months long, and any more tours after that would each be six months long. Johnny had been in Saigon for almost three months of his six-month tour. He had learned all the ins and outs of his job, and he knew his way around Saigon by day or night.

Johnny liked to drink at different bars so he wouldn't become attached to, or fall in love with, a bar girl as so many others had. Before coming to Vietnam he had worried that his relationship with his girlfriend would not be able to withstand an eleven-month absence. The "Dear John" letter he received early on had proven him correct so he decided to remain unattached until he returned home. He was stopping at this new bar because... well, let's just say he wasn't thirsty.

Johnny was riding in a motorcycle cyclo on the outskirts of Cholon, when he spotted a bar and told his driver to stop. He paid the driver and headed across the busy street to the bar. Just as Johnny had crossed the street he heard squealing brakes behind him. Johnny spun around to see an old Vietnamese woman lying in the street and a little motorcycle speeding away. It was a hit and run. Johnny rushed over to the old woman, asking if she was alright, but the woman was very mad and yelling in Vietnamese at the long-gone motorcycle.

When the woman tried to stand up she found that she couldn't put any weight on her ankle, so Johnny carried her to the side of the street. He sat the old lady on the curb and ran back to get her shopping bag out of the street. The old woman spoke no English at all, so Johnny found a passerby who could translate for him. He had the man who had volunteered to translate ask the woman if she needed to go to the hospital. She was very emphatic that she did not want to go to the hospital; she wanted to go home, and she pointed to a small side street just fifty meters away.

Johnny didn't see any way to get out of this "good Samaritan" task, so he picked the old woman up in his arms, and he and the translator went up the side street. This was the entrance to one of the many maze-like neighborhoods that the gun jeep teams were instructed not to enter without serious backup. There were too many turns for Johnny to remember how to get out on his own, so it was a good thing that the translator had come along. These neighborhoods were known to be Viet Cong strongholds because they were so very easy to disappear in.

When they finally got to the old lady's home her family came out and the translator and the old lady told the family what was going on, and they lit up. They insisted that Johnny and the translator come into their house, and they seated them at a small table by the front window. The interior of the house was very clean, but very stark and bare. The man of the family sent one of his boys out, who came back shortly with two sodas. They were Coca Cola, but the Vietnamese version that tasted kind of funny. The sodas were opened and set in front of Johnny and the translator, so Johnny took a drink and acted like it was delicious. He sipped his soda as the family made the grandmother comfortable.

Johnny happened to glance out the window, and what he saw made him jump out of his chair and hide from being seen through the window. He peeked out, and across the small street and two doors down was his captain, in civilian clothes, standing in an open doorway and talking to a very unsavory-looking Vietnamese man. They both looked very serious. The conversation ended, and the shady-looking Vietnamese man stepped into his house and closed the door as the captain came up the opposite side of the street, walked past the house where Johnny was, and disappeared down the first side street. Johnny didn't want his captain to see him because GIs never came into a neighborhood like this unless they were after drugs. Johnny was sure he had smelled opium on the way through this neighborhood, but it was hard to tell with all the other strange smells. Was the captain a junkie?

After he was sure the captain was long gone, Johnny drank the rest of the soda and thanked the family for their hospitality, and he and the translator left. Even the translator got lost on the way out but, luckily, he could ask someone for directions, and soon they were back on the main street where the whole thing had begun. Johnny had been surprised how an act of kindness had turned into such an adventure. He felt like he had risked his life going into the maze-like neighborhood, but he felt good about helping the old lady.

Johnny went into the bar he had originally started for and spent the rest of the afternoon drinking. He found one of the bar girls to his liking, and they stayed together until it was time for him to leave to get ready for the evening's work in the gun-jeep.

"You take me United States?" the bar girl asked Johnny in her broken English. Johnny gave her the same answer he always used. "I be here long time," he said as he walked out of the bar and headed back to his hotel to get ready for work.

On patrol a few nights later, Greg told Johnny that he should start calling him "short-timer" because his tour would be over in a few more weeks. Greg would be going home to Illinois because he was getting out of Vietnam and the army at the same time. The two soldiers exchanged stateside addresses and swore to look each other up back in the "land of the big PX." Johnny had just under four months left in his tour. He too would be getting out of Saigon and the army, so they both would once again be civilians after this tour of duty.

CHAPTER 5

THE NEW DRIVER

The next few weeks went by very fast, and then Greg was gone. Things just didn't seem as much fun without Greg, but Johnny's new driver was a good guy, and they got along fine.

Johnny's new driver, Bob Philips, was fast to learn and a good driver. Johnny taught him many signs of danger to look out for on the streets of Saigon. The big test for Bob was how he would react in an emergency, and Bob would pass that test with flying colors— numerous times, in fact.

One night they responded to a call where a GI was holding a prostitute hostage with a pistol at her head in a hotel bar. When they arrived on the scene the MPs wanted to wait for backup, but Johnny thought that more MPs would probably scare the GI and might push him over the edge. Johnny went into the hotel lobby by himself. The entrance to the bar was a big double door, and both doors were opened. Johnny peeked around the doorway, and there was the GI holding a pistol to the head of a very frightened bar girl.

As the GI looked up at Johnny, Johnny said, "Knock, knock!" in a very friendly voice, and he stepped into the open doorway with no weapon drawn. Johnny saying "knock knock" seemed to take the edge off the situation. "How's it going?" asked Johnny.

"Not good," replied the frightened GI.

"I just wanted to see if I could be of any help before this gets too far out of control," Johnny said. He could tell that the GI wanted a way out, so Johnny talked the guy into not pointing the pistol at the girl's head, because the girl was beginning to look like she might panic. Then Johnny came forward and asked where the GI was from, and a dialog was started to defuse the situation further.

"What would you do if your Mom and Dad were here right now?" he asked the GI. The GI's eyes began to stream tears, and the GI said that if they were here he would hug them. And he began to openly cry. "Well," said Johnny, "I'm the only one here, so you better just give me a hug." And with that the GI dropped the pistol and gave Johnny a big hug.

They came out the front door of the hotel just as the other MPs were arriving, but Johnny had his arm around the GI's shoulders and was smiling like they were old friends. The arriving MPs didn't even get out of their jeeps as Johnny led the GI to the back of his gun jeep and put him in the back seat. The situation probably would have gone bad if four MPs with weapons drawn had busted into that bar instead of Johnny. Many of the GIs that they had to deal with were combat veterans who had had all they could handle, and some had even run away from the military to go live in Saigon. Johnny respected these guys and thought that if he had to do a tour out in the boonies that he might have ended up just like they had.

They drove the GI to the MP station as they talked with him about where they lived in the US and what they planned to do when they got home. This got the soldier's mind off his troubles, and by the time they arrived at the MP station they were all laughing and joking.

After a few weeks, the new gun jeep team was truly a team. They both knew that the other could be trusted with both their lives and safety. In a combat zone, you may have to work with someone that you normally couldn't get along with in civilian life. The differences that would normally cause conflict are, in a combat zone, much less important. All that matters is how you react in an emergency; can you be depended on when the stuff hits the fan? Not only were differences ignored, but the bond that would be established in a few weeks, when you knew you could trust each other with your lives, would probably take decades to establish in civilian life.

The next call that night was to yet another hotel bar where there was a disturbance. Most GI disturbances at night were in the hotel bars because no one was allowed on the streets after curfew. However, all the people in a hotel could party in the hotel bar even after curfew as previously mentioned, when the hotel doors were locked. And party they did. When the MPs arrived, they waved the gun jeep in and had Johnny and his M60 back them up. It turned out to be a big argument between a GI, a bar girl, and the bar owner. The GI had discovered what was common knowledge to most: that the expensive "Saigon tea" drinks that the bar girl kept ordering were nothing but colored water. The GI had refused to pay his rather large bar bill, and the argument had escalated to the point where the GI had thrown a fifth of whiskey into the big mirror behind the bar. That's when the hotel owner had called the MPs.

The MPs opinion always seemed to have a lot of influence on any situation, but folks seemed to be even more cooperative when Johnny was standing behind the MPs with his M60 machine gun. They made the GI pay his bar bill and told the bar owner that they were arresting the GI for breaking the mirror because he didn't have enough money to pay for it. The MPs took the GI up to his room in the hotel to gather up his belongings, and Johnny went back out to his gun jeep and put his "60" back in its mount.

In a few minutes, the MPs brought the GI out and put him in the back of their jeep, and they all took off. Johnny thought they were going to the MP station to book the GI, but the MP jeep pulled up in front of another hotel and waved the gun jeep in. Bob pulled up behind the MP jeep and Johnny went to talk to the MPs and find out what was going on. It turned out that the MPs didn't want to book the GI for breaking the hotel mirror, so they banged on the new hotel's door until someone answered it} and the GI was freed to go in and rent a new room. He had promised the MPs that he would behave himself and that he now knew that when he bought a bar girl a Saigon tea he was not paying for the drink, but rather for the lady's company while he drank. Johnny and Bob were pleased to see that these MPs seemed to care about the American GIs.

A little over one month after Johnny and Bob became a gun jeep team, they were on patrol when the MP jeep pulled over and waved at Johnny and Bob to close in. The MPs were going to visit a friend of theirs who was CID.

CID is like the military version of the FBI. The MPs explained that they would be going to the Korean post snack bar, the only place in Saigon to get food at night, to buy dinner for their CID friends who were on a stakeout. They got the food, and drove to a part of town that looked run-down even for Saigon. They followed the MP jeep down an alley and parked right behind the MPs beside a dark entrance to a five-story building. The old building spanned a half a block, overlooking a rather shady neighborhood.

Johnny had Bob stay with the gun jeep in the alley, and he went with the MPs into the dark hallway that intersected with another hallway that they took to the left. This hallway was very long, and ran the entire length of the building. The MPs had flashlights, but they weren't allowed to use light in the building because if it were seen it could blow the cover of the stakeout. Everyone just walked dragging one hand against the hallway wall until they got their night vision. Johnny was surprised that he could see so well in the dark hallway once he got his night vision.

At the far end of the hall they entered a room that was also dark, and three CID guys were there. Two of them were sitting at a table and one was at the window, looking down at the street below with what looked like a telescope on a tripod with a camera on the end you look through. It was the biggest telephoto lens on a camera that Johnny had ever seen. The MPs put the food on the table. The two CID guys at the table handed the CID guy on the telescope his dinner and they all tore into it like they hadn't eaten in days.

The CID guys told them that they were watching some known Viet Cong who were involved in the black market to get supplies for the Viet Cong war effort. This wasn't beer and cigarettes. They were getting grenades, weapons, and ammunition from an Army compound, and they were supplying them directly to the Viet Cong to be used against American soldiers. The bad news was that so far, the CID had been unable to find out who the American traitor was who was dealing with the Viet Cong— the inside man. They had staked out the ammo dump where the supplies were turning up missing, but they only had observed underlings, and they wanted the main man.

The guy on the telescope offered Johnny and the MPs a look through the scope, and a line formed with Johnny at the end. When it was Johnny's turn, he was amazed. It was surprisingly clear for nighttime looking through the scope. The telescope was aimed at the doorway of a one-story building across the street. As Johnny was looking through the scope, the door across the street opened and two Vietnamese men stepped out. Johnny paused in shock before alerting the CID guy. One of the Vietnamese men was the man that Johnny had seen his captain mysteriously visiting the day he had helped the old lady home after she had been hit by the motorcycle. When Johnny alerted the CID guys that someone was in the doorway, things got very busy very fast. The CID guy moved Johnny back from the camera and started clicking pictures. The MPs grabbed Johnny by the arm, and they left. Johnny's head was spinning all the way back to the gun jeep, wondering what his captain would be doing with a known Viet Cong. Did his captain know that the man he had visited was Viet Cong? Should he be warned? Or was he the American traitor that the CID guys were looking for?

For the next three days Johnny was a mess, as he couldn't decide what to do about his captain. If he went to his captain and it turned out that the captain was knowingly dealing with the Viet Cong, Johnny's life wouldn't be worth a dime, and he would never make it home alive. He finally came to the conclusion that he had to do something because American soldiers' lives were at stake. Johnny knew an MP colonel who he felt was honest. Johnny had escorted him with the gun jeep, and the colonel had come back to the gun jeep and talked to Johnny for quite a while. He got up his courage and went to see the colonel.

When Johnny entered the colonel's office he began by saying that what he was there to talk about may be nothing at all, but that if it was real his life was probably in danger. The colonel listened intently, and even jotted down some notes on a pad as Johnny went through the whole story. He told the colonel about the old lady being hit by the motorcycle and how he had seen his captain talking to the same man he had later seen with the CID guys at the stakeout. After Johnny was finished telling all the details, the colonel told Johnny not to speak of this matter to anyone because it could interfere with the ongoing CID investigation. The colonel assured Johnny that he would make sure that Johnny was safe. Then he dismissed Johnny, and the meeting was over. Johnny was surprised that the colonel hadn't wanted to talk more with him about the matter, and this didn't leave Johnny feeling very safe. As Johnny walked back to the street to hail a motorcycle cyclo, he couldn't help wondering how good of friends the colonel might be with his captain.

CHAPTER 6

THE COLONEL

Days went by, and Johnny heard nothing from the colonel. His paranoia grew by the hour, and Johnny drank more every day. All he could think about was that he would be killed before he could get home to see his family. If the captain wanted him killed, he was in big trouble. The captain could have him killed at any time in his barracks, or at any military compound. If the Viet Cong were going to kill him, they could get him anytime on the streets of Saigon. There was no place where Johnny could feel safe. He was even afraid to tell Bob. Every night on patrol he had to fight the urge to tell Bob, but he knew that he may be putting Bob's life in danger too if he told him.

Every emergency call that Johnny and Bob responded to made Johnny wonder if this call was a setup for him to be killed. Johnny had less than two months left to complete his tour of duty, but he really didn't think that he would be allowed to live that long. Even if he was, he didn't think he could take all the pressure he was under for that long.

Then, one day before work, Johnny was riding in a motorcycle cyclo when the driver stopped at a red light. A long black French car pulled up next to Johnny and stopped. As the back window began to roll down, Johnny focused on the driver. It was the Viet Cong that he had seen talking to his captain. Johnny didn't hesitate—he dove out of the cyclo, taking cover behind the cyclo driver; but, as soon as he did that, the cyclo driver sped away, running the red light and leaving Johnny without cover. Johnny dove between two parked cars as a shot rang out from the back window of the black car. The shot was so close to Johnny's head that he could hear it cutting through the air as he slammed onto the pavement with his chest and legs. He could hear the screaming tires of the black car as it sped away. It was a setup. The fact that the cyclo driver had been part of the ambush became clear when he sped away in order to deny Johnny cover. Johnny was shaken. He was afraid to take a cyclo or a cab, so he ran three blocks back to his hotel. He would not leave the hotel except to work his shift the next night.

Johnny had no way to know, but the nice man who had been so grateful for Johnny's having helped his elderly mother after she was hit by the motorcycle was required to report any Americans who came into the neighborhood to the Viet Cong officer who lived across the street. However, Johnny did know that if the Viet Cong knew, his captain surely also knew.

When Johnny and Bob finished their night on patrol, Bob had dropped Johnny off and had gone to turn in the gun jeep. Johnny was going into the hotel when a very starched and spit-shined MP lieutenant approached him. Johnny recognized him as the colonel's orderly, but still did not trust him.

"The colonel wants to see you," the MP said, and Johnny was escorted to a jeep with his heart in his throat. The short drive from the hotel in Cholon to the Air Force installation seemed to take forever. Johnny thought that this day would probably be referred to by his parents back home as the day that he was killed in Vietnam. Johnny did not speak to the MP lieutenant, or the driver, the entire way.

Johnny Being Driven to the Air Force Base

When they arrived, the driver escorted Johnny to the colonel's office. Standing at attention in front of the colonel, Johnny saluted and said, "Sergeant Stone reporting as ordered, sir." The colonel looked up from some papers on his desk, casually returning the salute, and told Johnny to take a seat. He handed some papers to Johnny and told him to read them very carefully, and to sign them if everything was correct.

Johnny read the papers carefully. It was a deposition of Johnny's testimony, and it read exactly as things had happened. Johnny read and signed the papers and handed them back to the colonel. Then the colonel put his signature on the papers that Johnny had just signed, plus on a second set of papers that he handed to Johnny.

"You have done a great service to your country by stepping forward with much-needed information about an ongoing CID investigation," said the colonel. "These are your travel orders to go home. For your own safety we are ending your tour of duty now." And with that said, the colonel pointed to the corner of his office behind Johnny. Johnny was shocked to see all of his belongings stacked on the floor. The colonel told Johnny that he had had Johnny's locker cleaned out and his belongings all gathered up and instructed Johnny to put everything in the duffel bag lying by his belongings.

Johnny filled the duffel bag and closed the top by clipping the strap to it. The whole time Johnny's mind was racing. He had been told that he was going home, but he still wasn't sure if he would be allowed to leave the country alive. Johnny packed his belongings and returned to standing at attention in front of the colonel's desk with the duffel bag strapped over his shoulder. The colonel pressed his intercom button and called the driver back into his office. The colonel told the driver to take Johnny to the airstrip and to make sure he got on his plane safely. He told Johnny that all the out-processing had been taken care of, and all Johnny had to do was get on the plane and go home. The colonel smiled as he shook Johnny's hand—and thanked him again.

The colonel's driver not only drove Johnny to the airstrip but had clearance papers to drive Johnny right onto the runway where his plane was loading. Johnny was just now able to allow the thought of making it home alive to enter his mind. But still he wasn't sure if his being sent home was part of a cover-up, or to keep him safe like the colonel had said. Johnny thanked the driver and boarded the plane.

The other GIs going home thought that Johnny must be somebody special because he had been driven to the plane while the others had waited several hours just to get to the plane. As soon as the plane left the ground, the GI sitting next to Johnny pulled a fifth of Scotch whiskey out of his luggage and offered Johnny a drink. Johnny got drunk, and even had time to sleep it off during the twenty-two-hour flight back to the States. Johnny used the sleep to pass the time on the long journey home. He only woke up for meals because he hadn't had much good sleep for the last few weeks. Sleep was the only thing that could stop his mind from racing.

Johnny woke up to the pilot announcing that they would be landing soon in Oakland, California. Johnny felt a bit hung over, but he also felt something he had not felt in a long time—he felt safe. He thought that if the plane didn't crash on landing he was home safe. Johnny had a thirty-day leave before he was to report to Fort Benning, where they train soldiers to be paratroopers. Johnny, however, was assigned to be the driver for a lieutenant colonel. This would be a cushy job for Johnny, but something was wrong.

Johnny had PTSD from the terror he had seen in Saigon, and untreated PTSD only grows until it takes over your entire life. Johnny tried to get help from the VA (Veterans Administration), but their rule was that only soldiers in combat situations could get PTSD. As it turned out, this denial of benefits was done as a cost-saving method, and it was done with malice because it is common knowledge that policemen, firemen, EMTs and emergency room workers all can get PTSD from their work. Not to mention that victims of rape and other traumas also get PTSD. Even psychiatrists can get PTSD simply from hearing other peoples' terrible problems day in and day out and, as a result, psychiatrists have a very high suicide rate.

Because PTSD can often take years to become chronic, the number of Vietnam veteran suicides would eventually triple the 58,220 soldiers killed in the entire fourteen-year long Vietnam War. Johnny, luckily, would not be among the suicides because, thanks to the very good support system his family provided, Johnny's PTSD never became chronic. Johnny became one of those veterans who never spoke of the war. He put his Vietnam experiences in the back of his mind and fought daily to keep them there.

A few years after Johnny got out of the Army, he and Greg would be reunited. The Saigon Machine Gun Patrol gun-jeep team would remain friends for life.

IV - The Curse of the Buddhist Monastery

Bombed-Out Monastery Overlooking Tuy Hoa, Vietnam

CHAPTER 1

THE MONASTERY

Philip Turner grew up in Los Angeles, California, in a big house. His mother grew flowers all around her house, and Phil had fond memories of running and playing in a backyard that was a beautiful botanical garden. It even had a very small bridge that spanned a very small artificial stream that served as a watering station for the local birds.

As a child Phil always liked to play war, and this would come in handy because that's just where he ended up.

It was Sergeant Philip Turner's third tour of duty in Vietnam. It was 1966, and the war was at its peak. Phil had been through eighteen months of combat on his first two tours with the 101st Airborne Division and was having trouble with Post Traumatic Stress Disorder (PTSD). Combat PTSD is a disorder that ruins many lives. It happens when soldiers do things (normal combat) that are against their very nature. Brought up believing in rules like "Thou shall not kill" and many other laws of goodness that we are taught as children, the soldier, in combat, is put in a terrible situation. These basic rules must be ignored in order to take part in combat. The human mind's response to violating these rules is to become self-destructive and can even lead to suicide.

Phil had been in three firefights where over half of his side had been wiped out. He carried the M79 grenade launcher. One round weighed a half a pound. When fired, the round would spin from the rifling in the barrel. The round would arm itself after two hundred and fifty revolutions and then explode when it hit something solid. Phil's body count was big enough to garner respect from the other GIs in his unit—as well as from the officers. Phil was having a hard time not constantly thinking about an assault on a small village where his unit had been pinned down by sniper fire. The lieutenant had called Phil up to the front of the column and pointed out the hooch from which the hostile fire was coming. "Put one through that window," the lieutenant had told Phil.

The first round went right through the window, through the back wall, and out the back side of the hooch, exploding in the trees behind the it. The second round blew up inside the hooch, and the sniper fire did not happen again. Phil had to go check out the hooch, and after looking in the hooch he had never been able to get the sight he saw out of his mind. The sniper was long gone, but an old lady and a baby she had been holding were both horribly killed.

He had tried to put the sight out of his mind, but to no avail. It was like having a terrible test pattern in his mind. Every time his mind would slow down, there was the terrible test pattern again. Phil had built up way too many "test patterns" after two tours of duty in the jungle hunting Charlie.

Because he had been having a hard time dealing with his combat experiences, he had been assigned to a cushy job in Tuy Hoa to help him recover from his combat tours. Almost no one did a combat tour in the jungle fighting and then volunteered for another combat tour in the jungle like Phil had. But now, on his "safe" tour, he was having frightening dreams that would leave him sweating and trembling and easily startled, which wasn't like Phil at all. And sometimes a sound or smell would give him a flashback that seemed so real it made him question his own sanity.

He had been a fearless squad leader in the jungle who had earned the respect of all who served under him. Not to mention that Phil had earned two Purple Hearts and a Bronze Star during his two combat tours.

He had earned his first Purple Heart for a gunshot wound in his leg that was just a graze, but still needed hospitalization. Phil had gotten his second Purple Heart along with his Bronze Star, but he didn't remember anything about how he earned them. All he knew was that he would never see his best friend, Bob Lawson, again because Bobby was killed in the same ambush that Phil couldn't remember.

Now, he had decided to try to do something about his worsening condition. Phil had been talking to some short timers who were on their way home from their combat tour, and they had told Phil that helping others was good medicine for having been in too much combat. This sounded good to Phil, but he had no idea of how to go about helping others. For the past eighteen months, Phil had been doing more "killing others" than "helping others." He tried handing out money, but that ended up with a crowd of children following him everywhere he went, wanting more.

When he was in Tuy Hoa, he would buy his cigarettes one at a time from children. The kids made big business out of buying a pack of cigarettes and selling them one by one for a few cents each on the streets to make a profit on the pack. There were shoeshine boys everywhere you went in Tuy Hoa, so Phil kept them busy shining his boots every chance he could. These businesses were small, to say the least, but they provided much-needed income for the families of the children. Phil was looking for more ways to help others.

One day Phil went to the local hospital in Tuy Hoa and talked to a doctor who had told him that the hospital was always running out of things like tongue depressors, gauze, bandages. The next day Phil had gone to a friend in the supply tent and told him about the hospital's problem, and the friend had made Phil a "care package" for the hospital. The box of medical supplies was big, but not too big for Phil to carry out to the jeep by himself. He loaded the supplies in the back of the jeep and drove into town to the Vietnamese hospital. The doctor he had talked to was off duty, and Phil was reluctant to leave the supplies because they were very valuable on the black market. The doctor was summoned from his home and was at the hospital within ten minutes. He did not seem to be upset about being called back to the hospital on his day off, and everyone was very grateful for the supplies. This made Phil feel good about himself, which was very good medicine for Phil's PTSD.

On the top of a hill overlooking the Vietnamese town of Tuy Hoa was a bombed-out deserted monastery. Phil often climbed the hill to the monastery and watched the activity of the town below when he needed to get away from it all. But today Phil noticed the bright yellow and orange robes of Buddhist monks busy all around the monastery. Phil climbed the hill to see what was going on at his sanctuary from the army.

Phil spoke enough pidgin French-Vietnamese to find out what the monks were up to, although it was a long. drawn-out process involving a lot of hand gesturing and drawing in the dirt with a stick. The monks were very gracious and patient and told Phil that they were going to try to restore the monastery and turn it into an orphanage.

The monks gave Phil a tour of the monastery, making signs in each room for what the room would be used for. In one room they made an eating motion with their hands, and even Phil could tell they were eating with chopsticks, the sign was so clear. In another room they made a sign for sleeping, and Phil was surprised that it was the same sign that Americans/Westerners use—hands together as if to pray used as a pillow with the head tilted and the eyes closed. The most difficult part to understand was that they were going to build a wooden structure attached to the monastery that would serve as the school for the orphans. Everyone smiled broadly when they saw that Phil was finally catching on about the school, and they all had a big laugh about how hard it was to convey a simple message through the language barrier.

After the tour of the monastery, Phil noticed a monk using a fallen stone block for a desk and going over some papers. The monk looked up and saw Phil watching, and smiled at Phil and then went back to his work with the papers. Phil could see that the monk was working with numbers, so Phil pointed at the papers and made a face like he didn't understand. After the monk had made several attempts to explain what the numbers were all about, Phil caught on and understood that the monk was figuring out the expenses for the materials needed to restore the monastery. Phil saw this as a chance to help others, so he dug down into his pocket and gave the monk all the money he had. The monks seemed more grateful than a little under three dollars worth of Vietnamese dong notes would make anyone in the States, but the feeling Phil got was like medicine. Even though it was just a few dollars, Phil felt better immediately and the monks were delighted. Phil even slept through the entire night that night for the first time in a long while. This was the light at the end of the tunnel for Phil. This was the first time that he had found anything that seemed to help with the heavy depression that he had been experiencing. He felt that he could find some relief, or maybe even a cure, for the PTSD that had taken over his life. Phil had a new mission and he dove in head first, and for the first time in a long time Phil felt like he had hope.

Open Storefront Living Room in Tuy Hoa

CHAPTER 2

THE NON-COMBAT MISSION

In Vietnam there was a numerical system to define degrees of good and bad. Actually, there was only one number defining the term "good," and that was number one. Everywhere you went you would hear, "You number one GI." This meant that you were good. Then there was number ten that meant bad. If they would say "GI number ten," you knew that the GI had done them wrong. Then there was a number for very, very bad, and that number was ten thousand. When talking about the Viet Cong, they would say, "VC number ten thousand."

It seemed like everyone in Tuy Hoa was friendly to GIs. One day Phil was walking in Tuy Hoa when he came to a storefront living room. A family lived in a storefront right off the main street. The entire front wall was opened onto the street. Phil had stopped and asked if he could take a picture of their home, all with gestures, a few words in French and Vietnamese, and facial expressions. It seemed like everyone in Vietnam wanted to be in, or at least help with, any photo that was being taken. The father of the family invited Phil to stay and join them in a meal. It turned out that the family's uncle had owned the store, and he had been killed by the Viet Cong during the Vietnamese holiday Tet for being friendly with Americans. The father's name was Thao, which in Vietnamese means "courtesy, and he certainly was courteous.

Thao and his family had lived in the countryside outside of Tuy Hoa, and he had been a rice farmer. The problem was that they had lived on their farm so far out that they had no security. When American troops would come through the area they had to be very pro-American, and when the Viet Cong came through they had to be very pro–Viet Cong. It didn't matter which side was there, the Viet Cong or the Americans: if the soldiers got the idea that Thao was not on their side, the entire family would be killed and the farm burned to the ground. Normally a rice farmer outside a city could grow all the rice he had land for and sell the excess in the city. However, because of the war Thao could only grow enough rice to barely feed his family.

When the Americans, usually from the 101st Airborne, came through, they would assume that any large quantity of rice was being grown for the Viet Cong. So in order to keep himself and his family alive Thao had had to live in poverty, growing just enough rice to barely feed his family. Phil could tell that it had hurt Thao to abandon his rice farm. But when Thao's uncle was killed, Thao saw it as a chance to escape with his family to a safer place. No one would buy a farm that was not allowed to produce just to live in danger of being killed by either side in a war they wished wasn't happening, so Thao had had to sadly abandon the farm that had been in his family for generations.

It was evening, and Phil had spent all afternoon with Thao and his family. Phil said his goodbyes and went back to the apartment. The next day Phil went to the air base BX (Base Exchange or store) and bought a rotating fan and dropped it off to Thao at his storefront home. Phil, having visited through the hot part of the day, knew that it got pretty warm in Thao's living room even though it was open in the front. The entire family lit up like it was Christmas, and Phil could feel that he had, once again, found medicine for his PTSD.

Phil felt like he was on a mission: only this mission was meant to leave him feeling better about himself instead of feeling worse. He had made friends with the main monk at the monastery on the hill, whose name was Thanh, which means the color of the sky in Vietnamese. He was the one who seemed to be in charge, and they spent hours trying to communicate until Phil had a list of what was needed to restore and furnish the orphanage.

Phil was invited to join the monks in a meal one day, and Phil's bowl of rice was the only bowl that had meat in the rice. They had bought meat for Phil when they couldn't afford meat for themselves. Phil, being on his third tour in Vietnam, didn't let his mind drift into thinking about what animal the meat might have come from, and he enjoyed both the meal and the company of the monks.

Phil found that when he told his friends about the orphanage the end result would be a donation. It seemed that everyone wanted to help. However, after a while Phil had hit up everyone for whatever money they could spare for the orphanage numerous times. After he had depleted the donations from the enlisted men, he had even gone to the officers. Even though the officers made much more money than the enlisted men, they gave much less, and Phil was disappointed. He had noticed that his PTSD had gotten much better while he was working on this project. Phil knew that helping others was the medicine that he needed.

At this point Phil had pretty much worn out his fund-raising abilities, so he decided to ask the two "rich guys" in the next barracks, Johnson and Brooks. They had already donated generously both times he had asked them before, but Phil knew they could afford it. Johnson and Brooks pretty much hung out together and didn't hang out with the other guys much. They were always bringing things back to the barracks that they had bought at the PX (Post Exchange or army store). They had the best stereo equipment and electric fans, and they even had those little refrigerators beside their bunks. Phil could be sure he would be offered a cold beer whenever he would visit Johnson and Brooks. These guys seemed to respect what Phil was trying to do.

This time Phil was going to ask them not only for a donation, but also if they would ask their rich friends and relatives back home to help with the orphanage. The donation part went well—they each coughed up fifty dollars—but when Phil asked about their rich friends and relatives back home, Johnson and Brooks both cracked up laughing. When Phil wanted to know what was so funny, Johnson and Brooks looked at each other and appeared to come to some agreement with their facial expressions. Their faces became serious, and they swore Phil, or Turner, as they called him, to secrecy. Brooks told Phil that they did not come from rich families and they had no rich friends. Then Johnson explained that instead of rich relatives he had an uncle who was a bookie back in the States who had gotten a really good deal on some very poor-quality counterfeit money. The counterfeit money was so obviously counterfeit that it couldn't be passed in the US. However, Johnson explained, it could easily be passed in Vietnam. Then Brooks told Phil that the beautiful thing about this was that all the

US currency that was sold on the black market ended up in the hands of the Viet Cong.

"How cool can that be?" Johnson chimed in. "By the time anyone knowledgeable enough about American money gets it it's too late, and the VC are stuck with the loss."

Johnson and Brooks offered to turn Phil's orphanage money into much more money through their counterfeit money scam. Phil, considering that the VC would be the only ones to lose, and having been at the end of his donation-gathering rope, decided to try the scam.

One US dollar was worth over twenty thousand Vietnamese dollars, or dong, as the Vietnamese called them. Of course, the dong received for the counterfeit money was not worth a lot and there would be a ton of it. But by buying cheap Vietnamese gold with the Vietnamese money and sending the gold home to be sold by Johnson's uncle, they made an awesome profit.

Johnson and Brooks had friends in the air force at the air base in Tuy Hoa who would spread the counterfeit money all over South Vietnam. They were pilots, with friends in towns all around the country who passed the counterfeit money to the Vietnamese merchants.

Counting the one hundred dollars that Johnson and Brooks had just donated, Phil had over eight hundred dollars saved up. He gave eight hundred to Johnson and Brooks, and "Operation Orphanage" was underway.

Monsoon-Flooded Streets of Tuy Hoa

CHAPTER 3

THE MONEY ROLLS IN

About three weeks later the package came from the US, and Johnson and Brooks called Phil over to their barracks to see what had arrived. The package contained a small TV set that had no works inside. It was full of counterfeit money; twenty thousand dollars' worth of ten-dollar bills. It looked awesome all together but looking at the bills it was easy to tell that it wasn't exactly right. The color was off a little, and Alexander Hamilton looked more like George Washington. Nonetheless, in a few days the money was passed, and the resulting gold had to be packaged up and sent off to the US. Packaging the gold to be sent to the United States was, by far, the most time-consuming part of the operation, but everyone chipped in until it was all done.

A few weeks later when the next package arrived it was much smaller, but the money inside was real US currency. Johnson and Brooks gave Phil eight thousand dollars of the good money. They were getting more than that for the counterfeit money–generated gold, but Phil didn't mind them taking their cut. After all, ten times your money in less than two months was one hell of an interest rate; but when Phil mentioned that he didn't mind them taking their cut they laughed and told Phil that they were not taking a cut of the orphanage money.

"That cut goes to the CO." Johnson whispered. This explained why Johnson and Brooks never were called on for work details and why they had a jeep at their disposal.

This gave the whole operation a level of security that eased Phil's mind, so he gave the eight thousand dollars back to Johnson and Brooks and said, "Let's do it again!"

It was monsoon time, and you could set your clock by when it rained each day. It would be a perfectly normal day and within minutes the sky would turn black and it would dump rain like nobody's business. The streets of Tuy Hoa would flood because there was no drainage, and the children would play in the flooded streets like it was a stateside public swimming pool. The bicycle-powered cyclos would be out in force just in case someone didn't want to get their feet wet. Then, as quickly as it came, the rain would be gone, and everything would return to normal.

The monks were working on the monastery almost every day. They were doing the structural repairs and patching the roof to make the building habitable. The expenses for this were minimal, and fifty dollars' worth of dong had been plenty to pay for the mortar and roofing materials.

Phil was becoming friends with Thanh, and Thanh would go with him to buy the supplies. An American soldier walking into a Vietnamese store would mysteriously cause the prices to double or even triple. Everything was so cheap anyway that the GIs didn't seem to mind. However, when Phil walked into a store escorted by a Buddhist monk, the price gouging did not occur. Phil and Thanh would always stop at a restaurant and have a meal on their outings to buy materials. They would laugh and joke like old friends, and Phil felt safe in the company of a highly revered Buddhist monk.

Phil had told Thanh that he was expecting to receive a donation that would cover all of the expenses of restoring and furnishing the orphanage. Thanh seemed very happy to hear this news. Phil wanted to be sure that the monks would not feel that the donated money was spiritually tainted, so he spent over an hour trying to explain the counterfeit money scam to Thanh. He described each phase of the operation as Thanh listened intently, trying to grasp what Phil was telling him. Thanh finally understood the part about turning the dong into gold jewelry and he taught Phil that "vàng" meant gold in Vietnamese. After all that, Phil still wasn't sure if Thanh understood the concept of money that wasn't real, but Phil felt good about Thanh knowing about the scam and not objecting on religious grounds.

Johnson and Brooks had an apartment in Tuy Hoa which was the hub of activity for the counterfeit money scam. The folks who passed the counterfeit money would change the Vietnamese money into gold jewelry and send the gold, minus their cut, back to Johnson and Brooks, who would take it all to the apartment. They would open all the packages and dump all the gold, mostly in chain form, on the bed. The gold was much more hassle to send back to the US because of the weight. It needed to be sent in many small packages instead of several big packages. Johnson and Brooks had a man in the APO (Army Post Office) who, for a reasonable fee, would put all the packages of gold into the mail system after the "customs check" section, so the packages would appear to have already been through the inspection and were ready to be sent to the US.

When the counterfeit money came in it also would be dumped out on the bed at the apartment and counted into the small bundles that would be sent out around the country to the folks who would pass it.

Phil would bring his Vietnamese girl friend, Tuyen (To-yen), meaning angel in Vietnamese, to the apartment when nothing was going on there with the scam. One day she was turning down the bed sheets and a gold chain came out from under the pillow onto the bedspread.

Phil was fast thinking so he simply said, "Surprise!" and Tuyen assumed that it was a gift hidden for her to find. From then on she wore the gold chain as a cherished gift, and Phil had avoided involving her in something illegal and or appearing to have had another woman in the bed.

Tuyen was from a middle-income family by Vietnamese standards, and she had not known poverty like many Vietnamese. She was well- educated, spoke good English, and was strikingly beautiful. Their love was understood by both Phil and Tuyen to be of a temporary nature because Phil would be returning home and Tuyen couldn't imagine leaving all of her family and moving halfway around the world.

Tuyen's father was an officer in the local police department, and her mother and aunt ran a small family food store in downtown Tuy Hoa. Phil loved to look at all the exotic sauces and seasonings on the shelves at the store and, with Tuyen's help picking them out, he had an assortment of exotic sauces and seasonings at the apartment. Of course, Phil never had any idea about what exotic sauces and seasonings went on what food, but Tuyen would help him with that, too.

Tuyen's home, on the outskirts of town, was simple, but very well maintained, and the yard looked like it was a storybook garden. Phil and Tuyen spent many hours together in the garden. Tuyen never seemed to tire of hearing what it was like in the "land of the big PX" (USA), and Phil felt closer to home when he was talking about it.

The guys had run the counterfeit money scam several times, and all without a hitch. It was one of those things that seemed too good to be true, and yet it was happening right before Phil's eyes. Phil had not been without spending money, but that was all he had taken out for himself.

Phil was a short-timer (going home soon), and he was getting excited about finally going home to stay. He would be getting out of Vietnam and the army all at the same time. It would be sad leaving Tuyen and all of his friends, but he was ready to go home.

A few days later, Phil was back in his barracks when a guy from the next barracks came over to tell him that Johnson and Brooks wanted to see him. Another package had come in, and it was the gold payment in real US dollars. Phil had been giving the monks enough money to keep the work going on the monastery, but this shipment of cash would more than cover the entire cost of restoring and furnishing the orphanage.

"How much have you saved back for yourself?" Johnson asked, and when Phil told them that he had just taken spending money they told him that he should turn the money over one more time.

"That way, you will be set for life when you get back to the States." Johnson said.

"And you will still have more than enough to complete the orphanage." Brooks chimed in. This seemed like a good idea to Phil, so Johnson notified his uncle back home that they were ready to go again.

Phil spent most of his time with Tuyen while the package was slowly coming from the States. They both knew that their time together was short and that they both would miss each other very much.

The day that the package arrived Johnson and Brooks met Phil at the apartment and they had not one but three packages, and each of the three packages was bigger than the one they had expected. They all stared at the packages as if they were reluctant to open them, but when they did open the packages they found a note that said that this was all the rest of the counterfeit money and that it was just under a quarter of a million dollars. Everyone looked shocked because even in counterfeit money the amount was frightening. To get rid of this amount of counterfeit money was a problem, so they decided to distribute it in four waves, and they prepared the bundles of counterfeit money for the first wave.

For the next few weeks, the apartment was "off limits" to Tuyen because it was full of counterfeit money and gold jewelry, so Phil rented another apartment close to Tuyen's parents' house where they spent every possible minute together. The days went by too quickly for Phil and Tuyen until the last of the gold had come in. There was so much gold that it took almost an entire night to package it all and address all the packages. Johnson's uncle had sent them fifty PO Box addresses that they were to send the gold to, but with this many packages there would be a lot of repeat addresses. This was okay because the packages were moved past the inspection at the post office.

However long it took, they wanted everything to look normal as the many packages traveled through the mail system to the States. They had always added a note to each package that said who the jewelry was for— Mom, Aunt Lucy, etc.— so they would look like presents for folks back home. If they sent all the gold in one trunk, it would be illegal, and customs would stop it, but it was legal to send gold jewelry home as gifts. So, they made each package look like gifts for folks back home.

Johnson, Brooks, and Phil worked through the night. One guy would write the notes, another would wrap the jewelry, and the third guy would prepare the packages for mailing. When the guy writing the notes would get writer's cramp, they would all switch jobs and keep right on working. They had the labels, both address and return address, printed in town. The labels were peel-and-stick, but they had to cover them all with clear shipping tape, so the labels couldn't come off during shipping because the Vietnamese glue didn't hold well.

The packages were small and there were a lot of them, but all together they were very heavy, and they had to divide the load into two duffel bags for Brooks to drive to the army post office. After that there was nothing to do but party.

Vietnamese Police Arrive to Investigate the Murder Scene

CHAPTER 4

THE SKY IS FALLING

Brooks drove off to the air base post office with the two duffel bags, and Phil took a motorized cyclo to the other apartment where Tuyen was waiting for him. Phil was going home in eight days, so every minute he and Tuyen had together they were grateful for. Phil entered the apartment and went directly to Tuyen, who was standing by the bed. He embraced her, and they kissed.

"You make me very happy, Tuyen," Phil said as he spun around with Tuyen and fell backwards onto the bed with Tuyen held closely against his body, so she landed on top of him.

"You make me happy, too," Tuyen answered.

"I want to be with you always." Phil said, but Tuyen did not answer. They made love and Phil held Tuyen in his arms for more than an hour. He told her all about how life was back in the states. He described what life was like in Los Angeles, where they would live. Phil told her that his father was going to give the house to him because he and Phil's mom were getting too old to handle all the work keeping up a big house. They both wanted to buy a townhouse in the suburbs. Phil tried to make everything sound inviting. Then he tried again to talk her into marrying him and coming to the States to live.

"My heart is here in Tuy Hoa," said Tuyen softly, "and if I went home with you my heart would still be with my family here in Tuy Hoa."

"Maybe we could send for your family later." Phil suggested.

"They would never go," she answered. Then Tuyen looked into Phil's eyes and hugged him tighter. He could see in her face that she would never leave her family.

Phil was in that half-asleep, half-awake state when he heard the jeep screech to a stop outside. He thought it would be Brooks wanting Phil to go party in the bars, but Phil was going to turn him down to stay with Tuyen. The banging and shouting at the door was much more than Phil had expected, so he became alarmed as he rushed to open the door. It was Johnson, and he was panic stricken.

"Brooks is dead!" he said. "They shot him in the head and took all the gold!"

"What happened?" shouted Phil.

"The captain called me in and told me," Johnson continued. "They shot him right through the head!" And Johnson collapsed on the floor, crying. Tuyen ran to Phil's arms, crying, and Phil almost fell from her weight and had to sit down on the bed. Even after two tours of combat in the boonies, this was the worst day of Phil's life. Brooks was found by a GI, who was passing by, at an intersection on the road to the air base. The jeep was nosed into the southwest corner of the intersection and Brooks was slumped over the steering wheel and he had been shot one time in the side of the head. It appeared that after Brooks was shot the jeep had rolled into the intersection and come to a rest nosed into the corner of the intersection. It looked like someone on a small motorcycle had pulled up beside Brooks at the stop sign and just shot Brooks in the side of the head. They had to have known about the gold because both of the duffel bags were gone and there was no torn package paper or other signs of anyone having opened a package to see what was inside. Also, nothing in Brooks' pockets had been touched, and other things of value were not taken. Brooks always wore his .45 automatic hand gun, and it was still in the holster on Brooks' hip. No thief doing a random robbery would have left the .45 pistol, because it was very valuable on the black market. This was not just a random robbery; the murderer knew exactly what he was after and had no intention of asking for it.

The first to arrive on the scene had been a GI who had been driving a small, blue-green American pickup truck that belonged to his girlfriend's family. A Vietnamese crowd was gathering, but the GI had protected the murder scene from being looted. He had flagged down a Vietnamese police car that was passing by. The Vietnamese police were driving an American

Ford Falcon with a bubblegum machine (flashing red light) on top. When the MPs arrived they investigated the scene thoroughly, but they had come to the wrong conclusion about what had happened.

Brooks' death was blamed on the Viet Cong, which meant that there would be no further investigation. The only good part was that Brooks would receive full military honors, and his family would at least have that. The next week was a blur to Phil.

Phil had to tell the monks the bad news. Thanh took it all very well and seemed grateful that Phil was not hurt. Even so, Phil felt like he had let the monks and the orphaned children down.

For days it seemed as if everything was happening in a fog. Nothing seemed real to him as he went through the motions of his daily routine. He could think of nothing but who had killed Brooks and stolen the gold. He suspected almost everyone he knew and went over in his mind how each one could have or could not have killed Brooks and taken the gold. He even went to see the CO, and the CO told Phil not to ever talk to anyone about it again and that he would deny any knowledge if Phil ever did.

The murder of Brooks had undone any healing from his PTSD that Phil had achieved from helping others. He stayed drunk for the next eight days, but his mind kept going over each person that could have killed Brooks. Usually, a GI going home would spend this time getting addresses and phone numbers to keep in touch with his buddies back in the States, but Phil just kept to himself because he didn't know who the murderer might be. He made a list and crossed through the names that he knew could not have done it. Even the list would not reveal who the murder was.

The constant "heavy weight on the chest" feeling of PTSD was back. Phil was in bad shape as his PTSD overwhelmed his daily life. The terrible "test patterns" in his mind were back, and Phil's only escape was alcohol. The alcohol only dulled things, but that in itself was only a mild relief.

Too Much Traffic at the Crime Scene

CHAPTER 5

THE HOMECOMING

Phil had tried to go to the murder scene, but by the time he got to the road that led to the intersection where Brooks had been killed the traffic was so bad that he couldn't expect to find any clues, so he just kept on driving to the air base, where he stopped at a club and drank himself into a stupor. Phil didn't get belligerent or mean when he drank; he just got quiet and kept to himself. The MPs had brought Phil back to his barracks, so he would be safe, but Phil didn't remember much after the club.

The next day Phil found himself standing at the foot of Brooks' bunk. All of Brooks' belongings had been removed and the empty bunk was waiting for the next GI to move in. Phil didn't know how long he had been standing there, but it must have been a long time, because two soldiers came and took him back to his bunk. They sat Phil on the side of his bunk and reported back to the CO. One of the guys in Brooks' barracks had gone to Phil's barracks and told the few guys there what Phil was doing, and two of them had gone to the CO's office and told him about Phil. The CO had them go return Phil to his barracks. A few minutes later the CO came to Phil's bunk to check on him. Phil was very slow to respond, but he did seem to understand. When the CO asked if he was alright, Phil quietly answered, "Yes."

The CO was torn: if he put Phil in the hospital it would delay his going home; but if Phil really needed to be in the hospital the CO would have to commit him for psychiatric evaluation. The CO felt that going home might even help Phil get it back together, so he decided to give Phil one day and see how he was at that time.

Phil sat on his bunk for several hours until dark, and then he lay down and went to sleep with his uniform and boots on. When he woke he was noticeably better. He seemed a lot more coherent. So when the CO showed up he was greatly relieved to see a little improvement in Phil's condition. The CO thought that Phil would improve even more going home on schedule.

Phil did improve in the next few days, but he would never be his old self again. He went to the CO and tried to extend his tour in Vietnam, but the CO would not allow it, and Phil actually was disappointed.

Everything was a blur in Phil's mind until the day came when Phil was to go home. After a tearful goodbye with Tuyen, Phil packed all of his belongings and prepared to return to the United States. Saying goodbye to Tuyen left Phil numb, but soon he found himself on a jet, on his way home. He would never know if the orphanage was ever completed or not, and he would never see Tuyen again.

Phil felt nothing the whole flight home. There was a short stopover in Alaska, and Phil got off the plane and bought another bottle of whiskey and got back on the plane. When he reached California, Phil wanted to try to avoid the protesters at the airport, so he went into the restroom on the plane and put on his "civvies" (civilian clothes). This didn't seem to work, because as he passed through the crowd of war protesters he felt that they all knew he was military. He felt like all the shouting and jeering from the protesters was directed at him, and some part of him deep inside knew that they were right.

Phil headed straight to the nearest airport restroom and took a big drink of whiskey before going on to get his luggage. He was directed to a military bus that took him to the place for out-processing. He was drunk but could still maintain coherence through the out-processing. Phil was the last one in out-processing to finish filling out all the forms because his mind would not stop returning to his murdered friend, Brooks. He finished and looked up at the sergeant in charge, who was obviously anxious for Phil to get done. Phil handed in the papers, but he decided to skip the traditional steak dinner. He was out of the army and on his own.

The first thing he did was to stop in a stateside bar and have his first legal stateside drink. Phil had been too young to drink legally when he had gone to Vietnam. Of course, everyone could drink in 'Nam regardless of their age. But now it seemed to help Phil make it through each day. Phil sat down in a booth with his double shot of whiskey. There were two guys at the end of the bar talking to the bartender, and every so often Phil would hear a word or two of their conversation. After a short time, Phil realized that the men were talking about him. They were using terms like "draft dodger," and "commie," and then "pinko." When Phil realized that the men were talking about him, he was shocked. After three tours of duty in Vietnam this was the last thing that Phil had expected to hear. He approached the men at the end of the bar telling them that he was a Vietnam combat veteran and that he had a Bronze Star and a Purple Heart, but instead of convincing them that he was "on their side," this just seemed to frighten them. Phil had thought that the men would accept him as a Vietnam combat veteran when they realized that he was not a "draft dodger," a "commie," or a "pinko," but rather a highly decorated Vietnam combat veteran. But instead Phil went from being just someone that the men wanted out of their bar to someone they feared. The bartender reached under the bar and came out with a baseball bat. Phil left the bar in shock.

So far the only acknowledgment from the American people was the airport protesters and the men in the bar. This was not what returning home from serving your country was supposed to be like, and it accelerated Phil's downward spiral.

Phil had lived all of his life in LA except for his time in 'Nam. His parents lived in an upscale middle-class neighborhood, almost in Hollywood but still within the LA city limits. The house was beautifully landscaped and furnished, and it made you feel like you were in Hollywood. Phil had grown up pretty much without a care and with few hardships, so twenty-six months in Vietnam had had a very dramatic effect on him.

Phil's homecoming was wonderful, but somehow Phil felt numb to it all. It was as if he couldn't really feel anything—well, not like he could feel things before 'Nam. He felt as if he was just going through the motions. Phil's mom and dad were so happy to see him, but soon it was as if Phil were some other person to them. His PTSD had taken Phil over and it ruled his mind day and night, and he drank every day.

By day Phil was on edge and startled easily, and his temper was out of control. By night he would have nightmares and wake up trembling and covered in sweat. Then one morning it happened.

When Phil's mom tried to wake him up, Phil woke up with a start and had a gun in her face before he knew what he was doing. This pushed

Phil even further away from his family. After that, Phil really felt more isolated because he had made his family afraid of him, but he still kept the pistol under his pillow. He had made it home alive after three tours of duty, two of them in combat with the 101st Airborne, but Phil could tell that his parents felt like they had lost their son in the Vietnam War.

Within a few weeks this all became too much for Phil, so he packed a small backpack and left home. He had no place to go in mind, he just had to go. In the back of his mind Phil knew that his parents would have been better off if he had been killed in Vietnam. He actually felt bad about not having been killed, because then his parents would have been proud of him and they would have felt great honor. It was too painful for him to have made it home alive only to frighten those he loved. Phil felt jealous of his friends who had been killed in combat, because their families thought of them with love and honor, but Phil's family had actually felt relieved that he was leaving home.

Phil had money with him, but he didn't take a cab or bus; he just walked and walked, stopping occasionally to duck out of sight between buildings or in an alley to take a drink form his most valued possession— his whiskey bottle.

On his journey Phil stepped into an alley to take a drink and was confronted by two homeless guys as soon as he took out his bottle. They wanted his whiskey. One of them was a mousy-looking thin man that almost no one would fear, but his friend was a huge Native American man that looked very menacing, considering that he had a big piece of pipe that he held resting on his shoulder.

"We want that whiskey!" the thin man said.

"You're welcome to a drink." Phil had answered.

"That's not what we had in mind," said the huge man as he raised the pipe into striking position. Phil instantly handed his bottle to the mousy guy, and they moved aside to allow Phil to run out of the alley. They had been so into getting Phil's whiskey that Phil got away with his cash and his backpack. Phil had around seventy dollars, so he wrapped all but a few dollars up in a handkerchief, tied a piece of string tightly around the loose ends, and pinned it to the inside front of his pants. This turned out to be a smart move because not an hour later Phil was hassled by the police. They made him empty his backpack and pockets out onto the curb. They even made Phil pour out his new bottle of whiskey in the gutter, but luckily the bottle was over half empty by then. The good news was that the police had not found the money that he had pinned to the inside of his pants. They did, however, take the few dollars that Phil had in his pocket. Phil was shocked that the police could treat him that way without fear of legal repercussions, but then he realized that as a homeless person there was absolutely nothing he could do about it, and he understood.

It was early evening when Phil reached the outskirts of town. He felt less threatened because there were fewer people to run into. Just as he was feeling more relaxed, there they were again; the police were pulling over to check Phil out. This time Phil said the right thing. He told the police that he was trying to leave town. They didn't make Phil empty his pockets or backpack. They just put Phil in the back of their police car and drove him the rest of the way to the city limits and let him out. They pointed in the direction of leaving town and told Phil not to come back. Of course, he didn't leave town, but now he had to put some distance from where the cops who had told him to leave patrolled. He followed the access road along a freeway for the rest of the evening.

Like most cities in the US, the policy that the police were instructed to enforce was to harass the homeless into leaving the city and make the homeless become another city's problem. This was Phil's first day of being homeless and he had already learned many survival lessons, but not once had he felt welcomed home.

Phil's New Home Under a Bridge

CHAPTER 6

HOMELESS IN AMERICA

That night, Phil found a place to sleep behind a big factory. He found some cardboard boxes in a dumpster and made himself a three-layer-thick cardboard bed. Two hours later Phil woke up wet in the rain. He got under the top layer of cardboard box and lay there shivering for the rest of the night. Phil had spent many miserable nights in Vietnam, cold and wet, but he had never imagined that this would happen once he was safely back home.

He started out at first light and followed the freeway access road for the entire day. Around midday he spotted a fast-food restaurant in the distance. He was pretty sure that he wouldn't run into the cops who had told him to leave town and not come back, so he entered the city once again. Phil had a hamburger, french fries, and whiskey for his lunch. His bottle was getting kind of low, so he found a liquor store and bought a new one.

Within two weeks Phil could see that his money was running out, so he went further into town until he found an area where he could find enough deposit bottles and aluminum cans to keep him in whiskey and food. The problem was that there were many homeless people here, and Phil was beaten and robbed several times. Sometimes homeless guys would hang out at the recycle place and rob other homeless people of the items that they were bringing to cash in.

One evening Phil was looking for a place to sleep. He was pretty drunk as he climbed down the steep bank to go under a freeway bridge where he could sleep and drink in private. The police didn't appreciate his drinking in public or, it seemed, even his being in public. As soon as he rounded the corner to go under the bridge he saw four homeless guys sitting around a campfire. His first instinct was to turn and run and look for another place, but one of the guys waved at him and the others were all smiling, so he approached the campfire. A very good-smelling pot of beans was cooking on the fire, and the homeless guys invited Phil to have some. In return Phil got out his bottle of whiskey and passed it around. He had brought out his whiskey partly to share, and partly to see if they would want to rob him. They were grateful, and the bottle passed around the camp fire and returned to Phil.

It turned out that two of the homeless guys, Mondo and Johnny, were Vietnam veterans like him. Then there was Jack, who took care of Mikey because Mikey wasn't right in the head. Mikey needed to be told what to do at every turn. Jack had to tell Mikey to eat his beans six or eight times during the meal because Mikey would get distracted very easily by everything going on around him. Mikey could talk alright, but he was very childlike. If someone said something funny, Mikey would laugh and laugh but not because he got the joke—he would laugh when anyone else would laugh. Jack was very serious about protecting Mikey from himself and any outside threat, which made it possible for Mikey to live outside of an institution.

Since Governor Reagan had turned a lot of the institutionalized people out on the streets, many had died; but Mikey was one of the lucky ones. Even though many of them died on the streets, it did solve the problem of overcrowding in mental institutions. Jack never lost his temper with Mikey, no matter how many times he had to tell Mikey the same thing over and over again. It was amazing how patient Jack was with Mikey.

Although Mondo and Johnny were both 'Nam vets, they had not known each other in Vietnam. Mondo had been in combat with the 1st Infantry Division, more commonly known as the "Big Red One." Mondo would never talk about Vietnam except to tell what unit he was in and that he had gotten a dishonorable discharge—but he never did say why. Johnny had been in the rear area in Vietnam and had not seen combat. His job was to prepare the dead bodies of American soldiers who had been killed in action for shipment home. Johnny had PTSD as bad as Mondo or Phil from just seeing the results of the combat that Mondo and Phil had been involved in. Phil, for the first time, knew that there were some jobs in the Vietnam War worse than combat; he couldn't imagine handling all those dead and mutilated bodies.

Phil was still in his hometown, but the other guys were just in from Phoenix.

"Phoenix has been one of the best places for homeless people," explained Mondo, "as the winters are mild and the intense summer heat is just like 'Nam, except for the lower humidity.

They told Phil that there had even been a newspaper printed for homeless people to sell on street corners. "The newspapers cost fifty cents for a bundle of fifty papers, and the fifty cents all went to the driver who delivered the papers to the homeless. The drivers were all homeless people who lived out of their cars. It was good for everyone. The homeless even looked better as a result of selling that paper. They could rent a motel room once a week and wash their clothes and shower."

Mondo stood up to continue, "Not to mention they got to sleep, for a night, in a real bed, and watch TV." Mondo looked sad. "That's what I miss the most, TV."

When Phil asked why they had left Phoenix and such a good chance to get ahead and work their way out of being homeless, they said that the whole thing had gone bad. They told him that it had gone bad because the newspaper was a political exposé paper that openly talked about the political corruption that was rampant in Arizona. So, to protect the entrenched corruption, the legislature had passed a law that made it illegal for homeless people to sell or beg from the curbside along a road. This was followed by a police crackdown on homeless people.

They told Phil, "When a homeless person gets a ticket or is charged with a minor crime such as loitering, trespassing, shoplifting, or sometimes public urination, they have to leave town or face jail time because they can't afford to pay any fines that may be imposed. This technique is used by many cities to get rid of their 'homeless people problem' and force it to become some other cities' problem. This is what Phoenix had done." He asked if the authorities had known that two of them were Vietnam veterans, and they said that that was the last thing you wanted to tell them, because that made you a threat. Not only were Vietnam vets considered to be a threat of violence, but also a threat that the press would use the Vietnam veterans' high numbers among the homeless to garner sympathy from the general public for homeless people. Of all the homeless people sitting around the campfire, Phil knew that, including him, three out of five were Vietnam veterans.

Phil stayed under the bridge with the guys for several weeks. They would all go out each day to collect anything that would bring cash at the recycle center, and bottles to cash in at the store. Then they would spend the rest of the day and night under the bridge with plenty of food and whiskey for everyone.

One day they returned to the camp under the bridge to find all of their meager belongings gone or destroyed. The only thing Phil was interested in was the picture he had brought from home, and he found it torn into little pieces and thrown into the ashes of the campfire. Even the pot that they cooked beans in had been smashed with a river rock and ruined. All the footprints around the camp were smaller than adult prints, so they knew it had been done by kids. Phil was grateful that he kept his whiskey with him at all times because that's what he used to lessen the pain of losing his old photo of his mom and dad looking happy to be with their son.

It had been less than five years since Brooks had been murdered, and Phil had gone from being a highly decorated Vietnam combat veteran returning home to a homeless alcoholic living on the streets of LA. This was not the homecoming he had dreamed of through his three tours of duty in 'Nam. But because of the terrible mental images he kept getting day and night of his combat in Vietnam, some big part of him felt he deserved all that was happening to him.

After a few years of living on the fringe of the city in a camp situation with other homeless people, Phil now had to be in East LA to be near the places that helped the homeless. He had tried to go home, but a different family was living in his parents' house and they had called the police on Phil for knocking on their front door. Phil would never know that his father had died less than a year after Phil left home and his mother had died a year and a half after that. Phil doubted that his parents would even recognize him if they saw him because he had fallen and hit his face many times, and he had been beaten and robbed of his whiskey by other homeless people so many times he had lost count.

In fact, that was why he was where he was. He had been robbed, and they had missed a dollar that he had hidden in his sock, so he had gotten on a bus and had gotten off by an alley that looked promising behind several restaurants within two blocks of each other. He knew he could find food there in the dumpsters out behind the restaurants. He found a place to hide and sleep in an alcove behind a dumpster. He gathered cardboard to make a bed in the alcove. The alcove housed a door that was sealed shut by a business because they used the next door down the alley. This turned out to be a very good place for Phil, as he was well hidden and had a good food source, and there were no other homeless people around to compete with his panhandling. Even though he was eating from dumpsters, the quality of his food was greatly improved because the area's restaurants were all upscale.

The main thing that he had to do was to keep out of sight. He had to keep out of sight of the business owners, who would call the police if they saw him, and of the police themselves, who patrolled the alley at least once a day. To reduce the chances of being seen, Phil would try to panhandle enough for his whiskey, plus a little more for bus fare. Then he would be able to be gone from the alley throughout the day by riding the bus. The bus passed by the VA Hospital, and every time Phil went past the VA Hospital he would look the other way. It reminded him of the complete abandonment of combat veterans that had become US government policy.

Phil had been feeling sick lately, and it didn't seem to be going away as he had hoped. Then one day he was riding the bus when he became so ill that he got off the bus at the VA Hospital. He had been waiting in triage for over an hour and a half when they called him in. The doctors had him lie on a gurney. Phil was gasping for breath as the doctors began telling him to slow down his breathing. Phil tried his best and was able to breathe more slowly by breathing more deeply. Then they began walking Phil through a relaxation process, telling him to completely relax his legs, then his chest, arms and so forth until Phil was lying still on the gurney.

As soon as Phil was relaxed, the doctor said, "Ah ha! This proves that you were faking your condition to try to get drugs from us." Then they told Phil to leave the hospital. Phil was now in shock as well as very sick as he got off of the gurney and began walking down the hallway to leave the hospital.

He was feeling more disgraced than sick when he collapsed into unconsciousness before he reached the exit. Phil had no idea what happened after that, but he woke up in a hospital bed with clean sheets. He never saw the triage doctors again, and his doctor actually seemed nice. He was in pretty bad shape, but good food and rest had him feeling much better within a week. The folks at the hospital gave Phil a bus pass, and he rode the bus back to his alley.

The doctor at the VA hospital had told Phil that if he drank whiskey again it would kill him. Phil was afraid to die.

He tried not to drink, but that seemed to be beyond his abilities. He had panhandled enough money the day before to buy a small bottle of whiskey which he had sipped throughout the day and he was still alive, so he wanted to buy another bottle, mostly just to prove the VA doctor wrong.

By this time, he had severe liver damage, and that meant that it took less alcohol to get him drunk. His liver was unable to filter properly, and the alcohol just flowed right through it and into his bloodstream. It was hard to walk, but he managed to get out of the alley and around the corner before he staggered and had to sit down leaning against the building. He was two doors down from a fancy restaurant that had an awning that went out over the sidewalk to the curb. This was a good place to panhandle as people went in and out of the restaurant. Phil was feeling bad, and he was thinking that he might just need to eat some food when he saw a double-stretch limo pull up in front of the restaurant.

The driver jumped out and scurried around to open the limo door. A rich man stepped out with a beautiful lady on each arm. Phil felt a rush of adrenaline as he recognized the rich man. Speaking perfect English to his two companions was Thanh, the head monk at the Tuy Hoa orphanage. Thanh had to be the one who killed Brooks, because a Buddhist monk does not normally end up rich after taking a vow of poverty. Phil was filled with rage as he tried to get up, but he fell back to the sidewalk, his face once again bouncing on the cement.

But this time Phil did not feel the pain—he was dead.

Filing Into a C-130 for a Parachute Jump

V - I LIT THE MATCH

CHAPTER 1

I LIT THE MATCH

It was March 1967, and nineteen-year-old Jim Talleson was in parachute jump school at Fort Benning, Georgia. The back ramp of the C-130 Hercules slowly lowered until the end of it rested on the tarmac for the men preparing to board the plane. Finally, the long line of paratroopers began to move onto it. Jim had been having the time of his life being trained to be a paratrooper. He had been taught to drop ten feet and land, doing a parachute landing fall (PLF) without breaking any bones. He had been dropped from a big tower while hanging under his open parachute, and had parachuted to the soft ground below. He may as well have been at a huge amusement park.

Of course, someone was screaming at him most of the time because the harassment level was extremely high in airborne training. This level of harassment was too much for some recruits, but Jim's dad had been harassing Jim all of his life. Jim's dad was not mean; he truly thought that harassment was the way to build a strong man out of a weak child. As a result, harassment had very little effect on Jim.

Today was really exciting—this was Jim's first real parachute jump. As he walked up the ramp into the belly of the C-130, Jim had an ear-to-ear grin that wouldn't go away. The trainees sat on both sides of the plane, facing each other, for takeoff. The engines roared, and the plane raced down the runway and nosed up into the air as a cheer went up from the excited soon-to-be paratroopers. Then the order was given to "Stand up!" and everyone stood in a single line down the center of the C-130.

"Here we go," thought Jim as he went over the poem that had been brainwashed into his head. "Stand up, hook up, shuffle to the door, jump right out and count to four."

The order was given to hook up, and Jim tore the yellow strap loose from the back of the parachute on the paratrooper in front of him and snapped the locking clip to the metal cable that stretched down the center of the plane above their heads. Jim could feel the soldier in back of him hooking up his strap to the cable. As each soldier slid the strap to the soldier in front of them, each soldier would be holding his own strap and sliding it along the cable when he moved forward. This strap would pull the parachute out of the pack as the trooper jumped out of the plane.

The red light turned to green and the order "Shuffle to the door!" was shouted and the line started to shuffle toward the open side door at the back of the plane. They had been taught to shuffle (walk without lifting their feet from the floor) to reduce the chance of someone tripping and stopping the movement of the line going out the back door. As each soldier got to the door, he would receive the order from the jump master to "Stand in the door!"

Thus, they would stand with both feet on the doorjamb and their arms out to their sides with each hand on the outside of the plane. They would then wait for the jump master to bang on their helmet—the signal to jump. They knew well that if they did not jump when the jump master banged on their helmet that the next thing they would feel was a boot in the ass kicking them out of the airplane.

Jim shuffled toward the door until he was next soldier to jump. The jump master yelled for Jim to stand in the door, and Jim stepped forward and slapped his hands on the outside of the plane. Jim wanted to jump as far from the plane as he could because if he didn't he might bounce against the side of the plane—a common occurrence. As soon as the jump master impacted Jim's helmet, he leaped from the plane with all his might. He hadn't even gotten to two in his count to four when he felt the pull of his chute opening. Jim looked up to see a fully deployed parachute looming above him. He had never seen a more beautiful, or a more reassuring, sight in his life.

What a feeling! Jim felt like he was hanging motionless in the sky. Of course, this was just an illusion; the closer he got to the ground, the faster he seemed to be falling. He was trained to look at the horizon and not to look at the ground coming up at him because looking at the ground could make him tense up just before impact. Tensing up upon landing is a good way to break bones. A military parachute is only designed to slow you down enough so that if you do a perfect parachute landing fall you will not break any bones. Hanging in the air through a long, slow descent would make you an inviting target in a combat zone, so they dropped them in low and taught them to land hard.

The earth was rushing toward Jim at an uncomfortable rate as he neared the ground, ready to do his PLF.

Smoke Shows the Wind Direction on the Ground

He looked at the smoke at the end of the drop zone from a fire that was there to tell the direction of the wind at ground level. Five points, he thought, five points of contact: toes, heels, knee, hip and shoulder. It looked like he would have to do a rear PLF, but at the last minute he realized that he was on the forward swing.

The paratrooper and parachute can be moving in one direction, but that's not necessarily the direction the paratrooper will be approaching the ground. This is because the paratrooper is also swinging, like a pendulum, under the chute. So Jim waited for his toes to touch down, and he executed a forward PLF. He jumped to his feet immediately and began gathering in his chute. This was important because, after landing, if the wind caught your chute it could drag you along until you hit something, usually resulting in a broken neck.

Jim was elated. He let out a big "Yahoo!" and he carried his chute to the side of the drop zone. Jim had never been this excited; adrenaline raced through him like a freight train. The other paratroopers were as excited as Jim. Ear-to-ear grins were the uniform of the day.

Jim was doing his best in jump school. He had only gotten into trouble one time, because his shoes were not polished enough. He had been sent to an office where he was chewed out, and that was it. Nothing would go in his records about the incident, so Jim knew the chewing out was just meant to ensure that he shined his shoes every night—and that's just what he did.

After four more parachute jumps and a ton of harassment, the last day of jump school came. Jim's family was there in the stands on the parade grounds for the ceremony. They got to see Jim get his Parachute Jump Wings. This was the most wonderful day, and as soon as the ceremonies were over Jim joined his family, as a paratrooper, to show off his jump wings.

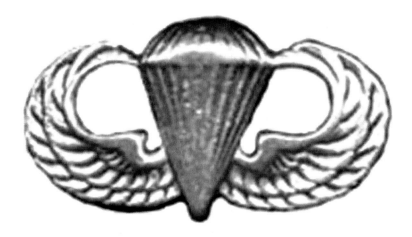

Jim's Parachute Jump Wings

They had all been told that they were on their way to Vietnam, and Jim knew that he would be assigned to the 1st Battalion, 327th Infantry Regiment of the 101st Airborne Division. But first, Jim would go home with his family for a thirty-day leave. He talked all the way from Georgia to Iowa on the car ride back home with his family. He wanted them to know all the wonderful, exciting things that he had done in training.

Tiger Force and 101st Airborne Patches

CHAPTER 2

TIGER FORCE

Jim's thirty-day leave went by with lightning speed, but Jim managed to show his paratrooper uniform and jump wings to all his friends and relatives. He was so proud. In a few months, he had been transformed from a gangling, clumsy teenager into a highly respected man. It was a dream come true for Jim to be looked up to by his peers and respected by his family.

For some reason, leaving his mom and dad was extra hard this time as he boarded the plane to Fort Dix, New Jersey. In his mind, peeking through all the accolades and honor that he had been enjoying, was the realization that he may not make it home from this duty assignment alive.

After a short stay at the in-and out-processing barracks, Jim found himself on another jet for a twenty-plus hour ride to the Republic of Vietnam. Everyone on the jet was a soldier going to Vietnam, yet there was an atmosphere of fun. They all were in their first "party like there's no tomorrow" in reaction to the fear state of mind. This reaction happens every time that combat troops return to the base camp from battle. A guy across the aisle said, "I hope if I die it is from this plane crashing instead of in battle, so Charlie doesn't get credit for my body count." Everyone laughed, even Jim, to his own surprise. Dark humor, Jim would learn, is very common among combat troops.

After landing, the door of the 707 jet was opened for everyone to disembark. Jim was about halfway back in the jet, but he knew exactly when the air coming in the door of the plane reached him. He had never smelled anything like it, and the air was almost of a different consistency because it was so thick with humidity. Jim had not known that countries could smell differently. Then, when he reached the door, he could see that nothing but the US Military stuff which all looked the same as he was accustomed to. Only the smell and thickness of the air was different.

After in-processing, the group Jim was in was loaded into a military C-130 troop transport plane and flown to the base camp of the 101st Airborne Division at Phan Rang, Vietnam. They arrived at the base camp at lunch hour, so they were all fed and then equipped with their combat gear.

For two weeks Jim went through extensive training on how to spot booby traps, and what to expect out in the jungle. He paid very close attention because almost everything they were teaching him could save his life out in the boonies.

Jim was assigned to work in the supply tent at the base camp of the 101st Airborne. This was not what Jim had wanted to do; he wanted to be out in the boonies. He hadn't volunteered for a tour of duty in Vietnam to be in a supply tent. For almost seven months he was the supply clerk, but Jim felt like he was missing out. He wanted to make his last four months in 'Nam something to be proud of. Although Jim knew the age-old recommendation to never volunteer for anything in the army, he volunteered for the most elite combat unit in the 101st Airborne—the Tiger Force.

Tiger Force was a small, highly trained unit of forty-five paratroopers, created to spy on enemy forces in the Central Highlands of South Vietnam. Established early in the Vietnam War as an experimental fighting unit, the Tiger Force was made up of soldiers who were the very best that the American military could produce. Their mission was to seek out enemy installations and radio in the coordinates for bombing missions, artillery attacks, or troop insertions. Jim thought this all sounded like just the job he needed to establish himself as a good soldier.

It took several days, but as soon as his replacement supply clerk arrived he reported to the CO of the Tiger Force. The CO told Jim that he would be going out in the boonies, but that his unit could not get to where a chopper could come in until the next day. Jim returned, somewhat disappointed, to his bunk. He wrote a letter home after moving outside into the sun because the paper felt damp. The intense Vietnam sun baked the paper dry in a few seconds. After dinner that night, he just hung out at the barracks. He laid down on his bunk sweating and wishing for a cool breeze until he fell asleep.

Jim woke up with a start, as this was to be his first day in the jungle. He got dressed and hurried to the mess hall. He ate quickly and went back to his bunk to gather his equipment; and then waited for about forty-five minutes until word was passed around to gather at the staging area. This was it. Jim was so nervous that his knees felt weak as he ran to the staging area. He was too excited to care about the stifling heat or his weak knees. As he joined the other soldiers everyone was unpacking their food rations and throwing the trash into a big bonfire. Jim had been assigned to carry the M16 rifle. He paused to slowly run his hand down the rifle. This was an amazing machine, and it was his.

Tiger Force members got to wear floppy camo hats instead of the heavy helmets normally worn in combat. When the backpacks were loaded up, they began painting their faces with sticks of black and green camo colored grease paint. Jim noticed that the others were painting their faces more to look fierce rather than for camouflage.

He was expecting to be exposed to horror time and again before these last four months of his tour in Vietnam were over, but he hadn't expected the horror to begin before they even started down the trail. His squad leader, Sergeant E-6 Antonio Valdez, had something strange about his face; his eyes were almost frightening to look into. They seemed to reflect something dark and horrible from deep in the soul of Sergeant Valdez. Jim was afraid of him, and he only spoke when his squad leader spoke to him. As Jim was watching his sergeant, he saw him reach into his pack and take a necklace out of his pack and put it around his neck. At first Jim thought it was made of potato slices and, just as his mind was wondering if this was a "boonies" way to dry potatoes to make potato chips, his eyes interrupted his thought—they were human ears, not potato slices. Jim looked around and saw several more GIs with ear necklaces. He quickly looked down at his pack, and said nothing. He decided to keep his mouth shut because this involved his squad leader. Jim, for the entire day, walking down the trail was no longer thinking of the extreme heat, and the painful weight of his backpack. He felt alone and very afraid, not only of the Viet Cong, but also of his own squad.

As they finished preparing for the mission, Jim heard the helicopter in the distance. Everyone put on their packs and moved to the edge of the landing zone. The chopper approached, and Sergeant Valdez, also standing near the edge of the landing zone, directed the chopper as it came in for a landing.

Jim was thrilled that they were going to ride in a chopper. They bent over, keeping low to avoid decapitation, and ran toward it as Sergeant Valdez led the way. Jim sat in the open doorway, like the others, with his feet dangling outside of the Huey helicopter. As the chopper lifted off, Jim found himself grinning ear to ear, just like in jump school. Then the helicopter went into a turn and, as it banked, the floor that Jim was sitting on tipped well past the point where gravity would have made Jim slide out of the doorway and fall to the ground. The only thing that was keeping him from falling out was the g-force.

"Oh, shit!" Jim yelled. He looked at the soldier next to him, who was grinning at Jim's discomfort. Now they were coming in for a landing. For some reason, the helicopter didn't actually land. As they started to approach the ground, the soldier next to Jim stepped out of the chopper and stood on the landing rail. Jim did the same, but his ear-to-ear grin was gone. Then they just swooped down near the ground, and everyone jumped off the rails. They hit the ground hard and ran, keeping low to make a smaller target, across the open landing zone to the edge of the jungle. The roar of the helicopter slowly faded into jungle sounds as the chopper disappeared from sight. A fresh feeling of fear and abandonment swept over Jim. The eight-man Tiger Force team was on its own.

Jim must have looked frightened, because Sergeant Valdez told him, "Relax, Charlie's not around here. The choppers would have announced our arrival. We still have a long walk to get to Charlie."

"Thanks," Jim muttered as he tried not to stare at the ear necklace around the sergeant's neck.

The Sarge was right. They walked for two days. After the first day's walk, they set up camp early, so they could build a fire and have a warm meal before dark. It was too dangerous to have a fire after dark, even though they were not in Charlie's current AO (Area of Operation). It was like a regular campfire, with everyone sitting around it in a circle because they weren't worried about Charlie yet.

Sitting around the campfire to Jim's left was Bo Johnson, a rifleman. Bo walked point (first man in the column) most of the time. He was a big guy who had grown up in the Deep South in Jackson, Mississippi. Bo had always been the big kid in school and he had always tried to help the underdog, using his size and strength to protect anyone being picked on by bullies. He had grown up being the enforcer of fairness and justice. There was nothing about Bo, or his childhood, that could explain the necklace of human ears that hung around his neck.

Next to Bo was rifleman Travis Hood, from Billings, Montana. Travis was very competitive. He always used to brag that Montana had more cows than people, but now he only wanted to talk about killing "gooks," as they called the Vietnamese. Nonetheless, Travis did not wear an ear necklace. Instead he had a body count that he kept close records of in a little notebook that he carried in a waterproof case. If Travis had had a necklace, it would have won the contest.

Next to Travis was the squad leader, Sergeant Antonio Valdez. Sergeant Valdez was from the Philippines. He had wanted to be in the military for as long as he could remember. His idea of being a good soldier was to follow every order he received without question. At first his orders were to recon and report, but for many months now the Tiger Force had been used for what most folks would call genocide, but what the military called "search and destroy missions."

Sarge was currently leading his squad to a village deep in the jungle. It was rice harvest season, and the US Military wanted to destroy the harvest before it could supply the Vietcong. The CO (Commanding Officer) had ordered Sergeant Valdez to remove this village from the Vietnamese map, and to destroy all rice stocks found. Then, almost as an afterthought, he had told Valdez to take no prisoners.

For every squad member he lost, Valdez would collect six ears. No one ever knew if he ever got caught up, because in combat he fought so fiercely that he appeared to be way behind in his ear count. Sergeant Valdez's human ear necklace was made of revenge.

Next to Sergeant Valdez was Mike Robertson, the RTO (Radio Telephone Operator), or radio man. He usually stayed close to Sergeant Valdez to keep the radio handy. Mike was from California. He was not a big talker, but he was very cool and calm under fire. He did not have an ear necklace; instead he wore a gold chain around his neck.

To Robertson's left was rifleman Henry Callahan. He rarely spoke to anyone. He had committed more than his share of atrocities. He was a religious person who had killed countless villagers and Viet Cong in the name of the Lord, but who now believed that he had lost his soul—he had given up, and was waiting to die and go to Hell. Callahan did not have a human ear necklace because he thought that the practice was not Christian. However, if Henry had had a necklace, it would have been collected proudly in the name of the Lord.

Martin Grant, or "Doc," as the guys called him, was the medic. He seemed to be the sane member of the squad. Probably because he spent much of his time keeping the squad patched up. He wasn't obsessed with a body count or ears; he was, however, obsessed with not losing any of his men. When he lost a man he felt like he had failed, even when, many times, no one could have done anything, even with the best medical equipment.

To Jim's right was Steve Hampton. Steve was called Papa Death because he was older than the other guys, and he was by far the most bloodthirsty member of the squad. Papa Death was the M79 Grenadier. He carried the M79 Grenade Launcher and a .45 pistol, and he was very good with both. An M79 HE (High Explosive) round explodes when it hit something solid, and it had a three–meter killing radius. One round weighed a half a pound and was 40 millimeters in diameter. For comparison, a golf ball is 42.67 millimeters in diameter. That's one big bullet. Papa Death could fire his weapon up into the air and drop a round behind a boulder to kill a VC that a rifle could not hit. He had more ears on his necklace than anyone.

Once he had been in an argument with Bo over who had shot a VC or, more importantly, who got the credit for their body count, and he had had to be restrained from killing Bo over it. Bo gave Papa Death the kill, and they were instantly friends again. That's how Papa Death was; he was a killer, but he could turn it off and on as the situation called for. Out here in the boonies it didn't matter if your boots were shined or if you had a neat, military appearance as was required in the rear area. The only thing a soldier was judged by was his body count.

Looking around the circle of soldiers, Jim thought: What a blood-thirsty group we are. Not one of them had started out that way. None of them tortured animals or were mean as a kid. When the Tiger Force mission had been changed from recon to search and destroy, it seemed like everyone was pulled down into the dark side of humanity. It was amazingly like Nobel Prize–winning author William Golding's Lord of the Flies, where the kids are stranded on a desert island and they revert to savages.

Usually, when atrocities are committed in combat, they are isolated events done by soldiers who know they are doing wrong, and that they could be caught and punished. This was not the case with the Tiger Force; they were being ordered from high up the chain of command to commit these war crimes. It was taking a terrible toll on the soldiers.

On the third day, about noon they set up a temporary camp where they would just hang out trying to get some rest before nightfall. Word was passed around to check for leaches because of the water they had passed through. Jim was amazed to find three leaches on his legs despite his pants having been tightly tucked into his boots. They would go the rest of the way under the cover of night.

CHAPTER 3

THE AMBUSH

At twilight, they began to break camp. They waited until it was completely dark, so the point man could use the night vision scope as they moved down the trail at a much slower pace than they would travel in the daytime. An hour before dawn, the small group left the trail and traveled through the jungle until they came to a hill. Sergeant Valdez led them up the hill, and they stopped about fifty meters below the crest.

"Get the night vision scope and follow me," Sergeant Valdez told Jim. Jim got the scope from the point man, and he and Sergeant Valdez climbed nearly to the summit and then low-crawled the rest of the way to the top of the hill, so they could get a look at the jungle on the other side. Nestled into a valley at the foot of a distant mountain was a village. Sergeant Valdez studied the village through the night vision scope, but after only a few minutes it was getting too bright to use it. The night vision scope, or starlight scope, used the faint light available at night, usually starlight, and amplified it so the user could see in the dark. It was, however, easy to have too much light with the scope, rendering it useless. The Sarge continued watching the village through his field glasses for quite a while.

Then, handing the binoculars to Jim, he said, "Check it out. NVA." (North Vietnamese Army) Jim was amazed at how close the field glasses made the village look.

"I see the NVA soldiers!" Jim gasped. He could clearly see that the NVA soldiers were throughout the village, and they were obviously directing the activities of the villagers. It was like watching ants as Jim watched as the villagers moved about. They were bringing big bundles down the rough foothills and through a strip of thick jungle at the foot of the mountain behind the village to a line of ten thin black bicycles on the path that led through and out of the village.

"What's going on with those bicycles?" Jim asked the Sarge.

"They use them to carry heavy loads. They don't ride the bicycles, they just load them up and walk them down the trail," Sergeant Valdez explained. "They load the bikes with three or four times the weight that one VC can carry, but one VC can walk the heavily loaded bike." Sergeant Valdez watched the village for quite a while longer, and the two GIs made their way back down the hill to the others.

Everyone gathered around for a briefing. Sergeant Valdez began, "We have NVA in the village. They are about to extract a large supply of rice grown by the villagers. They will be moving the rice on bicycles, and they will probably move by night. There are a number of trails coming from the village, several going up into the mountains, but only one trail can get those heavily loaded bicycles out of the valley. We will be waiting along that trail, in ambush, to stop that rice from getting to its destination." With that, Sergeant Valdez led the men back down the hill the same way that they had gone up. Then they skirted around the hill they had used to observe the village and headed due north until they came to a big, well-traveled trail. They walked down the trail for a short distance until they found a good ambush site.

"This is the trail coming out of the village," Sarge told the squad, "we will set up our ambush here." Sergeant Valdez sent Bo back to the hill to watch the village and report back when the bicycles started to move out. It had to be close to a two-hour walk from the village, but Bo could make it from the hilltop to the ambush site in less than fifteen minutes. This gave them plenty of time to prepare for the NVA convoy. Sergeant Valdez had estimated the size of the NVA force at thirty men. This helped him determine the length of the field of fire needed in the ambush. He had few men, so he ordered blocks of the plastic explosive C-4 buried every ten meters along the ambush site. Between the blocks of C-4, and two meters off the trail, he had the men set up claymore mines. They buried the claymores with leaves and then they concealed the wires running up to the ambush positions. The ambush positions were along a small rise running parallel to the trail. When they set off all the explosives, they would have to be ducking down in their foxholes because the ridge was only ten meters from the trail, and the air would be thick with debris. They secured their positions and dug in. With all these explosives going off in a matter of seconds, it would be a miracle if anyone on the trail survived.

Travis Hood laughed. "If there's anything left to shoot at after all this goes off, I'll be surprised." Then everyone laughed.

They had plenty of time to set up the ambush, because the NVA did not move out until that evening. All day long the guys were goofing off. They didn't need to be very quiet with Bo watching the village, so the day was fun and relaxed.

It had only been dark for twenty minutes when the cry of a jungle bird rang out and Sergeant Valdez stopped what he was doing and looked up the trail from his foxhole. He echoed the bird call, and it was surprising how well Sergeant Valdez had duplicated the call.

"What kind of bird is that?" Jim asked Travis, who was sharing a foxhole with him.

"It's not a bird, it's Bo," Travis responded. Jim felt just a little bit stupid. The Sarge passed the word around that it was Bo, so no one would be surprised and open fire. Bo came jogging up the trail with his equipment bouncing comically out of sync with his running. Bo came directly to Sergeant Valdez and reported.

"They have left the village," Bo gasped, trying to catch his breath, "It looked like all the NVA are coming; I counted twenty-six of them." Again, Bo took a few deep breaths, and continued. "There's an advance party of eight NVA traveling about one thousand meters ahead of the main column, with four NVA in front of the bicycles and four behind. They have ten bicycles, with one NVA walking each bike. They started moving out just before dark, and I waited until the end of the convoy left the village to be sure I knew what was coming, Sarge," Bo said, just before turning up a canteen for a long drink.

"Good job, Bo," Sarge answered. "The eight NVA in the advance party are an unexpected problem." Sarge took off his hat and wiped his forehead with an army green handkerchief and continued, "We have no extra men to set up another ambush down the trail for the advance party. We will have to let the advance party go by and hit the main column." Bo handed Sarge the canteen, and Sarge took a drink.

"It is very important that we don't set off the ambush until we are sure it will take out the entire rear of the column." Sarge continued, "Even if some of the main column gets by us, the most important thing is that no one is left at the end of the column because they would be behind us and we don't want to be caught in a crossfire." Sarge handed the canteen back to Bo, and went on with the briefing.

"As soon as we set it off, run forward to the trail, taking out anyone still alive, and then we will try to run down all who got past. Hopefully, just the advance party will get by, and we will need to move fast to catch them after the ambush." Sarge had everyone take their positions, and the long, silent wait began.

Just enough light from the moon filtered through the jungle canopy to barely make out someone moving down the trail without using the starlight scope. Everyone was straining their eyes into the darkness when the silhouettes began appearing on the trail coming from the village. It was the eight-man advance party, and they were moving cautiously up the trail toward the ambush. When they got closer Jim could see that they were carrying AK-47s. The Tiger Force soldiers froze as the NVA approached. As the NVA soldiers were passing right in front of Jim and Travis's foxhole, Jim stopped breathing. One of the enemy soldiers stopped and stood on the side of the trail, facing directly toward their position. Jim was horrified, as it appeared that the soldier had heard or seen them. Jim knew that if they were discovered he should set off the explosives in front of his position. Just then, Jim felt Travis's hand slowly cover the hand Jim had his detonator in, to indicate that Jim was not to set it off. Suddenly they heard the stream of piss splattering on the jungle floor at the feet of the NVA soldier. Jim and Travis remained motionless as the soldier on the trail finished his business and continued down the trail; and then the advance team was gone. Jim's heart sank as he realized how close to setting off the ambush too early and ruining the entire mission he had been.

Everyone's attention was once again directed down the trail toward the village, and it wasn't long before the main column began to appear. Everyone was ready, and they all were waiting for the position closest to the village to open up first, as soon as the four guards at the end of the column were in front them. The procession of NVA was moving slowly by, and bicycles had been passing Jim and Travis's foxhole for some time when the stuff really hit the fan. The first explosion was followed so closely by all the others that it sounded like one big, sustained explosion as the entire trail lit up below. There was no time to think as they rushed down to the trail. Jim tripped over something on the way down to the trail that he thought was a tree limb, but as he looked down he saw that it was a leg blown off an NVA. The first body that Jim came to beside the trail was horribly blown apart, but somehow still alive. Jim froze as Travis came running up and put a round from his M16 through the forehead of the dying man.

"My body count! Early bird gets the worm," Travis laughed as he ran to the next body. "Come on!" he yelled. "We have to get the forward guards!" They all ran up the trail after the eight-man team that they had had to let pass earlier. Within minutes they were engaged in a firefight with the advance guards, who were running back down the trail toward them to try to help the others in the main group. A firefight at night always tends to last longer than one in the daytime because of the limited visibility, but in the end five of the eight NVA were killed, and three escaped into the jungle.

Jim was surrounded by death, and yet he felt very exhilarated to be alive. They collected anything they could use from the five corpses, and destroyed anything they didn't want, but that Charlie could use before returning to the ambush site to do the same there. Jim found an NVA officer's helmet. On the front of the helmet was an NVA emblem.

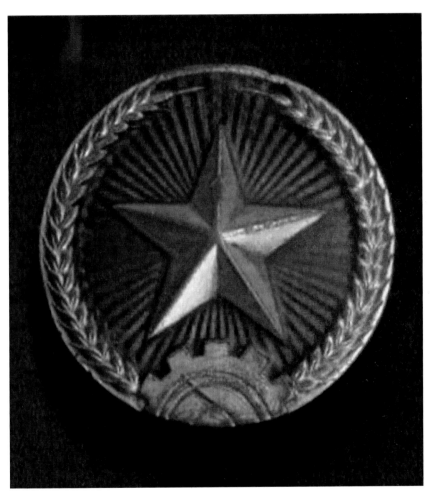

North Vietnamese Army Officer's Hat Emblem

Jim unscrewed a small nut from the threaded bolt coming out of the back of the emblem and hooked it onto his backpack strap. The others were gathering war trophies and ears, but Jim couldn't imagine himself cutting off someone's ear, even if they were dead.

Sergeant Valdez had the men burn, with lighter fluid, any piles of rice that could be gathered up by Charlie, and then they moved out toward the village. They followed the trail about half way to the village and set up beside the trail to get three hours of sleep.

CHAPTER 4

THE VILLAGE

Just before dawn they moved out. They were already able to smell the distinctive odor of the jungle village when they were still over a half an hour from it. As they came into view of the village, the remaining villagers did not run. Jim felt relieved that there was no resistance and that the expected firefight was not happening.

Then it happened: "No prisoners!" Sergeant Valdez yelled, and all hell broke loose. The guys started firing at the unarmed villagers and killing them where they stood or sat. The villagers started running and were gunned down as they fled. They were killing everyone, even the women and children. Jim was horrified as he stood there without firing his weapon.

Sergeant Valdez saw that Jim was frozen, and he came over and shouted, "Follow me!" and started running to the back of the village. Jim ran with him because running was the only thing that Jim could get his body to do. They followed the trail that was strewn sparsely with rice. Behind the village, the trail led into a strip of jungle. Sergeant Valdez and Jim proceeded slowly, on full alert, through the jungle until Sergeant Valdez noticed that the trail no longer had rice. They turned and went back toward the village and found where the rice left the trail. A bush had been uprooted and laid over the path where the rice forked off onto a small trail that the bush had been hiding.

"Here we go," Sarge whispered, and they followed the small trail until it broke out of the jungle and before them were the steep foothills of the mountain. The trail wound up to the entrance to a cave. Rice was everywhere around the cave entrance. They stepped into the darkness of the cave and waited for their eyes to adjust. Soon they could see that the cave opened up into a big room-like area a short distance from where they were. The "room" at the end was lit by a small hole in the top. No one was in the cave, and in the big room they found six big baskets, each empty except one that was about half full.

"This is what the NVA left for the villagers," Sergeant Valdez said. "Give me your C-4 and go guard the entrance to the cave." After a few minutes Jim was crouched down at the entrance of the cave, watching the foothills drop down to the jungle. Sounds of sporadic gunfire were still echoing from the village below as Sergeant Valdez backed by him, unrolling wire from a spool.

"Come on," Sergeant Valdez said as he backed out of the cave and moved off to the side of the entrance. Jim stood beside him as he cut the wire, separated the two strands, stripped the wire ends bare, and attached the wires to a handheld claymore mine detonator.

"Fire in the hole," said Sergeant Valdez calmly, with a smile, as he squeezed the detonator. A big puff of dust and smoke blew out the entrance of the cave, pushed by a huge explosion.

The sergeant led the way back to the village, where what had happened was way too obvious to ignore. It looked like the entire village had been killed—men, women, and children. When they reached the others, they all seemed to be mad at Jim, and they were giving him very unfriendly looks.

"Talleson didn't fire," Bo Johnson said in a loud voice.

"Cool it—and that's an order!" snapped Sergeant Valdez. "He just froze up, he'll be alright. It can happen to anyone their first time out."

Everyone was very upset with Jim because, by not taking part in the extermination of the villagers, he could be a threat if he decided to tell the wrong people what had happened. For everyone who was involved, keeping it quiet was in their own best interest. To have a witness who did not share the guilt was completely unacceptable to them.

"You guys make torches; we're going to burn it to the ground," Sergeant Valdez barked, then he turned to Jim. "And you will light the match." Within minutes they had made torches, and Bo was squirting the torches with a can of lighter fluid. Sergeant Valdez, trying to get the squad to feel better about Jim, handed Jim a book of C-ration matches. Jim knew that by lighting the torches he was taking part in burning the village, but he lit a match, out of fear, and held it out in front of him. Sarge thought that this might make the squad feel like Jim had taken part in the atrocities. He watched as each member of the squad stood in front of Jim while he lit their torches. Sergeant Valdez saw the looks that they gave Jim. The looks made Jim fear for his very life. This was unbelievable. With all the things to fear in the jungle, to fear your own men was too much for Jim. They lit each grass hut on fire and started down the trail out of the burning village. Jim heard the screams of someone in the corner hooch by the trail who was being burned alive but, as much as he wanted to try to save the villager, he kept walking with the others.

Following the villagers who had escaped they took a trail from the village that went through a mountain pass, and the trail was getting steeper as they went. The squad had only been walking for twenty minutes or so when Sergeant Valdez raised his hand to signal everyone to stop. Ahead, sitting cross-legged, right beside the trail, was an old Vietnamese man sitting alone. He had been left behind while fleeing the village because he could not climb any further up the mountain.

Everyone started arguing. "He's mine!" yelled Bo.

"I've got him. I saw him first!" yelled Travis, almost at the same time. Sergeant Valdez raised his hand for silence.

"Talleson will handle it," said Sergeant Valdez. He looked Jim in the eye and said, in a very serious voice, "Take care of it for me, and look out for an ambush and booby traps."

Jim knew he had lost the trust of his fellow soldiers and that he would be chosen for every dangerous "one-man job" until he was killed. His chances of making it home alive were almost gone.

Jim took a deep breath and marched up the path toward the old man. He marched with determination. Paying no mind to the possibility of an ambush or a booby trap, he went directly to the old man and stood right in front of him. The old guy was smiling broadly and nodding his head as if to bow, but Jim could see the fear behind the smile. Jim reached behind his head, pulling a machete from the scabbard on his backpack. Then, with one powerful, smooth motion, he lopped off the old man's head. Jim heard a cheer go up from his squad down the hill, but he ignored it as he severed an ear from the head lying on the ground. Jim marched back down the hill to his smiling comrades. When he reached his squad, he held out the ear to them.

"Who's got string?" Jim said, and another cheer went up from the squad. Jim felt great relief. He had earned his place in the squad, but what he had traded for it, he feared, was his soul.

Jim would never again be the same young man that his family knew and loved. Despite having just committed this terrible atrocity, and above the feeling of relief that his squad no longer hated him, all Jim could think of was the village. All the dead bodies, the children, the screams of the villager burning to death....

One thought kept repeating over and over in his head.

"I lit the match," Jim whispered to himself.

CHAPTER 5

THE FIREFIGHT

They moved through the mountain pass and climbed down the other side, and a valley stretched out in front of them. They had not seen any of the villagers who had escaped. Soon they found a defensible position and made a camp to spend the night before going into the valley.

Jim got out paper and pen to write home. He sat there a long time without writing a word. A tear ran down his face as he put the paper and pen away. The only good news that he could write to his mom and dad about was that he was alive, and he wasn't really sure if that was good news or not. He put the pen and paper away without writing a word. He was too ashamed to write home.

The next morning, they walked through the valley until they found a clearing big enough to land a chopper. Sergeant Valdez ordered everyone to dig in as he radioed in for the extraction helicopter. The guys grumbled about digging in just to leave a short while later, but they all dug in.

It wasn't long until the welcome sound of the helicopter grew near, and everyone was looking forward to a chopper ride. As the helicopter approached, Charlie opened fire with AK-47s, and the firing was coming from the jungle on two sides of the clearing. If the chopper hadn't come when it did, the Tiger Force would have come under a deadly cross-fire attack.

A large number of NVA had been on their way since they got word that their rice had been destroyed and the village wiped out. The firing was intense, and the chopper could not land and was driven off. As soon as the helicopter departed to a safe distance, the firing was redirected toward the Tiger Force. They were pinned down.

Sergeant Valdez yelled for everyone to only fire if they saw a target, and he got on the radio to call in the Cobra gunships. The problem was that the guys had to stay alive until the gunships arrived. They were out-numbered two to one, and they had not had time to dig in very deep.

The gunfire was intense when Jim heard the scream, "Medic! Medic!" and Doc Grant, risking his life, low-crawled past Jim's position. Henry Callahan was in the position next to Jim's. He had been hit in the only place exposed while firing from a foxhole—right through the head. His wait for death was over. There was nothing that could be done for Henry.

The enemy fire had become so heavy that Doc had to stay in Henry's foxhole with him. NVA were starting to move forward from the edge of the jungle. They were being shot down before they got far from the jungle, but the supply of ammunition would not last much longer. Sergeant Valdez passed the word from foxhole to foxhole to fire in short bursts and wait until you can't miss when they advance to save ammo.

Jim saw them break out of the jungle. Three NVA seemed to be running straight to his position. Jim had never done this before except in training, but he took a hand grenade from his pistol belt, pulled the pin, and paused just long enough for the grenade to explode as soon as it hit. The grenade was right on target; the three NVA were lifted off the ground and thrown to the side when the hand grenade exploded. Two of the NVA lay motionless on the ground, but the third was trying to crawl back to the edge of the jungle. Jim aimed his rifle and fired a short burst. The NVA soldier did not make it back to the jungle.

Now grenades were going off more frequently as the Tiger Force began to run out of ammunition. Jim checked his ammo supply, and was surprised at how fast he was using it up. He set his M16 to single fire and took careful aim at the spot where the three NVA had come out of the jungle. Sure enough an NVA soldier appeared, breaking out of the jungle right at that spot. Jim squeezed off a single shot and killed the NVA soldier three feet from the edge of the jungle.

They all heard it coming at the same time—two Cobra gunships were headed for them from the south. Sergeant Valdez was on the radio, and he yelled the order to throw white smoke at Charlie's positions. Soon white smoke was billowing up from the edge of the jungle on both sides of the clearing.

The gunships opened up with the deafening roar of rockets exploding. The Cobra gunship is a heavily armed helicopter. It is armed with rockets and two belt fed machine-guns that fire M79 HE rounds. The gunships lay down a wide path of these HE rounds, which exploded as they hit, and nothing in their path could survive. They do this with a weapon called the M75, a cam-operated, electric motor–driven, air-cooled grenade launcher that fires belt fed M79 HE rounds a rate of 215–230 S.P.M. (Shots-Per-Minute). The deafening hum of the two belt-fed M75s and the occasional earth-moving rocket explosions signaled the total destruction of the jungle across the clearing and everything in it. One gunship worked on each side of the clearing as everyone kept their heads down in their foxholes. The air was full of shrapnel and debris, to the point where no one could even peek out of their foxholes.

Silence was replaced by the sound of a million bugs unexpectedly as the gunships ceased their deadly assault. Not one round of incoming fire was heard from the NVA. Sergeant Valdez called the men together, and they rushed into the jungle to one side and discovered several bodies in the shredded jungle. Then they rushed across the clearing and entered the jungle. Everything was the same there. The bodies were shredded just like the jungle around them, but no one was alive, or even wounded—everyone they found was dead.

Suddenly, the Cobra gunships opened fire in the distance. They had spotted some of the NVA who were fleeing the battle. Sergeant Valdez led the guys back to the clearing, and the Huey helicopter started coming in to extract the Tiger Force. This time the chopper received no incoming fire, and it came in for a landing. They waited a few more minutes until a medevac helicopter came to pick up Henry. When it came, the guys carried Henry out to the waiting helicopter. As they carried Henry, Jim looked into Henry's blank eyes and was surprised at how young and childlike Henry's face appeared. Even with his war paint, Henry looked like a schoolboy. This was a shock to Jim because, even though Henry did not wear an ear necklace, Jim had always seen Henry as a very hardened killer with scary eyes.

As they approached the chopper, carrying Henry and keeping low under the blades, the medic jumped out of the Huey and came running up. He caught Jim's eye and made a questioning look as he nodded toward Henry. Jim shook his head, no, and the medic's question was answered— Henry was dead. After carefully laying Henry on the floor of the chopper for the medics, they ran back out from under the blades, keeping low, and then they all stopped and turned to watch Henry leave. Jim was shocked that he actually felt jealous of Henry for being choppered out of this hell.

They quickly loaded onto the waiting helicopter, and off they went to be dropped off at the far end of a long walk to another doomed village. In this village Jim killed everything living that he saw, as soon as he saw it. Here he learned the advantage of thinking of the Vietnamese as "gooks." Jim had thought it was meant as a racial slur, but now he saw clearly that it was an attempt to dehumanize the enemy in a not-always-successful attempt to avoid insanity. Jim was changing with every passing day, and the old Jim seemed to fade a little with each ear he added to his necklace.

CHAPTER 6

EXTRACTION

Thirty days, four villages, and about five tons of rice after the mission began, it was time to be choppered out to the forward base camp for a much-needed stand down (break from combat). It was time to party like there was no tomorrow, and in a combat zone that saying has an ugly ring of truth to it.

Everyone was in a good mood, and they laughed and joked as they waited for the extraction helicopter. Jim was now an accepted and respected member of the squad, and he even looked like he fit in. It's hard to explain, something about the eyes, but they all had it.

They all heard the sound of the helicopter blades at the same time, and they quickly gathered up their gear and stood ready as Sergeant Valdez had Bo bring in the chopper. Bo walked out from the edge of the landing zone and held his M16 rifle in two hands with his arms extended outward and upward and his rifle horizontal to the ground. He slowly lowered the rifle as the chopper got closer to the ground. He kept the rifle the same height from the ground as the landing rails of the chopper, so the chopper pilot could use Bo's rifle to tell how close to the ground his landing rails were.

Jim didn't get the thrill from riding in the open doorway like he used to. He felt like he was carrying a heavy weight on his chest.

The Forward Base Camp

That night, at the base camp, Jim got real serious about drinking. In fact, he drank himself into a stupor every subsequent night. The forward base camp had a club. Well, actually, it was a bombed-out farmhouse. Just inside the door of the club, in the only room left intact, was a big chest-type cooler that you could usually find the "bartender" sitting on. Outside the club was a parachute stretched out for an awning to provide shade. Jim spent most of his time under the parachute, drinking beer after beer. One night he drank so much that he had to crawl back to his pup tent. When Jim got to his tent he was too drunk to get over the sandbags, even though they were only stacked three high. He ended up lying on his back beside the sandbags.

While he was laying there, Bo, Papa Death, and Doc happened by. They all sat down in the dirt, forming a circle that included Jim's head. Bo loaded his pipe until it was overflowing with pot. They passed the pipe around the circle, and each time it came to Jim they would hold the pipe in his mouth while he took a hit. Jim learned that even if you are totally incapacitated, as long as you are not unconscious you can still party at the forward base camp. The party was going fine until, just before Jim's turn on the pipe, it started to rain. The guys got up and went to their tents, leaving Jim to sleep in the rain. Jim was not concerned that the guys had left him but, as he slipped into a deep sleep, his last thought was, "Hey, it was my turn."

Jim was in a serious downward spiral, psychologically, but he didn't understand what was happening to him. To confuse things more, Jim had arrived in 'Nam a boy and, in a few short weeks in the Tiger Force, almost all of the "boy" had been forcibly removed from him. Jim, never having been a man before, thought that this was simply the man that he had grown into.

The three–day stand down was soon over, and they all found themselves on a chopper ride back to the boonies. Jim looked around at the others in the helicopter with their faces painted fiercely, and all their combat gear, but now they didn't look so strange. Even with the ear necklaces they didn't look strange. They all just looked like his brothers.

They were receiving sporadic fire as they were coming in for a landing. This was another hot LZ. The chopper did not touch down, and everyone jumped out at the low point as the helicopter swooped down and back up again. They hit the ground and ran to the tree line for cover. Charlie had taken off and was not making a stand. They could see five or six Viet Cong in black pajamas and sloped hats, carrying AK-47s, disappearing into the jungle on the other side of a big clearing. When the squad got to the clearing, Sergeant Valdez held them up.

"This doesn't feel right," he said, "it could be an ambush." He led them into the jungle, and they followed the edge of the clearing all the way around to the end where the five or six VC had disappeared and where they now broke out of the jungle into the clearing. As soon as they broke out of the jungle, the VC opened fire from across the clearing. Sarge was right, it was an ambush. If they had chased Charlie across the clearing, they would have been caught in an ambush with no place to hide—no cover. They ducked back into the jungle, and Sergeant Valdez got on the radio to call in artillery. Within minutes a white smoke artillery round came crashing through the jungle canopy, surprisingly close to the Tiger Force and nowhere near Charlie. Sarge radioed in the correction on the coordinates, and another smoke round landed across the clearing where the Viet Cong were firing from.

"Fire for effect!" Sergeant Valdez shouted into the field phone, and momentarily a barrage of explosions began across the clearing. After the artillery attack, they quickly skirted the jungle running along the edge of the clearing, so that if Charlie opened fire again they could duck back into the jungle. When they reached the spot from which the firing had come, they went into the jungle on full alert. They found one dead VC and one that needed a little more help to die. Travis put an M16 round into his forehead. Travis then took out his little notebook from its waterproof case and carefully added one more VC to his body count. He kept separate records for VC and NVA—of course women and children counted as VC.

Jim felt a sense of comfort to at having Sergeant Valdez as his squad leader. Any other member of the squad would have led the team right through the middle of the clearing and into the ambush had they been the squad leader.

Sergeant Valdez led them further into the jungle to try to catch up with the VC who had gotten away. He knew that the amount of firepower coming from Charlie in the ambush could not have been laid down by two men. Soon they came upon a trail, and Bo went ahead to check for foot-prints to see which way Charlie went on the trail. Bo was a hunter back home, and he could track anything that left a trail. This was why he was the point man for the squad. Bo went to the left, following the trail, but staying off to the side while he studied the prints.

"This is where they came onto the trail," Bo said, "and there are four of them. One is wounded, and two others are helping him along, one on each side." Bo stopped moving down the trail and bent down to get a closer look. "Look here," Bo exclaimed, "the guy in the middle's feet are dragging intermittently as they go down the trail. He must be going in and out of consciousness." They began moving down the trail to catch up with the Viet Cong. They hadn't gone two thousand meters when Bo came upon the dead VC.

"Here's the one they were carrying," Bo announced.

As Jim passed the body of the dead VC, he bent over the corpse and placed an ace of spades on the dead man's chest. This was a form of psychological warfare. The Vietnamese believed that an ace of spades on a dead body would prevent the spirit of the dead person from going to heaven and would attract many bad spirits.

Psychological Warfare Secret Weapon

The US Playing Card Company back home was sending decks of cards that were all aces of spades for the soldiers to leave on the dead bodies. When the VC came back later to bury their dead, if an ace of spades was on the corpse they would not even touch the body, let alone bury it.

They moved fast, but on full alert, down the trail as quickly as Bo could follow the tracks. Just after a curve in the trail, Bo put his arm up in a signal to stop.

"The tracks have left the trail," he yelled, "hit the dirt!" They all dove for cover just as the enemy fire began. The three VC had set up a hasty ambush when the Tiger Force was getting near. The guys opened up with everything they had, and the enemy was overwhelmed by the fire power of seven against three. Papa Death had a clear shot and he landed two HE rounds from his M79, and they went off right where the VC fire was coming from. That was it. As they moved in on Charlie's position they received no more incoming fire. There was no doubt about it. Papa Death's M79 spoke with a loud voice.

"I got 'em all!" Papa Death yelled as he removed an ear from each VC. Jim could tell by looking at Papa Death's ear necklace that he was going to need a longer string before he could add three more ears.

Sergeant Valdez decided to check out the trail in the direction the VC were headed to see if they could find where Charlie was going. They had followed the trail for over an hour when things started getting dangerous. The trail they were on intersected with a big trail. This big trail, considering that it was deep in the jungle, was like a superhighway. It was covered with footprints and thin bicycle tracks. The Tiger Force was deep in Charlie's territory, and it looked like a seven-man squad was not a sufficient force to deal with this situation. Nonetheless, they proceeded down the big trail on full alert.

They hadn't gone far when the single shot rang out and Bo spun around and fell to the ground.

Doc Grant ran past Jim and yelled, "Come with me." They ran up to Bo and they grabbed him, one on each arm, and drug Bo back to a safe place while Papa Death pumped HE rounds into the tree from which the sniper was firing. As soon as an HE round hit a branch thick enough to set it off, an explosion happened within the tree limbs and a VC came tumbling down out of the tree. Bo had been grazed along the side of his head, and they had almost drug him back to safety when he woke up.

"I'm okay!" Bo said, and he jumped to his feet. Doc and Jim had to make Bo stay so Doc could treat the wound. Bo wanted to join the others on the way to the sniper tree.

As the others moved in on the tree, they set up a defensive position to secure the area around it. They were in Charlie's territory, and the gunshots would alert every VC within ear shot. A few minutes later, Doc, Bo, and Jim joined the Sarge and Papa Death in standing over the dead VC at the base of the tree. Then something happened that blew them all away. Papa Death was very glad to see that Bo was alright.

"You can have the ear," he told Bo, "but I get the body count."

"I can't take your ear," replied Bo, "but thanks, brother." Papa Death and Bo smiled at each other.

Sergeant Valdez got on the radio to report the situation. As he handed the receiver back to Mike he gave the order to move out. Bo took the point again, and they all started down the big trail. They were now looking for a place that was easy to defend and where they could get a chopper in. Within minutes they found a low hill, flat on top, that was big enough to land the helicopter on. They took up positions around the top of the hill and dug in. Soon they heard the Huey coming, and they gathered up their gear and waited. The helicopter was still some distance away when they heard sporadic firing far off in the direction of the chopper. As the Huey got closer, so did the firing.

"Be ready to load fast!" Sergeant Valdez yelled as the chopper came in for a landing in the center of the hilltop. There didn't seem to be any incoming fire as they ducked low and rushed to the chopper. Just the same, when they lifted off no one was dangling their feet out the door. Sure enough, they received the occasional ping and thud as rounds grazed or hit the helicopter body.

"Are we going in deeper?" Papa Death shouted to Sergeant Valdez with a grin.

"No," Sarge shouted back, "they are sending in the 1/327th as they said there are too many VC for us." Everyone was pissed. They felt like they had been ripped off by a regular "grunt" (combat) unit, the 1/327th, of the 101st Airborne.

After a fifteen-minute ride, they were dropped off once again in the jungle with orders to "take out" yet another small village.

Jim was getting used to the killing, but now he had Henry Callahan's memory to encourage him to extract an even higher price from Charlie. Jim was also becoming more and more withdrawn. He rarely spoke to anyone, and he denied himself fun. For instance, he would volunteer to guard while the others bathed and frolicked in a stream.

CHAPTER 7

THE HOMECOMING

Jim had only been with the Tiger Force for three months and one week. He was a "short-timer" with only three weeks left in country. As hard as Jim tried not to think about going home, that was all he could think of. He was so torn between wanting to make it home alive and being too ashamed to go home. What could he tell his family…? If only he had refused to light that first match.

"That match started it all," he thought, "the match led to arson, the arson led to murder and then atrocity after atrocity. My God, what have I done?"

Jim appeared fearless as he began taking unnecessary chances. If they were pinned down by a sniper and they didn't know where the sniper was, he would stand up and look. When the sniper fired at him he would either have the location of the sniper or be dead. Somehow, as hard as he tried, he couldn't get himself killed. It only gained him more respect within the squad. The guys started respectfully calling him "Crazy Jim." And everyone left him alone.

In the next week Travis went home, and Bo was killed by a Bouncing Betty land mine. He was walking point—it all happened very fast— and Bo was gone. A Bouncing Betty mine has two explosions; the first throws the big explosive charge up into the air where it, too, explodes. This cannot be avoided by diving to the ground because the shrapnel rains down from above.

When Travis and Bo's replacements arrived, Jim did not talk to them. Well, it wasn't personal, because Jim was not talking at all, and he looked like he was staring all the time. He had watched Bo get zapped (killed), and there had been nothing he could do. Jim insisted that he take point for the rest of his time in the field. And still he couldn't get himself killed. Getting killed in the boonies seemed to be his only hope for honor and respect. Folks always honor the fallen soldiers of every war, and Jim wanted very badly to be one of them.

At the end of Jim's last week Sarge tried to get him to go to the rear area three days early, but Jim wouldn't go. He stayed to the very last day. They sent him in to the rear area on a re-supply chopper. While Jim was high in the air over the jungle, he took off his ear necklace and threw it out of the Huey.

Jim was like a zombie in the rear area. He just sat on his bunk staring straight ahead. The captain assigned a soldier to help get Jim through the out-processing center. Jim's helper got him through out-processing and turned him over to a flight attendant who helped Jim onto the plane and even had to fasten his seat belt for him. He had to be escorted through the entire process. Then he was on the flight home, where his family would be at the terminal.

Jim slipped further and further into his own mind and became even more unresponsive. He no longer knew what was going on around him as his mind relived the atrocities he had committed one after another, over and over again. Being in the military had made Jim a man. The only problem was Jim could not live with the man he had become.

Jim's family was waiting for Jim when his plane landed at the Des Moines, Iowa airport. They were very excited to have Jim back safely at home. They all watched as the passengers disembarked, looking at face after face, but Jim did not come out. When it was obvious that everyone else was off the plane, Jim's dad went to the attendant and asked about Jim. The attendant checked the roster and saw that Jim should have been on that plane. The attendant and Jim's dad went down the long hallway to the plane, and the flight attendant inside the doorway of the jet nodded to the passenger section. She was pretty sure who they were looking for, even without an exchange of words.

Jim was rocking forward and back in his seat, staring straight ahead, clutching tightly to an old book of C-ration matches, unable to face his family with the guilt of what he had done.

"Speak to me son!" his father tearfully asked Jim.

Jim tried to speak; his father bent down for Jim to talk in his ear, and Jim, almost too quiet to hear, whispered something to his father. Jim's father's eyes streamed tears as they helped Jim off the plane.

Jim never did respond again after that; he had to be institutionalized for the rest of his life. His father would never understand what Jim had whispered and would carry that with him to his grave. Jim died in the institution, an old man, never having spoken since he had confessed to his father, whispering to him, "I lit the match."

Jim's C-Ration or "Boonie" Matches

Ancient Shaman's Ceremonial Dagger

VI - The Dagger

CHAPTER 1

THE CURSE

Late at night Steve and Joanna were startled out of their sleep by men's voices chanting. They sat up in bed, holding each other in fear. This was not the first time, but this time the chanting was louder than ever before. Then they were horrified when the bed started lifting off the floor several inches and crashing back down repeatedly with a loud bang, over and over.

Steve shouted angrily, in his best army voice, "Get out of our home and leave us alone!" Steve had no sooner finished yelling when right through the wall came five or ten small round balls of light. They all flew around the room, swooping very near Steve and Joanna each time around. Joanna began to scream, and then Steve cried out in pain. In that second the lights flew back through the wall that they had come out of and were gone.

It was finally over, but Steve was holding his shins and grimacing in pain.

"What's wrong, Steve?" Joanna shouted.

"My legs," Steve groaned, "something scratched my legs." Joanna was horrified as she pulled up Steve's pajama pant legs and saw the three deep cuts running down Steve's shins on both of his legs.

"Get dressed," Steve said, "we're getting out of here." They both quickly got dressed, threw some things together, and ran down the stairs. They didn't slow down to gather any of their belongings. They ran right through the living room, fled the house, jumped in the car, and drove to a nearby motel.

One Year Earlier:

It was 1966, and Master Sergeant (E-7) Steven Dunlevy was on his seventh month of duty in Vietnam. He had four more months to go in his tour. He had been assigned to the base camp of the 101st Airborne Division at Phan Rang, Vietnam. A few short months ago the base camp had sandbag bunkers around the perimeter road, but now the bunkers had been replaced with armor-plated guard towers.

Sandbag Bunkers Were Replaced with Armor-Plated Guard Towers

Being so far from his wife and home in Phoenix, Arizona, was not easy for Steve. They had gotten married knowing that Steve was going to Vietnam, so they had been torn apart while still in the honeymoon phase of their marriage. Steve kept a calendar for each day of service, and every day he would "X" out that day. He always knew how many days it was until he would get to go home.

He was a cook in the army and he was the mess sergeant at the base camp. He loved to cook. As a child, he had watched his mother cook and bake, and the end result was always so delicious that Steve wanted to know how to create things that were a delight to eat. Of course, this desire was pretty much wasted on the volumes of food that were mass-produced for the enlisted soldiers (peons)—after all, what can you do with powdered eggs and shit on a shingle (chipped beef and gravy on a slice of bread)? But the food that Master Sergeant Dunlevy personally prepared for the officers and the occasional VIP was a different story entirely. He planned to go to chef's school when he got out of the army, but he was already cooking on a professional level.

Steve worked three days on and one day off, but he usually dropped by the mess hall on his days off just to make sure everything was going well. He had always been aware that being a cook often led to being overweight, so he exercised regularly. He would jog along the perimeter road on his days off. The perimeter road circled the compound inside three rows of concertina wire that skirted the outer perimeter to keep out the enemy. Along the way Steve would jog past a guard post every so often, but most of the way he was alone with his thoughts. He enjoyed the solitude, and it allowed him to sort out things in his mind and plan for his future back home with Joanna.

From one guard position, you could see the next position, but it was far away. As Steve jogged passed each guard tower, the guard would wave at him. Even though this eventually became a hassle, he would always wave back. Steve figured that since the guards were alone in the guard tower they were probably waving out of boredom.

The run was a time of solitude for Steve, but one day he did have a bit of excitement. As he was jogging that morning, he had to move to the side of the road to let a two-and-a-half-ton truck pass. The truck was replacing the guards at each tower with new fresh guards. The truck came to a stop at tower five, and the fresh guard jumped out of the truck as the tired guard was climbing down from the tower. Steve was coming up behind the truck, so he started walking so he would not pass the truck while it was stopped.

As the tired guard was climbing into the truck he threw his ammo can into the center floor of the truck. From twenty meters away Steve heard the soldiers begin to shout and evacuate the back of the truck with amazing speed. The soldiers were yelling "Fire in the hole!" which Steve knew meant an explosion was about to happen. Steve dove to the side of the road and landed lying flat on the ground just as the explosion happened. The guard who threw his ammo can into the truck had forgotten to replace the caps to the tops of his hand flares. To fire a hand flare the soldier would take the top off the flare cylinder and put it on the bottom of the flare. Then, by striking the bottom of the flare the soldier would drive a firing pin into a detonator and the flare would be launched. The problem was that the guards also kept their five hand grenades in the same ammo can as the flares, so when the guys in the truck heard the flare go off inside the ammo can they knew that a very serious explosion was about to happen. And, of course, it did. One grenade would be enough to kill everyone in the back of the truck, but five grenades going off at once was a serious explosion. After the explosion Steve ran to the truck to help, but everyone was fine. The guards, despite being very tired, had evacuated the truck in record time. There was a huge hole in the wooden floor of the truck, and the only thing that had survived was the drive shaft below the hole; so, the troops loaded back into the truck and they drove on.

About halfway around the 101st Airborne side of the perimeter, Steve would stop between two of the guard positions. There was a small, two-foot-high hill, or mound of dirt, that was just right to sit on for a break. It was about halfway through the run, so it was where Steve always stopped for a break.

When Steve first got to Vietnam the base camp was still being built, but now the 101st Airborne was all moved in. The compound was divided in half, as the 101st Airborne shared it with the Air Force, but Steve had never been to the Air Force side. The two sides were completely different. The 101st Airborne side had dirt roads, and tents without cooling. The tents were being slowly replaced with wooden barracks, but they were still without cooling. On the Air Force side, there were cinder-block barracks with an air conditioner in every window, and not only had they paved the roads, but they had lined both sides of each road with white-painted decorative rocks. The two sides looked like the difference between night and day.

Master Sergeant Dunlevy had a second-in-command in the mess hall, First Cook, Staff Sergeant (E-6) Eli Harris. Then there were six cooks under Staff Sergeant Harris. These six cooks did most of the cooking. Sergeant Harris was a strict taskmaster, and he shouted orders and chewed out cooks and kitchen workers all day long. He was always threatening people with court-martial. Steve knew that the bottom line with Staff Sergeant Harris was that he had never really had anyone court-martialed, he was fair, and he ran a very smooth and efficient mess hall.

Staff Sergeant Harris was from a small town in Indiana called Martinsville, south of Indianapolis. He had visited Indianapolis many times with his family while he was growing up, but he had never been out of Indiana until he joined the army. Staff Sergeant Harris was counting the days until he could go home. Mild racism was a way of life in his family; they didn't hate, they just believed that they were superior to all other races.

Early on, Staff Sergeant Harris had used the term "gooks" to refer to the Vietnamese people while reporting to Master Sergeant Dunlevy. Steve had stopped him short, telling him that racism would not be tolerated while he was in charge. Back home the country was ablaze with racism and protests against racism, and Steve would not tolerate it under his command. Sergeant Harris was shocked, because he did not think he was a racist. He was the kind of racist who thinks that because he spoke, laughed, and joked with minorities that this somehow exempted him from being a racist. Steve having stopped him from using a racial slur had opened his eyes just a little, so he became a silent racist and would never use a racial term unless he was sure that he was alone with other racists. Harris never again showed any signs of racism around Steve, and they worked together well running the mess hall.

Steve was not only against racism, but he was also faithful to his wife, Joanna, back in the States. They had a wonderful family life with very supportive in-laws. They had only been married for a year and a half when Steve was ordered to Vietnam. Steve and Joanna had decided to wait until Steve got home from Vietnam and out of the army before having children, but they both looked forward to starting a large family when he got home. Joanna was a homebody, and she was very good for Steve. She encouraged him and wrote every day while he was in Vietnam. In the short time they had been married, the only hard time was when they found out that Steve had been assigned to his tour of duty in Vietnam.

She was outfitting a room in their new home as a nursery, and she wasn't even pregnant. She was so much a positive thinker that she advanced Steve's and her plans and goals even in his absence.

Most of the guys would go to the "strip" every chance they got. They could go to the city of Phan Rang, but the military had set up a little block-long "city" closer to the base camp than Phan Rang that consisted of nothing but bars, and each bar was also a whorehouse. The entire strip was patrolled by the South Vietnamese police, and all the prostitutes were checked regularly for venereal disease. When a soldier got a day pass to go into town, a condom was issued along with the pass. Steve had never been to the strip, but he had gone into Phan Rang several times. Phan Rang was a big city, by Vietnamese standards, and Steve enjoyed visiting with the people and learning about their culture.

In the poor families, which were the majority, every member of the family had to do something to earn money. There were two main businesses that the children operated—the shoeshine business and the cigarette business. They would buy a pack of cigarettes and sell them individually, for a profit. The bad news was that most of the children from poor families were addicted to smoking cigarettes from a very young age.

CHAPTER 2

DINNER IN THE BOONIES

It was Thanksgiving, and even though it was Steve's day off he came in anyway because today they were delivering a hot meal to the troops out in the boonies. Steve had never been anywhere near actual combat, and he figured that this may be the closest he would ever get. He also wanted to make sure that it was a first-rate meal for the guys who risked their lives every day out there. He showed up early and personally directed the preparation of the food. He wanted this meal to be as special as any that he had ever prepared for the officers and VIPs.

A long table ran all the way across the back of the kitchen, and it was completely covered with thermal food containers with clamp-down hinged lids. These containers would keep hot things hot and cold things cold and, when the lids were clamped down, they were spill proof. Of course, being official army equipment, they were all painted OD (Olive Drab) green. This meal had to be prepared, transferred to the thermal containers, loaded onto helicopters, and flown out to the troops in the jungle. Once there, a long serving table and a chow line would be set up.

This was not a regular meal: these 101st Airborne Division, combat-hardened troops only ate C-Rations out in the boonies, but for Thanksgiving they would enjoy a complete Thanksgiving dinner with all the trimmings. There were even Thanksgiving dinner menus for the soldiers to keep as mementos.

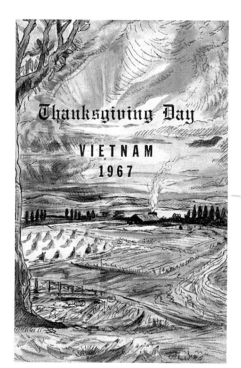

THANKSGIVING DAY DINNER

Shrimp Cocktail

Crackers

Roast Turkey

Turkey Gravy   Cornbread Dressing   Cranberry Sauce

Mashed Potatoes   Glazed Sweet Potatoes

Buttered Mixed Vegetable

Assorted Crisp Relishes

Hot Rolls   Butter   Fruit Cake   Mincemeat Pie

Pumpkin Pie w/Whipped Topping

Assorted Nuts   Assorted Candy   Assorted Fresh Fruits

Tea w/Lemon   Milk

Thanksgiving Day Menu

Steve went over the meal plan. It consisted of shrimp cocktail, crackers, roast turkey, turkey gravy, cornbread dressing, cranberry sauce, mashed potatoes, glazed sweet potatoes, buttered mixed vegetables, assorted crisp relishes, hot rolls, butter, fruit cake, mincemeat pie, pumpkin pie with whipped topping, assorted nuts, assorted candy, assorted fresh fruits, and tea with lemon or milk. For those brave guys that spent their time trudging through rice paddies and chopping their way through the dense jungle just to end up in a gun battle, this meal was more than well deserved.

"Where the hell are my shrimp?" shouted Sergeant Harris in his "army voice." An army voice in civilian life would only be used while committing an armed robbery. It is loud, authoritarian and frightening.

"It just arrived out back and the Vietnamese are unloading it right now," one of the cooks yelled back. The frantic hustle and bustle of the kitchen went on with clockwork precision, and each part of the meal was prepared and packed into the thermal containers.

When everything was ready to be moved to the landing zone and loaded onto the helicopters, Steve told Harris that he was going to ride along in one of the choppers and see what it was like out in the boonies.

"You're kidding, right?" Harris said as he looked at Master Sergeant Dunlevy with a new respect.

"No, I'm serious," Steve replied. "I'll be going out with the chow for the 1/327th."

The food containers were taken out the back door of the kitchen and loaded onto "army mules" to be driven to the helicopters. An army mule is a four-wheel, half-ton vehicle that is basically a four-foot-wide by eight-foot-long platform mounted on two axles. Designed for combat use, it will carry a load of one thousand pounds, and that's more than its own weight.

Steve had a jeep waiting, so when the mules took off his driver fell in behind and they all drove to the LZ (Landing Zone). As they arrived, the choppers were approaching the LZ in a "V" formation, six of them in all. Combat soldiers that were going out to join their units, some coming back from the hospital, were out on the LZ. Steve held his M16 above his head with both hands, and as the helicopters came close to the ground he lowered his rifle. The distance from the rifle to the ground reflected how far the helicopter landing rails were from the ground. The chopper pilots couldn't see the landing rails under their choppers, so the troops would bring them in safely with their M16s.

Steve ran out to the chopper, keeping his head down to avoid the helicopter blades, and he jumped in with all the food containers for the 1/327th. Fear swept over him as the realization that if he got killed out in the boonies, this would have been the worst mistake he ever made. But he "shined that thought on" and enjoyed the ride. It was awesome up above the jungle, and Steve grinned at the very young door gunner, who smiled back. They were flying in formation with two of the other helicopters with the Thanksgiving dinner for the ground troops.

Suddenly there were two thud sounds very close together, like something had hit the chopper.

"What was that?" Steve shouted to the gunner.

"Incoming fire," the door gunner shouted back without taking his eyes off the jungle below, and he opened up with two long bursts from his M-60 machine gun.

This was not as much fun as Steve had thought it would be. Steve looked at the young door gunner and wondered how he could be so calm, dragging on his cigarette like he didn't have a care in the world.

Soon they were coming in for a landing. The combat troops on the ground directed the helicopters in, and the landing rails had barely touched down when eight soldiers came running up, keeping low under the chopper blades, and began to unload the food containers.

Two of the helicopters carried all the food and the replacement soldiers returning to the boonies, and the third chopper was full of high-ranking officers. These officers, all majors and colonels, were here to serve the food to the combat troops as a sign of great respect.

Steve was amazed at the faces of these hardened combat soldiers. They looked like young boys, but something about their faces showed the deep horror of what they were going through. Something about their eyes that made them seem to stare right through him. And yet, they were friendly, and always ready to help when needed.

Soon a mess tent was set up. Then the chow was all laid out on a long serving table, and the officers took their places along the table to serve the food.

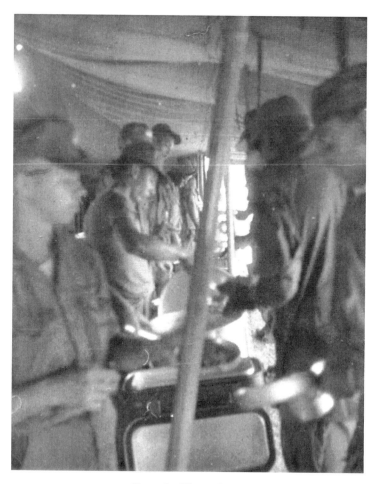

Boonie Chow Line

Once the chow line began to move Steve was able to relax a little, so he went over to a guard position and struck up a conversation with the two soldiers manning that position. Steve met Wayne Cox from Indianapolis, Indiana, and Phil Johnson from Boston, Massachusetts. They must have been five or six years younger than Steve, but he felt like he was talking to two wise older men. They faced death every day for a living; every day of their lives could turn into a nightmare, and many days did. But not today, and Steve was proud to be part of making that happen for them.

The cleanup was easy: everyone just put their serving spoons and dishes into the empty thermal food containers and the soldiers loaded them back into the waiting choppers. Steve went to say goodbye to Cox and Johnson, and they were actually washing their mess kits by rubbing dirt in them.

Cox saw Steve's face and said, "This gets them clean enough for army purposes." They all laughed. They both had written a letter home, and they asked Steve to mail them in the rear area. Steve took the letters and felt an almost religious compulsion to get the letters safely mailed. He could see that level of seriousness in the eyes of the two battle-worn kids as he put the letters inside his shirt.

Steve boarded the chopper to return to the base camp having to fight back tears for these brave young men he was leaving behind.

CHAPTER 3

LOST ANCIENT TREASURE

Steve had been unable to do his perimeter run for several weeks because it was monsoon season. Even when it wasn't raining, the dirt road was too muddy for jogging. You could set your watch by what time it started to rain each day, and to Steve it almost seemed like the rain was messing with him personally. He had put on several pounds during this monsoon season. Steve was very excited the first day that it didn't rain. He waited two more days without rain to let the sun work on the dirt road, and then he began his regular exercise regimen once again. The dirt road still had puddles but going around them was no problem. Steve, however, was a little out of shape. He had to walk the last thousand meters to his halfway point rest area. He was still winded, even after having to walk, when he arrived at the mound of dirt for his rest break. There was a puddle on the side he usually sat on, so he walked around to the other side, so his feet wouldn't be in water and mud.

"Holy shit," Steve exclaimed as he looked at the mound of dirt.

He knelt down, and there was what he thought was a tombstone that was round on top and had what looked to Steve like Chinese writing on the front face of it. He cleared the dirt away from the stone until he could see the entire stone and all the writing. There didn't seem to be any birth and death dates on the stone, so Steve was curious. This stone had been completely covered by dirt until the monsoon rain had exposed it. Steve dug more dirt away from the top left of the stone and got his fingers behind the it. With one big pull the stone moved forward, exposing a dark chamber behind the it.

Inside the chamber Steve could see a bright red color even in the dark. He reached in and pulled out a very highly decorated pouch with an intricate woven pattern on the front and a very old book with writing, just like on the stone, inside. Steve reached back into the chamber and pulled out the most beautiful garment that he had ever seen. It looked like a sleeveless shirt, but it looked like it had been made for a king. The front of the vestment had two golden dragons facing one another. Between the two dragons was a highly decorated gold circle. Below the decorative dragons were row after row of tiny little men, and they were all praying.

Steve decided that he needed something to carry all these items in, and because they looked so valuable he put them all back in the chamber and pushed the stone back in place. He jogged back to his room in the barracks and brought back an army laundry bag and a flashlight. Back at the treasure site, Steve was removing all the beautiful items and putting them into the laundry bag when he pulled out something wrapped in a bright red silk cloth. When he removed the cloth, he found a beautiful ornate dagger. He shined the flashlight into the chamber and found a necklace with a round silver amulet. The last item was an intricately braided cord with a tassel, a tiger tooth, and a small bell attached to it. With all the treasures in his laundry bag, he secured the string ties around the top. He then replaced the stone and repacked the dirt around it until it was hidden.

Steve's Trove of Treasures

Back at the barracks, he closed the door to his room and dumped the laundry bag's contents onto his bed. He thought he would send everything to Joanna, so she could use them to decorate their home. They looked very old, but in good shape. Steve put everything back in the laundry bag— except the dagger. He really liked the feel of it, so he put it in his footlocker.

The next morning, Steve was at the mess hall bright and early. He brought the beautifully decorated pouch with him to work so he could show it to Sergeant Harris. The kitchen was a madhouse, with cooks and assistants running about preparing breakfast for hundreds of hungry GIs. In the dining hall, the Vietnamese workers and GIs on KP (Kitchen Patrol, or kitchen duty) ran about setting the tables up and getting everything ready for the onslaught. To get put on KP, a GI either had to be new to the unit or have messed up and been assigned there as punishment.

It wasn't until after breakfast had been served that things slowed down enough for him to show Sergeant Harris the pouch. He and Sergeant Harris were standing in the kitchen when Steve brought out the decorative pouch. Two Vietnamese workers were moving a big pot full of water onto the stove. When they saw Steve bring out the pouch, they both dropped the big pot, and water went everywhere. The faces of the two Vietnamese reflected absolute horror, and they chattered in Vietnamese as they backed away from the pouch.

One of the Vietnamese workers pointed to the pouch and said, "Number ten! Number ten! You no have, very bad." And the two workers fled the kitchen. "Number ten" meant that something was very bad, just as "number one" meant very good.

Steve was a little disconcerted, but he and Sergeant Harris just laughed while Steve told a nearby worker to mop up the water from the floor. Sergeant Harris checked out the pouch and told Steve that he thought that it might be valuable. One of the cooks came and told Steve that the two Vietnamese workers had left the entire compound and that they needed replacements from the KP staff.

The remainder of the work day went smoothly, and the troops were fed their three squares and the evening cleanup was completed. Steve had returned to his room and was writing a letter home when a banging started on the wall. The man in the room next to Steve's was hammering in a nail to put up a picture on his wall. Steve shocked himself by becoming totally enraged. He found himself in a heated argument with the supply sergeant next door, to the point where their friendship was permanently damaged.

Back in his room, Steve was almost in shock; nothing that trivial had ever upset him so much. He tried to return to writing his letter to Joanna, but he could only think of negative things. He never was negative with Joanna, so he was unable to complete the letter that night. Steve explained it all away by attributing it all to his being tired, and he went to sleep early.

The next day Steve was called to the CO's (Commanding Officer) office, and there were three Buddhists monks dressed in bright orange robes, with the two Vietnamese workers who had fled from the pouch the day before. The CO explained that the monks were interested in the pouch that Steve had shown Sergeant Harris. Steve told them the whole story, and the CO told him that the things he had found were very important to the monks' religion.

Steve wanted very much to do what was right, so when the CO asked him to go get the articles he had found, he happily complied. Back in his room he gathered up all the items he had found in the hidden chamber. When he opened his footlocker, and picked up the ornate dagger, he decided to keep it, and he put it back in the footlocker which he then closed and locked. He put the rest of the items into his laundry bag and returned with it to the CO's office. Steve handed the bag to one of the monks, and the monk opened the bag and the three monks peered down into the bag. Two of the monks began to chant with their eyes closed while the third monk removed the items from the bag one at a time and placed them on the CO's desk. As soon as the last item was out of the bag, the monk started putting them back into the laundry bag. The monk asked in perfect English if they could see where Steve had found the precious items. The CO had a jeep brought around, and they all drove to the perimeter road and to the dirt mound. When the monks saw the stone, they immediately dropped to the ground and began to chant. The CO, Steve, and the jeep driver stood together for a good five minutes before the monks stopped praying and stood up. Their faces reflected fear, and they wanted to leave the dirt mound at once. They drove back to the CO's office, where the monk who spoke English explained that the items Steve had found had belonged to a very powerful shaman who had lived in the fifteenth century and that he had been feared by all because of his great powers. He explained that the stone in the door of the chamber was an ancient curse on anyone who disturbed the chamber. The monk told Steve that he had done a great service to the Buddhist community in Vietnam, and that he was sure that the curse would be canceled because Steve had returned the items. Then the monks left with the precious artifacts.

The CO was very happy with Steve for having helped the Vietnamese community recover artifacts that were important to their religion. He told Steve that he would be putting him in for a promotion to First Sergeant E-8, and that Harris would also be promoted to E-7 to take over as Mess Sergeant when Steve went home.

Back at the barracks, Steve opened his footlocker and took out the dagger. He felt a little bad about keeping it, but the monks had not missed it and he knew just where he wanted to keep it; above the mantel, over the fireplace, back home.

Steve had two months left until his tour of duty was over, and he would be getting out of Vietnam and the army at pretty much the same time. Steve did not have to worry about making it home alive like the combat troops did, but he missed Joanna so much that it made the time drag by slowly.

During his next regular jogging session, he stopped at the dirt mound to rest, but he didn't feel comfortable there; so he began walking through the middle of his run to rest instead of stopping at the mound.

Eventually, the time for Steve to go home came, and before leaving he knocked on the door of the room next to his where the supply sergeant that he had argued with lived and gave him his stereo reel-to-reel tape player because he couldn't take it home. He knew the staff sergeant had a radio because he had heard it playing, but he had never heard stereo sound coming from next door. The sergeant smiled and accepted the gift, but he was still a little cold with Steve. Steve couldn't really blame the guy, so he shined it on. He packed his duffel bag and buried the dagger in the middle where it would be safe. Then he said his goodbyes and was soon aboard a commercial jet flying home.

They landed in Oakland, California, where Steve went through out-processing. After out-processing, the group he was with went across the street to the mess hall, where they were treated to a steak dinner. Then, after the steak dinner, they were free to go home as civilians.

Steve took a cab to the airport and got his ticket to Phoenix. He called Joanna and told her the time of his arrival in Phoenix and his flight number. Despite the fact that the flight to Phoenix was very short, all the family, on both sides, was waiting for Steve when he got there. What a wonderful reunion. The entire family had reservations at a fancy restaurant for a welcome-home dinner with Steve. Joanna would not let go of Steve's arm all the way out to the parking lot. She was so glad to see Steve that she was crying for the first five minutes. When they got to the parking lot, Joanna and Steve's dad and mom, Mike and Edna, led Steve to a brand-new Corvette Stingray. Steve's parents had bought him a car as a welcome-home present.

"This is your new car," Mike said, "for your new civilian life." They all hugged, and Steve got behind the wheel of the 'Vette and just sat there for a minute before Joanna noticed a tear in his eye.

"What's wrong?" she asked.

"Nothing; don't worry," Steve said, "I just thought of two Boonie Rats that I met on Thanksgiving Day when we served them dinner out in the jungle. I hope they get to have a wonderful homecoming like I am having." Joanna leaned over and gave him a hug, and they drove to the restaurant in their fancy new car.

The tour in Vietnam had seemed endless, but now it just seemed like a bad dream. Steve was toasted with raised glasses, and he received much honor and respect from his family. They made him feel welcome in a way that every veteran coming home needs. A big family picnic was planned for the next day with the extended family at Encanto Park in Phoenix.

CHAPTER 4

FAMILY LIFE

The house seemed bigger to Steve after having lived in a single room for eleven months in Vietnam. After making love "to welcome him home properly," Joanna took him to see the nursery first, which resulted in a big kiss in the nursery doorway. Then they toured the rest of the house while Joanna pointed out all the improvements and changes that she had made while he was gone.

Steve had bought Joanna an ornate silk jacket with a dragon motif and a beautiful matching silk blouse. When she opened the gift, she was delighted. She put them on right away and, to Steve's amazement, they fit her perfectly. Joanna embraced Steve for a big thank you kiss.

In the living room, on the mantel, was a very highly decorated bronze statue of a dancing figure with its arms extended to the sides and a tall pointy spiked hat. Steve had mailed the bronze statue as a gift to Joanna before he had left Vietnam. This reminded him of the dagger.

Bronze Statue of a Dancing Figure

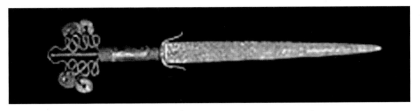

The Shaman's Dagger

Then he held it against the wall above and behind the dancing figure, and Joanna smiled and nodded her approval. Steve laid the dagger on the mantle, went and got his tools, and mounted the dagger on the mantle wall behind the dancing statue.

They slept in the next day and had a leisurely morning. Then they were off to the big family picnic. Trees all around, children running and playing everywhere, more relatives than Steve had known he had, plus an amazing amount of good food. With all of this, Steve could only feel Joanna's hand that he was holding. He really hadn't known how much Joanna meant to him until he had to be away from her for eleven months. This was truly the homecoming that he had dreamed of while in the 'Nam.

Everyone at the picnic wanted to talk to Steve, so through the entire picnic he was constantly being drawn away from Joanna. Then, at his first opportunity, he would return to her side. The end of the picnic looked just like the beginning, except that the picnic table looked like it had taken a direct hit from a mortar round. The goodbye process took some time with so many relatives, but Steve didn't want to miss thanking anyone for such a wonderful welcome home.

Back home Steve pulled into the driveway, and they went into the house and plopped down on the couch. As much fun as the picnic was, they were glad to be alone.

"Wow, look," Joanna said, "the statue is turned the wrong way." Steve looked up, and sure enough the dancing figure was turned toward the wall and toward the dagger behind it.

"You probably put it back wrong," Steve laughed, "or maybe it wanted to look at the dagger." They had a good laugh and watched television until bed time.

That night Steve woke up with a start. He sat up in bed for a minute, hearing voices chanting. Then he reached over and touched Joanna to wake her up, and just then the chanting stopped.

"What's wrong?" Joanna asked, alarmed that Steve was breathing heavily like he was out of breath.

"Did you hear that?" Steve asked.

"No, what?" Joanna responded.

"It sounded like men's voices chanting, but I couldn't understand what they were chanting." Steve said. "I must have been dreaming."

"Are you alright, honey?" Joanna asked with concern.

Steve looked into her eyes and was touched by her concern. He smiled at Joanna. "I'm fine; it was just a dream," Steve said, and they went back to sleep.

The next few days went by quickly. Steve signed up for a culinary school that would start in three weeks, and Joanna kept busy decorating the house. Then one night Steve woke up frightened again by hearing the chanting. Joanna was very worried that something was wrong with Steve.

The next morning, she went to visit with her Aunt Mary, who had been married to a Vietnam combat veteran who had taken his own life. Aunt Mary was now married to Uncle Lenny. Joanna told her aunt about Steve hearing the chanting men, and that it had happened twice. Aunt Mary thought it might be PTSD (Post Traumatic Stress Disorder), and she advised Joanna as to what symptoms to look out for. Joanna's aunt went upstairs and brought down some pamphlets on PTSD.

"Oh, another thing," Joanna said, "he keeps turning the statue of a dancer on our mantel around backwards to face the wall." She looked serious as she continued, "He denied it the first time and said that I must have done it. But every morning when I go downstairs to start the coffee and make breakfast, he has turned the statue around to face the wall. I just turn it around and never say anything about it."

Joanna decided to talk to Steve that night and see if there was anything she could do to help.

When she told him that she thought he might have PTSD, he laughed and said, "Do you think I have PTSD because my soufflé fell in Vietnam? You have to have had something bad happen to you to get PTSD, and nothing bad happened to me during my entire tour of duty."

Then she asked why he kept turning the dancing statue around to face the wall. He thought she meant that first time, but when she told him it happened every night, he reassured her that it was not him. She could see in his eyes that he was telling the truth.

The next morning, they went downstairs together and, sure enough, the dancing statue was facing the wall. Steve suggested that maybe a car going by on the street at night could have caused the mantle to vibrate and made the statue turn. Still, every morning, the statue was turned one hundred and eighty degrees—facing the dagger behind it. After several days, Steve bought some superglue and glued the statue to the mantle. Late that night Steve woke up hearing the chanting voices. The room was unnaturally cold for some unknown reason. He shook Joanna and asked her if she heard the voices chanting and, to his shock, she did hear them. They held each other as they both listened, and within a few minutes the chanting voices faded away.

It was frightening and yet reassuring for Steve to have Joanna hear the chanting too. The chill in the room was gone, and Steve turned on the light and they went downstairs together. The statue was turned to face the dagger, despite Steve having glued it down. The most amazing thing was that when Steve tried to turn the statue back around, he found it glued in place and had to break the superglue loose to turn the statue back around.

"I know damn good and well that I glued that statue to the mantle facing the right direction!" Steve exclaimed.

"I know you did, I saw you," she said, "and you even checked to make sure it was glued tight when the glue dried; and it was." Joanna and Steve talked until it was getting light outside, trying to figure out what to do about these strange occurrences. They thought that if they told other people, whoever they told would think that they were crazy.

In the next few days, the strange occurrences increased. Lights would turn on by themselves, and the television would come on in the night. Steve and Joanna seemed to both have short tempers, and they had several arguments. They had never done this before, so they sat down and had another long talk.

They decided to try to get some kind of evidence of the strange occurrences before telling anyone. That day Steve went out and bought a small reel-to reel-tape recorder that was voice activated. You could set it to turn itself on and record when a sound occurred. Steve put the tape recorder on the nightstand beside the bed, and they checked the tape each morning. Nothing showed up on the tape for a few nights, but within a week they both woke up in the night hearing the chanting. Steve reached over and felt the tape recorder. He could tell by the slight vibration that the tape was turning. Joanna was holding him tight, and he whispered in her ear that the tape recorder was running.

As soon as the chanting faded away, Steve turned on the light and rewound the tape. There it was, so clear that if the voices hadn't been chanting in a foreign language, Steve and Joanna could have understood every word.

"We got it!" Steve shouted.

CHAPTER 5

EVIDENCE

They talked for the next few hours, trying to decide what to do with this evidence. Joanna suggested that they try to get the tape translated to begin with, to see what they were dealing with. Steve thought that was a great idea, and they went to bed to try to get a little more sleep before time to get up.

The next day they went to Arizona State University where they had located a professor who was an authority on Asian languages. They took the tape recorder and met with Professor Li Chan in her office. Upon hearing the recording, she looked very serious and listened intently to the chanting until it faded away. There was thirty-eight seconds of chanting on the tape. She listened to the tape two more times, taking notes.

"Where did you get this?" she asked.

Steve didn't want to tell her the truth, so he said that he had gotten the recording in Vietnam. "This is an ancient Chinese dialect that is no longer used today." She explained. She told them that, in ancient times, Buddhists monks were used as a powerful weapon of war, and that they would chant curses on the enemy.

"This is what the voices are doing," she said; "they are trying to destroy their enemy through prayer."

She warned them that, like voodoo and other religions or practices that get their power from the dark side, it could be very dangerous. Then she said something that frightened Steve and Joanna.

"I must have my translation wrong, because it doesn't make any sense," she continued, "but they seem to be cursing an enemy for dishonoring a dagger. But that must be wrong, because I'm not sure how a dagger can be dishonored. Maybe it's not 'dagger'; it could be the name of a deity."

I'll try to find out and let you know." They let her copy the tape, and Joanna gave the professor their phone number, and then they took their recording and returned home. All the way home they discussed what would be their next move.

"I think we need help." Steve said. "This is way over our head."

"I agree," Joanna responded, "but who in the world can help us, and not think we're crazy?"

"What about that psychic we pass on the way to the mall?" Steve suggested.

"You mean the palm reader?" Joanna asked.

"I guess," Steve replied. "Do palm readers know about that sort of thing?"

"I don't know," Joanna said, "but if she doesn't, she may know some-one who does."

Instead of going all the way home, they drove to the house that they had often passed with the palm reader sign out front. Inside, the lady palm reader said that they needed to have the house blessed and cleansed, and that she could do that for one hundred and fifty dollars. Steve wrote her a check, they made the arrangements, and they left for home. The psychic was to come to the house at two o'clock that afternoon.

The psychic was dressed very much like a hippie, Steve thought, but she showed up at the house right on time. As soon as she stepped in the door, she stopped and closed her eyes.

"Yes," she said, "I feel a presence." She reached into a cloth bag that she had slung over her shoulder like a purse and brought out a small glass bottle of water and a small bundle of sticks all tied together. She explained that the water was purified salt water and that bad spirits didn't like it, and the sticks were sage, which bad spirits liked even less. She held a match to the end of the bundle of sage until smoke was streaming from it. Then she removed the lid from the small glass bottle and began walking through the house.

"In the name of Jesus Christ, I command you to leave this house!" she repeated over and over as she walked through the house, sprinkling the pure salt water and making sure the sage smoke got in all the corners of each room. After going through the entire house, including the attic and the basement, the psychic was finished with the purging of the bad spirits.

Steve and Joanna felt relieved that the house had been blessed and cleansed, but events would soon change all that. Joanna was in the kitchen preparing dinner that very evening when the room became very cold for no apparent reason. Then, suddenly, the cabinet doors began to shake so violently that it rattled the dishes inside.

"Steve!" she screamed, but as she screamed Steve's name, the dish drainer full of clean dishes flew across the room, leaving a trail of silverware and dishes crashing to the floor behind it, and smashed into the wall. Steve came running into the arched kitchen entrance way and stopped. Broken dishes and silverware were strewn all over the floor, and Joanna looked absolutely panic-stricken.

"What happened?" Steve asked. "Are you alright?" Joanna was crying, and he led her to the living room and tried to comfort her. When she told Steve what had happened, they both knew that the blessing and cleansing had not worked. Then Steve took her to a restaurant for dinner and to talk. They sat in the parking lot of the restaurant and talked to give Joanna some time to compose herself.

In the restaurant, they decided that things were very much out of control and that they needed to seek professional help, if any such thing existed.

"I'll ask my sister, June, she reads all those psychic books on that guy—" Steve paused to think. "—oh yes, Edgar Cayce. I'll ask June tomorrow." That night they both woke up hearing the chanting, so they moved down to the living room for the rest of the night.

The next day Steve and Joanna drove out to June and Allen's house in Apache Junction, Arizona. Allen was at work, and the kids, Julie and Aaron, were at school.

June came out on the porch as Steve was pulling into the driveway. She had a grin on her face to see her big brother coming to visit. They hugged on the porch and went into the house.

"Can I get you two some coffee?" June asked.

"That sounds great." Steve answered.

When June came back with the three cups of coffee, she sat on the couch next to Steve and Joanna and they sipped their coffee.

I don't know how to ask this, so I'll just jump right in," Steve began. "Do you know anything about what to do about a haunted house?" June could see that Steve was very serious, so she didn't make light of the question. "What's going on?" she asked. They told her the whole story from the first time Steve heard the chanting to the turning statue and the lights and TV turning on with no one around. They told her how things seemed to be escalating and becoming more violent.

Much to their relief, June took them seriously. She had read an article recently about a psychic investigator in Jerome, Arizona. This sounded good, and June said that she would check it out and get back to Steve and Joanna as soon as she could.

They walked to the front porch, and Steve and Joanna thanked her for her help and for her understanding. Joanna was relieved to know that they may be able to get help. She had become afraid to be alone in her own home. Steve decided to put off chef's school until this was resolved so he could be with Joanna and she would never have to be alone.

The next day they got two calls. One call came in the morning from Professor Chan, who told Steve that she had researched the tape and found that she had been correct and the voices on the tape were putting a curse on an enemy for dishonoring a dagger.

"The important thing," Professor Chan said, "is that there are some monks in Vietnam who speak this lost dialect." The professor continued, "It would be very important to science if we could interview these monks. They could provide pronunciation and even words that we are unsure of today." Steve assured her that he could not give her even a clue as to where these monks were. She thanked Steve, and said that having the recording was very helpful.

The second call was from Steve's sister, June, who had located the psychic investigator in Jerome. She had the phone number of the investigator, and she made Steve promise to call her as soon as he talked to the medium. The psychic's name was Philip Robinson. The couple was a little bit intimidated by having to call a psychic. After finding that neither of them wanted to do the talking, they decided to both call Phil with Joanna on the kitchen extension. The psychic sounded very reassuring on the phone.

CHAPTER 6

THE PSYCHIC

Steve and Joanna talked to Philip Robinson for a long while. Steve told the entire story of the occurrences that they had been experiencing in their home. Mr. Robinson agreed to come to the house with his team of psychic investigators and see if they could find out what was going on. They made an appointment for the team to arrive at Steve and Joanna's house at three in the afternoon in two days. Joanna called June and told her all about the call to the psychic, and when she told her that the team would arrive at three o'clock Friday, June said she would be there at two o'clock.

That night was the horrifying night that they were violently chased from their home to the nearby motel. Steve was worried about Joanna; she seemed very shaken and jumpy from the frightening events, and especially frightened by the violent nature of the poltergeist. The chanting voices, the sprites, the bed jumping up and down with them in it, and the deep scratches on Steve's shins—it was all too much for her. Steve, however, was anxious for the psychic to come while they still had the physical evidence of the scratches on his legs. Somehow the scratches seemed valuable to him as evidence. Actually, the scratches were the only physical sign that whatever it was haunting them was not a good or friendly spirit.

The next day they stayed at the motel and called everyone to let them know where they were. They weren't about to go back to that house until the psychic investigators arrived on Friday. They wanted to get their minds off of everything for a while, so they went out to a shopping mall and bought a Scrabble board to play at the motel. They had the same game at home, but going there was not an option. That night Steve woke up in the motel room hearing the chanting voices, but he was careful not to wake Joanna up, and he didn't tell her about it. He wanted her to feel safe in the motel.

They stayed at the motel until Friday without further incident. Then they drove back to the house to meet the investigators. June was already there, sitting in her car at the front curb. Steve parked behind her, and he and Joanna went and sat in June's car to wait for the investigators to arrive.

It wasn't long until a van pulled up and Philip Robinson stepped out and met Steve, Joanna, and June on the sidewalk.

"I'm glad you called me," Phil said, "I can feel it from here." He stood facing the house with his arms out to his sides and his elbows bent upwards like he was being robbed before introducing two of the members of his team, who went inside to the living room with Phil, while the two remaining team members brought equipment into the house.

Phil stood quietly facing the fireplace, again with his arms raised to the sides and upward.

"This room…I feel a strong presence here," Phil told the couple. "May I walk through the house?" Steve and Joanna followed Phil through the house from the basement to the attic.

Back in the living room, Steve and Joanna told Phil about the chanting. Steve was telling Phil about the statue, and as he spoke Steve noticed that the statue was once again facing the wall and he went over to the mantle and turned it around to face the proper direction. They told Phil about the balls of light, and showed him the scratches on Steve's shins.

Phil asked them to leave him alone in the living room for a few minutes, and they waited out on the front porch. They sat on the porch swing and held each other as they quietly waited. Ten minutes later Phil came out on the porch, and he looked pale.

"We have a serious problem here," he began, "and it is all centered on that dagger above the mantel. This is not a haunted house," he continued. "We are dealing with an active curse directed at Steve, and it has something to do with the dagger."

Steve told Phil all about finding the buried hidden chamber in Vietnam with the shaman's belongings inside, and how he had returned all the artifacts except the dagger.

"Wow!" Phil said, "The pieces are all falling into place. This curse must be stopped, and it must be stopped soon."

"Shall I take the dagger and throw it away out in the desert?" Steve asked.

"That would be the worst thing that you could do," Phil explained. "The dagger must be returned; not to a person, but rather to the rest of the shaman's belongings."

Phil told them that they should just leave the dancing statue facing the dagger, and that the spirits were using the statue to show them that the dagger was not supposed to be there. He told them that it wasn't the house that caused the problems; it was the act of bringing the dagger here. When Joanna mentioned that they had been staying in a motel, he said that would not help. He said that the curse would probably follow them wherever Steve went. Then Steve confessed that he had heard the chanting in the motel, but that he had not told Joanna. Joanna gave him a frown.

The two assistants put the equipment back into the van, because it was not necessary to check the house. It was, however, necessary to do something about the dagger. They decided to contact the local Buddhist monks. Steve found a Buddhist monastery, and they called the monastery to try to get them to help. The monk that they talked with spoke very good English but didn't seem to grasp what Steve wanted. Then Steve told him that he wanted to donate the artifact to them. The monk said that someone would come to the house to receive the donation. The monks showed up in a small white car that was so plain that it looked generic. They were very cordial, but the visit lasted less than a minute. As soon as they went in the house and saw the dagger, they looked frightened and said that they would not take it. It seemed as if they couldn't get out of the house fast enough, and then they were gone.

"Wow," Steve said, "that was no help at all." Steve took Joanna's hand and said, "Did you notice that those monks were Japanese, not Vietnamese? I wonder if that matters."

"Phil said that the dagger must be returned to the rest of the shaman's belongings." Joanna reminded Steve.

"That's right," Steve said, "we need to contact the monks in Vietnam who I gave the other artifacts to."

Steve had no idea how to get back in touch with the Vietnamese monks who he had given the artifacts to. Then Steve realized that he had Harris's information in his address book. Sure enough, there it was in his 'Nam address book: Staff Sergeant Eli Harris and his APO (Army Post Office) address at the Phan Rang base camp.

Steve worked on a letter to Sergeant Harris. He started off with personal stuff, catching Harris up on his homecoming, and he asked Harris to say hi to all the folks in the mess hall. He didn't want to tell Harris about the curse, because he was afraid that Harris might think he was crazy, so Steve just wrote that he felt bad about keeping the dagger and he wanted to return it. He asked Harris to talk to the Vietnamese mess hall workers that had dropped the big pot full of water when they saw the pouch that he had brought to show him. Steve asked Harris to ask the Vietnamese workers to contact the monks that had come to the base camp to get the relics and ask them to contact him, because he wanted to return the dagger. He put his address in the letter in case the return address on the envelope got smudged going halfway around the world to Vietnam.

"Let's hope this works," Steve said seriously, "because I have no idea what to do if it doesn't." The couple drove the letter to the post office to mail so they could find out how much postage it would require going to Vietnam.

The soldiers serving in Vietnam did not need to worry about postage when they wrote home. They simply had to write the word "FREE" on the envelope where the stamp should go. To send a letter or package to a soldier in Vietnam from the United States, it only cost the regular postage rate to the APO in San Francisco or New York, whichever was closest. It seemed strange just putting a single regular postage stamp on the letter going that far.

Now there was nothing to do but wait, and Steve was good at that, having been in the army. They also had to endure the haunting curse of the Buddhist monk. Things did slow down a bit. The chanting continued, but nothing flew across the room, and the sprites, as Phil called the little balls of light, did not return.

Whenever they awoke to the chanting, Steve would say in a loud voice, "I am trying to return the dagger. I am sorry for taking it." Saying that didn't make the chanting stop, but nothing other than the chanting was happening, so they felt that it had helped.

CHAPTER 7

THE VISITING MONKS

Two and a half weeks later, the letter came. Steve and Joanna were excited; the letter had five Vietnamese stamps on it and looked like it had been through a lot getting to them. The letter was hand-printed and very easy to understand even though it had a few grammatical errors. You could tell that English was not the primary language of the monk who wrote it. The letter was a great relief to them both. The monks were coming to Arizona to retrieve the dagger. They would come in three weeks and take the dagger, and Joanna and Steve would be rid of it, and hopefully rid of the curse.

Joanna was a sound sleeper, so she slept through most of the night's chanting, and Steve got used to pretty much ignoring the chanting. If it woke him up, he would just roll over and go back to sleep. The chanting was subdued from what it had been before, and Steve felt that the chanting monks somehow knew that he intended to return the dagger.

Steve and Joanna were already getting their lives back on track. Steve signed up for chef school and Joanna got plenty of rest because she didn't feel very well, especially in the mornings.

The days went by quickly, and Steve and Joanna spent a lot of time with Steve's parents, Mike and Edna. They were worried about Steve and Joanna, so they tried to keep them busy. Joanna and Edna took a ceramics class where they each picked out a pre-made figurine that was not glazed yet but had already been kiln fired. Then they painted the figurines with glazes that would then be kiln fired to make the glaze permanent. They got to take home the finished figurine. Joanna enjoyed most talking with Edna. She especially enjoyed hearing about what Steve was like growing up.

Meanwhile, Steve's dad was trying to turn Steve into a golfer. They started off with golf lessons for Steve, and he and his dad would go, several times a week, to a driving range and hit a bucket of balls, and then they would play a nine-hole municipal golf course that was very easy and good for beginners. Within a week Steve was able to hit the ball and have it actually go in the direction that he had intended.

Both Mike and Edna, and June and Allen invited the couple to dinner three or four times a week. Steve had a great support system, and they were very well organized. A good support system is what every veteran returning home from a combat zone needs; but now Steve and Joanna both needed support.

Soon the day came for the monks to arrive from Vietnam. Steve and Joanna drove to Sky Harbor Airport. They stopped at a long line of television sets on the wall that had the arrivals and departures all listed. They found the incoming flight, and soon were on their way to gate seventeen. When they were approaching the gate where they were to wait for the plane to arrive, they were surprised to see eighteen or twenty Buddhist monks all dressed in bright yellow who almost filled the entire waiting area. The only monk not wearing yellow was dressed in bright orange, and he seemed to be the leader. He came up to Steve and Joanna and, in perfect English, asked if Steve was Mr. Dunlevy.

Steve chatted with the monk and found out that many of the monks were from California. The monks who were arriving from Vietnam were very important in the Vietnamese Buddhist community.

Steve told the monk that he did not bring the dagger, because they were afraid to touch it. The monk didn't question why they were frightened; he seemed to understand. Just to be sure, Steve told the monk about the things that had been happening. The monk listened without seeming surprised, but he did look concerned. Steve wanted to hear that when the dagger was returned the curse would be over, but just then, before the monk could answer, the monks all rose and the passengers began to file out of the aircraft jet way and into the terminal.

Three monks dressed in bright orange disembarked, and the waiting monks surrounded them until Steve and Joanna could not see the orange robes anymore. Then the mass of yellow robes parted, and the monk that Steve had been talking to approached Steve with the three other orange clad monks following behind. The three visiting monks all shook Steve's hand, and one of them surprised Steve by speaking in perfect English.

"I understand we get to visit your home," the monk said. "We look forward to that." With that, they all went to the parking lot across the street from the main terminal. And what a procession they made with Steve and Joanna leading all the monks through the terminal! Everyone stopped to watch them all go by.

The monks had three white vans, and all the yellow robe–wearing monks loaded into two of the vans and the four orange-robed monks took the third van. Steve had the monks wait for him and Joanna to go get their car and lead the monks to their home.

When they arrived at the house, Steve and Joanna went to the front porch and all the monks lined up on the walkway to the porch in a line two monks deep, with the orange-clad monks in the front. The monks began to chant, and Steve could tell that the chanting frightened Joanna. Steve squeezed her hand and looked into her eyes with a smile, and that seemed to give her comfort.

Steve unlocked the front door and motioned for the monks to come inside. Most of the neighbors were out on their front porches to see the unusual visitors.

"Show them the dagger," Steve said, and he ran upstairs. Joanna motioned toward the dagger as the chanting monks entered the living room. The monks gathered around the dagger, and the chanting stopped. Steve came running down the stairs and went over to the main monk that he had talked with at the airport and held out a bright red silk cloth.

"This is what I found it wrapped in." The monk smiled and took the red cloth. Then he approached the fireplace and stood in front of the dagger. He prayed for a moment before he reached up and removed the dagger from the wall. Holding the dagger out in front of him, he slowly turned to the other monks and said something in Vietnamese. The monks began chanting again as he wrapped the red cloth slowly around the dagger. The monk turned again to Steve and Joanna and thanked them sincerely. He smiled and reached up on the mantel and turned the dancing statue around to face the right way. He then held the dagger out in front of him and started for the door, and the other monks formed their column of two and chanted their way back out to the front sidewalk. Out on the sidewalk, the orange-robed monks turned to Steve and Joanna and shook their hands, and the two English-speaking monks bid them a pleasant goodbye.

As the three white vans drove away, Steve and Joanna waved and went back into the house. As soon as they stepped in the front door, they were elated. The heavy feeling in the house was gone. The sun seemed to be brighter coming through the windows. They could feel that the spirits were gone. They enjoyed the heaviness in the house being gone, but they were a little apprehensive about the chanting when they went to bed that night. Steve set up the voice-activated tape recorder, just in case.

In the morning Steve and Joanna woke up from the first peaceful night's sleep they had had in a long time. Even though they hadn't been awakened by chanting, Steve rewound the tape recorder, and they were excited that it was already almost completely rewound already, and that there was no chanting on the tape. They went downstairs together and were very happy to see that the dancing statue on the mantel was still facing the right way, just like the monk had placed it. That morning they called Steve's parents, as well as Allen and June, and told them the good news.

That day Joanna told Steve that she was pregnant with their first child. Steve was elated, but not very surprised because of the morning sickness that had been so consistent lately. Steve and Joanna were very happy, and they went out for lunch and to shop for Steve's culinary equipment. They both felt like their life together was just now starting.

VII - The Life of Thanh Trung

CHAPTER 1

THE VILLAGE

He was born in a small village deep in the jungle in Vietnam. In the remote villages, old customs were closely adhered to, thus new parents would do their best to make their new baby seem unappealing to evil spirits. They believed that evil spirits liked to steal babies, especially the attractive ones. They would never compliment their newborns. Instead, they would call the new baby the most unflattering name they could think of to trick the spirits into leaving their baby alone. So, for the first month of his life he was affectionately called "Cứt," which means "shit" in English. Even though they called the baby shit, they would say it in the most endearing and loving way.

Because infant mortality was so high, tradition dictated that only close family members would visit a new baby before its one-month birthday. By this time the baby's chance of survival was thought to be more secure, and it could be brought into society and openly named.

At one-month old he was named Thanh, which means the color of the sky; it is a very popular name for boy babies in Vietnam. The family name was Trung, which means loyalty to one's country or king.

Thanh's early life in the village was a fun learning process. His father taught him many useful things. Thanh followed his father everywhere and tried to help from the very moment that he could walk. As he grew older, the jobs that he could do became more and more important to the village. At three years old, he could carry bundles of long grasses when his father fixed their thatched roof, and he would work in the rice paddies just like a grownup.

Thanh's favorite chore to do was gathering firewood, because he could do that all by himself and it made him feel important. After Thanh had gathered all the firewood for his family, he would gather firewood for an old lady in the village whose husband had died of old age. He would do any other chores that the old lady needed him to do, and he often checked on her to see if she needed him to do anything. Even if the old lady didn't need anything, she would make something up because she enjoyed having someone to talk to. She had a hard time eating without spilling and dropping food on her dirt floor. The other villagers would prepare and deliver her meals to her, and when Thanh had finished his meal at home, he would always check on her. He knew that he would need to clean up any bits of food from the dirt floor, so they wouldn't attract insects into her home.

The old lady would tell Thanh stories from her life, and he was always interested in how things were in ancient times. To Thanh, however, ancient times were anything that happened over five years ago. Even though the old lady had never left the little village her entire life, her stories were full of knowledge and lessons about life in the village. Thanh listened closely when she told her stories, even when she rambled on a bit and sometimes even dozed off for a short nap right in the middle of a story. But she never slept long, and when she woke up there would be Thanh, patiently waiting for the story to continue.

Thanh always tried to do all he could for his family and his village. When one of the village men fell from a tree while gathering vines for a village project, Thanh brought firewood to the family and offered each day to do any chores that needed to be done. When the man was able to work again, he and his family brought a special dish of fish heads and rice to Thanh's family to show gratitude for Thanh's help. When Thanh's father served the meal, he made sure that Thanh got the biggest fish head sitting right on top of his rice.

Heavily Armed Jet

The villagers had been aware that a war was going on, but it did not seem to have any effect on the village. They would see the occasional American heavily armed jet fly over, but the jets were usually just a dot in the sky and they always kept going until they flew out of sight. So, life in the small village remained very busy with the daily routine of constant work required to insure the survival of the village. But even if the work was hard, everyone in the village would pitch in and have fun with each other while doing it. Laughter was often heard throughout the village and, when it was, everyone wanted to join in. Village life was good.

There were three other boys in the village near Thanh's age: An, which means peace or peacefulness; Bao, which means protection; and Chinh, meaning correctness or righteousness. An and Bao were brothers, and they were two years apart in age. An and Bao were inseparable. The boys did many chores together and played every chance they got. An was a creative boy; he never had trouble thinking of a game to play, and this came in handy when the boys were bored. An didn't even know how to be bored, he was too creative. Bao was a follower, but he was into details. If the boys were playing in the dirt, Bao would insist that everyone had the same amount of dirt and all the little piles had to be lined up straight or he wasn't happy. Chinh was the smallest, as well as the youngest, and he just wanted to do whatever Thanh wanted to do. He followed Thanh around and wanted to be just like Thanh. Chinh was too small to do many chores, but he would always try to help Thanh with his chores. Thanh would always let Chinh help and tried to teach Chinh how to do each task. If Thanh was gathering firewood, he would come back with his load and Chinh would bring a small load—together they brought more than Thanh could have brought on his own.

Up until about a year ago there were five boys, but Hien, meaning nice, kind, or gentle, had become very sick; and after a month he had died. Hien had been the youngest, but his passing left Chinh the youngest. The villagers knew it was Hien's time to go because all of the prayer and chanting that they did had been to no avail. The boys were very important to the villagers because they represented the future of the village. The boys were also considered to be the wealth of the village, and the villagers were very grateful to be so wealthy. Hien's death had been a terrible loss to the entire village. When the men of the village grew too old to work, the boys would continue providing for the village and the circle of life would be unbroken and the survival of the village would be insured. The elders said that good spirits cared for and protected the village, and that the village had been blessed so that the evil spirits could not enter.

Thanh was twelve years old when the signs of war became an almost daily event. The sky became very busy. More jets flew over now than ever before, but now the villagers could hear the terrible explosions in the distance as the jets delivered their gift of death to those below. Helicopters flew over in formations like migrating birds, and the villagers became more and more frightened with every passing day. The village elders were sure that all that was needed to keep the village safe from the war was chanting and prayer. The villagers spent many hours chanting and praying, but none of it turned out to be as powerful as war.

One day a man from a remote village to the east was found lying in the trail leading to Thanh's village. The man was near death, but he managed to tell the villagers what had happened. He told them that his village had been burned by the Americans, that many of the villagers had been killed, and that only a few of them had managed to escape into the jungle. The man went in and out of consciousness for two days until he died without having spoken again. This was a very bad sign to the village elders. The village elders had a meeting to decide what to do.

From this meeting on, the villagers decided to have two guards, day and night, on the trail that went through the village. One guard went down the trail to the east, and one up the trail to the west. They set up positions where they could see very far down the trail so they could run to warn the village if anyone was coming. They also went out the back of the village about a half a mile, where they set up a safe hiding place in a cave. They put rice and water and all the things they would need to hide in the cave for several days. They transplanted nearby bushes to the front of the cave entrance, so it couldn't be seen, and they erased all of the footprints leading to the cave.

Even with the new village security measures in place, life had changed and was full of fear for the villagers. Thanh could no longer run about in the jungle playing while he gathered firewood. He had to sneak about looking and listening for danger like a small animal. It frightened Thanh when the helicopters or jets flew over the village, and he often prayed for the safety of the village. He knew that the harder one prayed, the more good spirits would be attracted to protect the village from the evil spirits, so he prayed very hard and very often.

MACV COMMAND INFORMATION PAMPHLET 6-66 JULY 1966

Plane Dropping "Chieu Hoi" (Surrender) Leaflets

CHAPTER 2

WAR REACHES THE VILLAGE

Early one morning, when the villagers were just beginning to awaken, they heard an airplane fly over the village. It was not the sound of a jet or a helicopter, but a rather strange sound that they had never heard before. The villagers ran out of their homes to see something very strange. It was raining brightly colored papers that were falling by the hundreds on the village and the surrounding jungle. Thanh ran out and picked one of the papers up and brought it to his father. Thanh's father went to the only one in the village who could read, An Dinh, who could read mostly Vietnamese and French, but was able to read a little English as well. He said the papers said "Chieu Hoi," or "Surrender," and said that if they surrendered with these leaflets that they would be treated well and not killed. The idea of surrendering was something you might think of if you were at war, but the villagers didn't feel like they were at war; they felt like they were, however, in the middle of one.

Chieu Hoi (Surrender) Leaflet

This "free pass" to surrender was not reassuring to the villagers. In fact, it was very frightening. The villagers had many questions. What would happen if they used the leaflets to surrender? Would they be taken from their village? Or was it a trick, and would they all be killed despite the leaflets? But An Dinh had no answers. Most of the villagers felt that the leaflets were dangerous, especially if the Viet Cong came and found them. But several villagers thought that the leaflets might be lifesaving if the Americans came. So, they decided to gather all of the leaflets they could and burn them. One leaflet for each villager would be kept well hidden, only to be brought out if the Americans came.

Three uneasy days went by before their worst fears happened. The guard from the west end of the trail came running into the village in a panic. The Americans were coming! They were crossing the river and would soon find the village. Everyone was frightened and didn't know what to do. They decided to run to the cave and hide from the Americans, but one old woman refused to leave her home. It was the old lady that Thanh had been taking care of. She was too old to flee, so they gave her the Chieu Hoi leaflet and left her sitting in her home.

When the Americans arrived, they went from house to house carefully searching and being very cautious of booby traps. When the first American GI stepped into the old woman's "hooch," as the Americans called the bamboo and grass huts, there she was sitting on a bamboo mat on the dirt floor, cross-legged, with a big smile, holding the Chieu Hoi leaflet under her chin. The GI did not hesitate. He was holding a .45-caliber pistol in his hand and he discharged one shot into the old lady's chest; so much for Chieu Hoi.

Much later the villagers sent one man to check to see if it was safe to return to the village. When he returned to the cave he looked as though he had seen a ghost. He told them that the village had been burned to the ground. They stayed in the cave for two more days to be sure that the Americans would not return, and then they began the task of burying what was left of the old woman and rebuilding the village. Thanh cried at the burial ceremony because he had grown close to the old woman. He had learned much from the old woman's stories, and he would miss visiting her every day.

It was a horrible time requiring much prayer, but their prayers seemed to have been answered. The activity in the sky was greatly reduced within a week, and they could no longer hear the terrifying explosions from the jets. The Americans had moved to another area of operations, and the villagers felt less fear as the days went by. In two weeks' time the village was rebuilt, and the villagers returned to a more or less normal life.

Doing daily chores again gave Thanh a sense of security, and he worked even harder than he had been used to. Thanh was out gathering firewood a good distance from the village when he came upon what he thought was a bomb fallen from an American jet. It was actually a rocket launcher that had fired all its rockets and been ejected like a spent round from a rifle. Thanh was afraid to go near it, so he slowly backed away, fearing that it would explode. He made a mental note of where the "bomb" was so he could tell the other villagers not to go there. He even counted his steps back to the trail to the village so he would know exactly how to find the bomb if the village elders wanted to see it.

Discarded Rocket Launcher from an American Jet

When he got back to the village he told his father, and he and his father spread the word throughout the village for the children gathering firewood or playing in the jungle to stay away from the place where the bomb was and to not touch anything unusual that they might find in the jungle. They told everyone that they must not go far from the village and to always be cautious when they left the village. This was yet one more thing that increased the underlying fear in the daily lives of the villagers. They had to leave the village every day for firewood since all the firewood near the village had been used, so they were to try to bring back as much as they could carry so they would make fewer trips each day. The elders had the older children go out into the jungle and break limbs that would dry and provide a closer source of firewood to the village when the dead limbs dried. Some of the villagers thought that the gods were upset with the village and arguing among the men was an almost daily event. Some of the villagers even blamed the old woman who was killed because the gods were obviously very mad at her. Thanh had never seen his village this divided.

CHAPTER 3

THE VIET CONG

Early one morning, just at first light, the lookout from the east side of the village came running into the village in a panic. The Viet Cong were coming, and there was very little time to decide what to do. The villagers thought that since the Americans obviously considered them to be the enemy that the Viet Cong would consider them to be on their side, so they decided to stay and welcome the Viet Cong. Everyone ran back to their homes and stood out front to wait for the Viet Cong to get to the village. As the Viet Cong squad entered the village, the villagers all cheered and clapped. But the Viet Cong remained very serious and ordered all the male villagers to line up in the center of the village. The leader of the squad, a lieutenant, walked down the line of men like it was an inspection, closely looking at each man. Two very old men were told to leave the line, as were the children. Then the lieutenant announced that the remaining men were now Viet Cong soldiers and they would be leaving with the squad to be trained. One man left the line and approached the lieutenant, saying that the village needed the men to survive. He had barely finished his sentence when the leader pulled out a pistol and shot the man cleanly right in the forehead. No one spoke after that except the soldiers who went through the village and took everything that they wanted. This was much worse than when the Americans had burned down the entire village. Now the women and children would have to survive on their own.

Thanh's father was suddenly gone, as were all the fighting-age men of the village. His mother was hysterical, and Thanh thought that she might be killed also because she tried to follow the Viet Cong down the trail, screaming for them to give her back her husband. She remained in shock for several days.

No one knew what to do. There was talk of abandoning the village, but no one knew where to go, so everyone just performed their daily duties for survival. Thanh and the other boys took over their fathers' duties as well as their own.

The old people of the village knew that before the Americans there were the French, who had been fighting in Vietnam for forty years. But when the French left the Americans seemed to take their place. They also knew that when villagers were taken by either side they were rarely ever seen or heard from again. This news was not what Thanh wanted to hear—it made him cry.

This was the hardest time that Thanh had ever experienced in his life. He was unable to comfort his grieving mother, and he had no idea how the damage done to the village could ever be repaired. His father was gone, and for the first time in his life Thanh felt despair.

Not two weeks from when the Viet Cong came to the village, they were back again. This time it was a different unit, and they came without warning because the boy guarding the east trail had fallen asleep. They lined up everyone left in the village and had Thanh and two other boys move off to the side. The two other boys were brothers and Thanh's good friends that he had grown up with, An and Bao Nghiem.

After the soldiers took all the food in the village, the leader ordered his men to leave, taking the three boys as Thanh's mother begged and screamed for her son back. Thanh could hear his mother for some distance down the trail, and though his eyes streamed tears he dared not say a word. He was now a Viet Cong soldier.

The Viet Cong took Thanh further from his village than he had ever been in his entire life on his first day with them. They walked for three days, traveling only at night, until they arrived at a jungle training camp, just in time to get a couple of hours sleep. The three boys curled up under a tree and fell asleep. At daylight Thanh woke in a forest with a very high canopy. Thanh thought he might see his father here, but it was not to be. The training camp was at the foot of a big hill and was undergoing some serious construction. When finished, the camp would accommodate a battalion of training soldiers.

They had already finished building the classroom. It had a bamboo frame with a thatched roof and no walls. There were rows of bench seating facing a bulletin board–type structure at the front of the classroom. There were about thirty people at the camp, and they used five campfires to cook the food for them all. The five campfires were spread along the foot of the big hill and spaced far apart. Each one was cooking the same thing, rice. If they used one big fire to cook all the rice together, the smoke from the big fire would breach the forest canopy above and would be spotted by American aircraft, which would promptly call in an airstrike on the camp.

Even though the training camp was not completed, classes had already begun. Thanh went through classes all day for four days with his two friends An and Bao and eight other "new recruits." They learned how to use many things from the jungle as weapons of war. They learned to make punji steaks by splitting and sharpening bamboo sections into sharp stakes that were stuck into the ground at an angle with the sharp end pointing toward the enemy. This would give a puncture wound or scratch to the leg of the enemy. Of course, a puncture wound or a scratch to the leg is not such a big deal in combat, so they were taught to put water buffalo dung on the sharp end of the punji stake. Then even a scratch would cause a life-threatening infection requiring the victim to be medevaced out of the jungle for medical treatment in a hospital. They learned many things in those four days, and became more accustomed to their new life.

Everyone in the training camp was talking about the very important NVA (North Vietnamese Army) officer who was coming to take charge of the camp construction. He was an engineer who had been educated in Hanoi and France. He arrived during the night with three Viet Cong soldiers. Two of the soldiers were carrying the engineer's belongings and equipment, and the third soldier was heavily armed with an AK-47 automatic rifle and grenades.

First thing the next morning the engineer picked eight helpers from the new recruits, and Thanh was one of them. They were going to build an oven big enough to cook all the food for the training camp. This didn't seem to make sense to Thanh because of the smoke problem—but he didn't say anything.

The engineer brought out a big bundle of string that was wrapped around a bamboo stick and had a knot every meter for measuring. He gave the end of it to Thanh and told him to go up the hill. When the string was fully extended, the engineer directed Thanh to move to the left and then to the right until the string was just where he wanted it. He then told Thanh not to move. The other workers were instructed to hammer bamboo stakes into the ground along the string about five paces apart. They were told to hammer in the stakes so that they were touching the string, but not moving it. Then they moved the string about three meters and had stakes driven along it again in the same manner. This created two rows of perfectly straight stakes marking the sides of a great ditch that was to be dug all the way up the hill.

The other workers were already digging the ditch when one of the engineer's assistants began rolling up the string. Thanh, at the top of the hill, was to keep enough tension to prevent the string from touching the ground and slowly come down the hill as the string was rolled up. When Thanh got to the bottom of the hill the engineer was there, and he told Thanh that he wanted him to be one of his permanent helpers. This was a very prestigious job that removed Thanh from the pool of laborers who did all the hard work. The engineer, whose name was Colonel Hoang, took Thanh to the case with all the colonel's tools and took the time to tell him the name of each tool; what each tool was used for; and how important it was that the tools always were to be put back in the case exactly where they came from. Thanh paid close attention because he knew if it weren't for the colonel, he would be up on the hillside digging the ditch with An and Bao.

When the workers had finished the ditch to the colonel's satisfaction, an arched bamboo framework was constructed over the ditch and covered with broad leaves. Three-inch-diameter hollow bamboo pipes were placed every few meters, first on one side of the ditch cover and then the other all the way up the hill. Thanh laughed and said that the smoke stack looked like a dragon lying on its back with its legs sticking up. These bamboo "pipes" would serve as many small smokestacks so the smoke from the big oven would be dispersed up the hillside and no smoke would rise above the jungle canopy. After that, the entire framework was covered over with mud that had a heavy clay base. Some of the workers brought the clay-laden mud from a stream bed that was a twenty-minute walk from the camp while the others packed the mud over the bamboo-and-leaf dome over the ditch. At the bottom of the covered ditch they built the oven, mostly cut back into the hill. Thanh now understood how one big oven could be used without giving away the camp's position with the smoke. The construction job continued, and all the construction materials came right from the jungle.

The colonel had another group of workers making stacks of bamboo poles about two inches in diameter, each about one meter long and split in half and tied into bundles of ten, and they also made countless bundles of the one-meter-long stakes. No one knew what these were for, but they knew they weren't for the oven because the oven project was done.

Every day a work detail had to be sent to the far side of the hill, where there was a natural spring, to bring back water. They went up over the top of the hill, but they didn't have to go very far down the other side to get to the spring. The morning after the oven was completed the colonel and Thanh went on the water run with the soldiers who had been sent to get water, and the colonel had Thanh count the steps. Thanh could only count to twelve, so the colonel had him gather a bunch of small stones. Then he gave Thanh a pouch and instructed Thanh to count ten steps and then put a stone in the pouch. When they got back to the camp, the colonel had workers pick up as many of the bamboo bundles as they could carry.

The colonel then led the way, taking steps of about one meter each, and every twenty paces he would have a bundle of bamboo placed on the ground. They did this all the way around the hill, gradually getting closer to the top, until they reached the spring on the other side. The colonel explained that they were making a very long trough to bring the water all the way around and down the big hill. They started at the spring, but they did not install the first section that would catch the water from the small waterfall. The stakes were driven into the ground in an "X" and tied together where they crossed. These "X's" held the bamboo troughs that were placed in the top "V" shape of the crossed stakes and tied into place with vines. The bamboo troughs were pointed toward the next bundle of troughs lying on the ground twenty paces down and around the hill. Each new trough would start directly under the end of the trough before it so that the water would run out the lower end of one bamboo trough into the high end of the next. They continued this all around and down the hill but stopped just short of the camp so that the water runoff would not go through the camp. The colonel had them dig a channel to take the water to a nearby ravine.

Then they went back to the spring and installed the first section that caught the water from a tiny waterfall where the water came out of the hill. They followed the water all the way down and around the hill, adjusting any trough section that was spilling water on the ground and not into the next section. They weren't halfway around the hill when they heard a cheer go up from the camp as the water came running off the end of the last section of trough. The colonel looked at Thanh and smiled. As Thanh smiled back, he knew more than ever before how very important the colonel's job was and how very good the colonel was at doing his job.

The whole camp was in high spirits, but the colonel's work was done, and it was time for him to move on to his next assignment. Colonel Hoang told Thanh that he would be going with him as his assistant and that Thanh should try to get some sleep because they would be leaving as soon as it got dark, thus traveling at night. Thanh tried to get some sleep, to no avail. At sunset Thanh gathered his belongings, which all fit into one small bag, and he was ready to leave. He said goodbye to An and Bao and asked them to look for his father and, if they saw him, to tell him that Thanh loved him very much. Then he joined the colonel and his guards, and they left the camp. This was the last time that Thanh would ever see anyone from his home village.

For the next four years, Thanh and the colonel traveled around South Vietnam. They supervised the building of several more training camps, but most of their work was supervising the refurbishing of the old tunnel networks left from fighting the French and Japanese, and constructing new ones for even larger numbers of Viet Cong to hide in. The entrance to the cave complexes needed to be concealed as well as possible because to find the entrance was to find the entire complex. These complexes were very important in jungle warfare. Large numbers of Viet Cong could appear, attack an American unit, and then disappear very quickly. Even the advanced technology, used from the air to detect enemy troops through the jungle canopy, could not find them when they were underground.

These tunnels were much more than just tunnels. Some of them were like underground cities. The tunnels would lead from one chamber to the next. Some chambers were for storing food, some for weapons and ammunition; there were sleeping areas, and each big complex would have a hospital section. One day the officer in charge of the workers digging a complex came to the colonel and said they were running into large rocks and the digging had slowed because the boulders had to be moved all the way to the entrance of the tunnel and hauled away. The colonel was busy working on some papers, so he sent Thanh to see what he could do about the boulders.

If the boulders were too big, they had to dig around them, but they were running into a lot that were small enough to need to be taken all the way back through the tunnel and hauled away. This was time consuming and was slowing the project down considerably.

The workers welcomed Thanh with much respect and escorted him into the cave. They seemed to have total confidence that Thanh would solve their problem. Thanh was surprised that the workers were giving him as much respect as they would give to Colonel Hoang. This made Thanh realize how lucky he was to have been chosen to be the colonel's assistant.

When Thanh got to the boulder in question, deep in the cave, he could see what a problem it would be to move it all the way back to the tunnel entrance. He thought about the problem for a few minutes, and then he had an idea that was so simple that the workers laughed at themselves for not having thought of it on their own. Thanh took a stick and made an "X" on the side of the tunnel wall. He told the workers to dig a compartment for the boulder in the wall of the tunnel and just move the boulder into the compartment and out of the way. Thanh stayed until the boulder was moved into its compartment and out of the way, and then he left the tunnel. The colonel was waiting at the entrance with a broad smile. Thanh's idea had been passed from worker to worker all the way out to the colonel, and he was very pleased with Thanh. Colonel Hoang promoted Thanh to lieutenant on the spot—Lieutenant Thanh Trung. Thanh was very proud and wished his mother and father could know of his success.

CHAPTER 4

TRAVELING BY NIGHT

Their next job was a five-day journey that took over two weeks because the US Army was very active in this region. The first few nights were uneventful. They traveled slowly enough to make as little noise as possible. They spent a lot of time motionless because of unidentified sounds. Then, on the fourth night, they were moving down a trail when they smelled the stench of rotting flesh. For hundreds of meters the smell grew stronger with each step they took. They all pulled their shirts up over their noses to try to filter out the smell. They thought it must be a water buffalo because of the intense smell, but as they turned a bend in the trail they saw it. It was the body of a Vietnamese man, and it was swollen to three times its original size. The moon was shining on the body through a hole in the jungle canopy. As they got closer they saw it; on the chest of the dead man was an ace of spades. The colonel gasped, and Thanh's knees felt weak, and two of the colonel's helpers ran up the trail away from the body and began to chant prayers. The ace of spades was an evil sign. It not only prevented the dead man's spirit from going to heaven, but it attracted evil spirits. No one wanted to stay there, but the colonel found a stick and flicked the ace of spades off the body, an act of bravery that very much impressed Thanh. They didn't walk away from the dead body; they ran away, even the colonel. Soon they found cover, and they stopped to pray that the evil spirits would not follow them.

This was psychological warfare sponsored by the U.S. Playing Card Company. Decks of nothing but aces of spades were sent to Vietnam and passed out to American combat troops. They were meant to terrorize and did have the effect of terrorizing any Vietnamese who saw a dead body with an ace of spades on it. It was as if the Americans had taken not only the life of the dead man, but also the man's soul.

Psychological Warfare Weapon

The other soldiers from the dead man's own unit would not even go near a body with an ace of spades on it. Under normal circumstances they would have waited for the Americans to leave and then they would have buried the body and prayed over it to help it on its way to heaven. All this was canceled by the presence of such an evil sign. This was the only thing that could prevent a fallen soldier's comrades from helping the spirit get to heaven. To leave the body to rot was unacceptable under any other circumstances.

Walking the rest of the night felt more like fleeing the dead body and the evil spirits than heading for their destination, so they all walked a little faster than they normally would. Just before dawn they climbed up a hill strewn with big boulders that provided a safe hiding place to sleep through the daylight hours. They did more praying than sleeping that day to try to cleanse themselves of any evil spirits that may have followed them from the dead body. The colonel could see that Thanh was very frightened and upset from the ace of spades incident, so he called Thanh over to talk to him. The colonel knew that Thanh was from a small remote village where they still believed in the old ways, and that it would take more than talking to ease Thanh's mind. He had Thanh sit down with him. Then the colonel reached in his personal items bag and brought out something in his hand. As Thanh stared at the colonel's closed hand, the colonel explained that he was holding a very powerful and magical good luck charm. He told Thanh that the charm had been blessed by one thousand monks and that whoever possessed it would attract many good spirits. Then he opened his hand very slowly, and there lay an old North Vietnam five-dong coin equivalent to an American nickel.

"Magic" Coin from North Vietnam

The colonel placed the coin in Thanh's hand and closed Thanh's fingers around it. He told Thanh to never be without the coin and that it would protect him. Thanh held the coin tightly in his hand as he returned to his sleeping place, and he didn't open his hand until he woke up that evening. The coin was very old, but you could still make out the five-pointed star of communism. Thanh knew this to be a very powerful symbol and it gave him great comfort, just as the colonel had planned.

CHAPTER 5

THE MOUNTAIN SIDE

On the thirteenth night of their five-day trip, they were getting ready to start out when they heard noise from the trail below. Everyone froze, and Thanh even held his breath as he squeezed the North Vietnamese nickel tightly in his hand. It was an American unit moving down the trail. After the unit passed, the colonel sent one of the guards to see where they were going. Within an hour the guard returned to tell the colonel that the Americans had set up an ambush along the side of the trail, about four thousand meters down the trail.

No one was going anywhere that night, so they remained very quiet and tried to get some more sleep. The next morning the American troops passed by again as they were going back down the trail after their uneventful ambush. When it was safe they went up the trail and found the ambush site. They looked for anything left behind by the Americans that they could use. They dug up every spot where the Americans had dug a hole. Most holes that the Americans dug were for going to the bathroom, but occasionally they would find something of value to them. Thanh found a LLRP (Long-Range Recon Patrol) meal bag with American writing on it. The bag was made of cloth and lined with aluminum coated with plastic to make it waterproof. He had never seen anything like it, and it seemed almost magical to Thanh. He had never seen cloth woven so tightly, and the plastic-coated aluminum was totally alien to him.

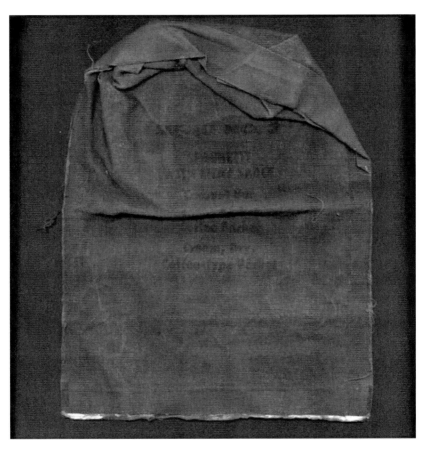

Long-Range Recon Patrol Meal Bag

Thanh could now keep things in this bag to keep dry even when they crossed rivers and streams. Thanh put the magical coin that the colonel had given him into his waterproof LRRP bag. They returned to their safe hiding place to sleep through yet another day. That night everyone was anxious to move on, so they left shortly after dark. They made their way slowly and quietly down the trail.

The colonel had taught Thanh to hold raw rice in his mouth as he traveled and gently chew it once in a while. The outer surface of the rice kernels would soften, and the chewing would allow the softened outer surface to be eaten. After a while the rice would be completely gone, and it would be time for another mouthful of raw rice. This kept their strength up and allowed them to travel all through the night without having to stop for meals. This was also an advantage because they ate even though they could not make a fire to cook on at night.

They arrived at their destination just after midnight, but it was very dangerous to safely find the trail guard. One of the colonel's men would make a jungle bird call every five hundred meters until the call was answered by the trail guard. Anyone who lived in the jungle would know that the bird whose call they were imitating never made a sound at night unless disturbed, but the Americans didn't know the jungle sounds very well, so it was safe to use the bird call. When they heard the trail guard answering the bird call, they knew they had found their destination. The guard took them into a small, rice-producing village, but they went right through the village to a hillside with a secret entrance to a tunnel network where basket after basket of rice was hidden. The tunnel network was so full of baskets of rice that there was barely any room left for them to relax. The rice was grown for the Viet Cong, but delivering it was a big problem with American troops operating in the area.

At first light, a villager came to talk to the colonel. They talked for quite a while, and then the colonel called Thanh to go with them, and the three left the tunnel. They were in a beautiful valley that ran up against a sheer cliff that rose eighty meters above the valley almost straight up. From the very top of the cliff, a waterfall fell all the way to the floor of the valley. Then it gracefully wound through the valley as a life-giving stream. It was a very beautiful and scenic spot. The village elder told the colonel that the rice had to be moved five kilometers (one kilometer equals about five eights of a mile) along the face of the cliff before coming to a place where they could climb up the cliff. The colonel had been called in to make a shortcut to get the rice to the top of the cliff and on its way to the Viet Cong.

They walked along the bottom of the cliff as the colonel studied the face of the cliff above. Soon they stopped because Colonel Hoang had found his spot. The colonel went up to the base of the cliff and looked up to the top with his cheek touching the cliff face. Then he backed away from the cliff face as he looked up to the top, all the while making notes in his book. Thanh couldn't imagine what the colonel had in mind, because this sheer cliff was so obviously impossible to climb, even without rice to carry to the top. Thanh knew the colonel well enough by this time to have a great deal of confidence in the colonel's opinion, so Thanh was anxious to see what the colonel was going to do.

All the work, of course, had to be done at night, and only when the Americans were not in the area. The village had a very good security system, with guards in every direction from the village who could spot anyone coming toward the village and run to warn the villagers while remaining completely undetected. Because of this, the villagers knew of any troop movements in the entire area before the troops could get anywhere near the village.

Work had to begin at the top of the cliff because a bulge in the cliff face had to be removed. Just to get to the top of the cliff took two and a half hours. It took one hour walking along the bottom of the cliff to get to the place where they could climb to the top of the cliff. Then a thirty-minute climb and another hour walk to get back to the work site on the top of the cliff.

Four workers in rope harnesses had to be lowered over the cliff edge and down to the bulge where they worked. Every day before nightfall the colonel would go to the base of the cliff and look up and study the progress of removing the bulge. They slowly chipped away at the bulge for twelve nights until it was gone. They had to stop working each night a little over two and a half hours before first light, because each night when the work was done, and the workers were climbing back down, others from the village would clear all the fallen debris from the base of the cliff so that if the Americans were to come, it would not look like anything was going on.

Once the bulge was completely removed the work could be done from the bottom of the cliff, so more hours of actual work could be done each night. The colonel had a worker bring a bamboo pole, and he cut a short piece from one end. He had the worker pound the small stake into the ground at the base of the cliff, and then he paced off thirty meters and had another short stake hammered into the ground. Then he had a worker hand him the long pole. He measured the long pole and made a mark about a half a meter from one end and had a worker cut the pole at the mark. The colonel told the workers that each new cutback would be measured at the wide end with this pole. Then the workers began cutting a path into the side of the cliff face that started at the ground and ended thirty meters later one measuring pole higher than it started. They made and followed marks on the cliff face to the tall end, and they were able to finish one section of the path in about four nights of work. Then they made the path go back the way it came, but always higher, creating a series of cutbacks that were to go all the way up the cliff to the top. The assent was so steep that the cutbacks had to be very close together. The workers, standing on the path, could work on the cutback directly above the one they were standing on even at the wide end.

As the work went on slowly night after night Thanh's duties were few, so he spent a lot of time with a girl named Cam Lo (meaning mountain sunset) that he had met in the village. Cam was small in stature, with silky black hair that fell to her waist. She was soft spoken and very polite. They got along like old friends right from the start, and Thanh, having never heard the term, experienced love at first sight. Cam was Thanh's first love, and he vowed to return and take her to his village to be his wife after the war.

They loved to take long walks in the moonlight, and had no trouble finding things to talk about all night long. Cam knew all the nicest spots around the outskirts of the village, like a seven-foot waterfall about fifteen hundred meters behind the village. The waterfall had a big "room" behind the falling water that was big enough to escape the splashing at the rear wall. The sound of the falling water covered their talking, and they felt safe here. This was their love nest.

The work continued for weeks without a problem or an accident until, one night, one of the workers fell from about nine meters, or about thirty feet up. He had stepped too close to the edge of the cutback trail and it had given way. The worker lived for three days, but never regained consciousness. The village elders took over, and all the ceremonies and customs were followed for the worker to be buried. The worker's family was devastated, and Thanh and Cam's heart went out to them. Although Thanh didn't know the worker who died, he was upset because Cam knew him and his family well and she was very upset.

After the cutback trail up the cliff was completed, the colonel and Thanh walked the cutback path to the top of the cliff and then back down. It was monotonous going back and forth over and over again, but at no time did the assent or descent become a hard climb. The colonel and Thanh smiled at each other in satisfaction. Their work was done, and now it was time to go to their next assignment in the same region. Thanh and Cam went to their love nest behind the waterfall until it was time for Thanh to leave. It was a tearful goodbye, and Thanh held Cam in his arms for a long time before he could tear himself away. They walked slowly back to the village, trying to make their time together last as long as possible.

When they got back to the village the colonel was waiting for Thanh, but Thanh asked for a few more minutes, and Cam took Thanh to her home to say goodbye to her family. Cam's mother cried to see the young couple so sad to have to be separated. Then Cam walked Thanh back to where the colonel was waiting for him and they said their final goodbyes. As Thanh said goodbye to Cam, she cried, and she waved to him until he disappeared down the trail. This made leaving even more painful to Thanh because it reminded him of his mother crying as he had left his village back home. Thanh's eyes were streaming tears, so he kept his face turned away from the colonel so he wouldn't see that he was crying. The village soon disappeared behind them. Thanh's heart was broken and with every bit of his being he wanted to stay with Cam, but that was not to be.

CHAPTER 6

BURIED RICE

Lieutenant Thanh, the colonel, and the three guards traveled for three nights further into this rice-producing region. They were headed for another village that also was plagued with a rice-storing problem. This village also had a hidden cave that was overflowing with baskets of rice. They arrived at the village just before dawn. It was harvest season, and this village also had more rice for the Viet Cong than they could hide.

The colonel wasted no time getting started. He had the villagers start making a basket. The villagers made baskets all the time, but they had never made or even seen a basket as big as this. The basket was to be two meters across and four meters high. At the same time, the colonel had a hole dug that would hold the basket with plenty of space around it for air circulation. The hole, to accommodate the basket, had to be four meters across and six meters deep. The basket took the most time to complete, but when the workers told the colonel that the hole was finished, he had them dig three narrow trenches going out from near the bottom of the hole to the surface like spokes. These trenches sloped up and out from about one meter from the bottom of the big hole. Then the colonel had three four-inch-diameter hollow bamboo pipes made, and they were laid in the trenches. One end of the bamboo pipe would be sticking out into the big hole, and the other end stuck up out of the trench above ground level into a bush so it couldn't be easily seen. When the pipes were laid in the trenches, the workers packed the trenches with dirt. When the pipes were buried, both ends stuck out; one end stuck out into the bottom of the hole and the other end stuck out above ground so that the bamboo pipes provided air circulation for the big hole. When the basket was done, the colonel had five bamboo poles as big around as a newborn baby's head laid across the bottom of the hole. These were to provide air circulation under the rice basket. Then the big basket was lowered into the hole. Thousands of small baskets of rice were then brought from the cave and poured into the big basket. After two hours, the big basket was full. A bamboo false floor, which would easily hold the weight of a man, was built over the basket and covered with a woven bamboo mat. Then the false floor was covered with dirt and the dirt was packed very hard. The colonel had had the hole built right in front of the front door of one of the village homes. The final touch was to build a roof over the hidden rice, so they built the roof like a covered porch, with no walls, coming out from the front of the grass hut. The colonel and Thanh walked through the porch and over the hidden rice, and they were pleased with the work. The villagers were elated. They felt safe that the rice would not be found by the Americans, because if the Americans found it that would mean the end of the village and everyone who lived there.

The villagers had a big feast for the colonel and his men. This was a wonderful meal with all the traditional Vietnamese dishes. The villagers, wearing colorful costumes, performed traditional dances for the entertainment of their special guests. To Thanh this was quite different than his normal daily routine of hiding by day and sneaking down a trail by night. After the wonderful meal and the festivities were over, Thanh followed the colonel and the guards out of the village.

Their next job was in yet another village with the same problem: too much rice. They moved out that night to begin a four-night journey to the next village that needed their help. They traveled by jungle trail for the first two nights without incident even though the American helicopters flew over constantly as they tried to sleep through the days. On the third night, just a half an hour before first light, they came to a vast stretch of rice paddies. They would have to spend the day there because they dared not be caught crossing the rice paddies in the daylight. There was no cover, no place to hide in the rice paddies, and they spanned a great distance. The colonel found some thick bushes on a hill overlooking the rice paddies. The bushes would provide cover for the day, so they crawled under them to get some rest.

Thanh was tired but was having trouble sleeping. Every time he thought of Cam, he would cry. He tried to occupy his mind with other thoughts, but his mind kept coming back to Cam and her village. Thanh wished he could sleep for an escape from his pain, but that was not to be.

It was still morning when the guard came crawling toward Thanh and the colonel's bush. "The Americans are coming!" he said in a whisper. They were coming right for the very hill where the colonel's men were hiding. They had no choice; they would have to cross the rice paddies in broad daylight. If they left right away, the Americans wouldn't see them until they reached the hill that the colonel and his men were hiding on. They started running immediately across the rice paddies on a dike. 'This is not good,' Thanh thought as he ran.

They were a thousand meters into the rice paddies, about a third of the way across, when the American soldiers reached the hill overlooking the rice paddies and saw the small party of Viet Cong running across the paddies. Thanh saw the Americans reach the top of the hill, but the Americans were not pursuing them. For a while Thanh thought that they may escape being captured or killed. Then they heard the terrifying sound of a jet in the distance. There was no place to hide from the jet. It was coming in low, and very fast. Thanh had never seen anything move so fast. It flew over once, and Thanh dived into the rice paddy water beside the dike. A huge explosion followed that left Thanh half conscious and with ringing ears. The explosion erupted on the other side of the dike from where Thanh was lying. The colonel and the guards were all on the other side of the rice paddy dike, where the explosion had occurred. Thanh lay very still in the rice paddy water with his head turned to the side so he could breathe. The jet flew over once again for damage assessment, and this time there was no explosion. Thanh lay there listening to the jet noise fade into the distance, and then the jet was gone. He slowly raised his head and turned to look behind him at the American soldiers who he thought would be coming to kill him if they didn't think all the Viet Cong had been killed—or maybe be just coming for a body count. Thanh hoped that the Americans did think that all the Viet Cong had been killed.

Thanh was unable to move more than just his head for quite a while, but when he did try to get up and run he saw the terrible damage that the rocket had done to the others. It was a morbid sight. Thanh got to his feet, but as soon as he stood up he collapsed onto the rice paddy dike, unconscious. The colonel and the guards were all dead, and their bodies were horribly blown apart. Thanh had no idea how long he was unconscious, yet he was pretty sure it had been too long.

American Soldier Calling in an Airstrike on Colonel Hoang's Squad

Thanh woke up as he was being pulled to his feet by two American soldiers, one on each arm. As his eyes opened, the first thing he saw was the dreaded "Screaming Eagle" shoulder patch of the 101st Airborne Division. Thanh's heart sank, because among the Viet Cong the 101st Airborne was one of the most feared American units. The soldiers were very serious as they tied Thanh's hands behind him and took him back the way they had come, toward the hill. The Americans stopped on the hill to eat their noon meal, but no food or even water was offered to Thanh. Then they continued on until they came to a well-traveled trail, and they followed the trail in the hot Vietnamese sun. The American soldier behind Thanh would hit Thanh with the butt of his rifle every time Thanh walked too slowly for the soldier.

Hour after hour they walked in the sun, and Thanh was not given any water or even so much as a hat. He grew weak, and several times fought off passing out. His mind wondered back and forth from thinking of Cam and of his village back home to the terrible reality of being captured, and to the pain that he felt. He thought of his work with the colonel. He wondered where his father had been taken and if he would ever see his family again. Then he started thinking over and over, "I am Viet Cong, I will show no weakness. I am Viet Cong, I will show no weakness." Finally, Thanh suffered no more as he fell to the ground dead from heat stroke. Lieutenant Thanh Trung had shown no weakness, and the colonel would have been proud of him.

This story is dedicated to the Viet Cong soldier that my unit of the 101st Airborne captured, denied water and a hat to, and purposefully walked to death in the hot Vietnam sun, making us all accessories to murder. Although I was just a private and had no say in the matter, I will never forget him. ~ Sarge ~

The End